Nightmare

CURSE OF FATE

BOOK THREE

SAMANTHA BARRETT

To my parents, this is for you.
Thank you for all that you have done and continue to do.
Your love and support, means the world to me.
"Which beach?"

I was at my breaking point. They're torturing me—daily. Vampire blood may heal my bones and wounds but it doesn't take the pain away. Which basically means they know they can make me suffer as much as they want without ever allowing me to just die.

I thought my mother's treatment was bad, but oh God, how wrong I was. Living with my mother was a picnic in the park compared to this.

They draw my blood three times a day and inject me with something; it knocks me out for God knows how long. When I wake, I always wish I hadn't.

Lucian, my jail buddy who is in the cell across from mine, tries to draw the guards' attention so they will focus on him, instead of me. Sometimes I think it just gives them twice the fun.

I'm lying here on the cold hard ground, nursing what I'm sure is a broken arm. No doubt they will be down soon to give me blood to heal my broken bone. I can't take deep breaths either, so I guess my ribs are broken—again.

"Are you awake?"

"Unfortunately." There is nothing I want more than for everything, especially me, to just be over. But I deserved all this pain for what I did at the chapel. I was a coward and getting weaker by the day. What you see on TV isn't what happens in real life; you don't drink vampire blood and become a superhuman. All the blood does is heal your wounds and bones.

They give me the blood daily, so I'll heal, and then they torture me again. It's a cycle I have been living for weeks now. I can't do this for much longer.

"Don't say that, you can't die! You owe me a trip around the world." Lucian and I spend our days—when I'm not being beaten or unconscious—talking about what we're going to do when we get out of here.

He has never seen the outside world, except for once when he was about ten.

Lucian was raised in the cells by a woman who died when he was ten years old; he doesn't remember who she was, but he says she was kind and cared for him. The first and only time Lucian was able to be outside was to watch Randall Cane kill the only mother he'd ever known. She was trying to set Lucian free and got caught.

I sighed. Lucian was trying to keep my spirits lifted, but they were wearing me down. I hurt all over, breathing was becoming a chore, and no one was coming for me or Lucian. We were stuck here at the mercy of the vampire king and my sister. "Don't give up Smurfy, please."

I could hear the panic in Lucian's voice: he wanted me to fight and make it out of here. I didn't want to let him down; he needed me just as much as I needed him. We were each other's only saving grace in this fucking nightmare of a place. I may be physically hurt, but Lucian has had it a lot harder than me. His mother died giving birth to him, he doesn't know who his father is, and the woman who raised him was killed trying to help him.

I need to woman up and think of a plan to save myself and Lucian; I couldn't leave here without him.

"I won't give up, Lucian, I swear. We will make it out of this hell hole, even if it's the last thing we do. I refuse to die down here." Lucian didn't get a chance to answer. We heard a creak and bang; that meant someone opened the door at the top of the stairs. We both remained quiet as we listened to the stairs groan. My stomach sank. I couldn't handle another round of torture, not this soon and not without the vamp blood to heal me.

I knew they weren't coming for Lucian. They never did. Whoever was making their way down the stairs wasn't very big. I could tell from the sound of the creaks. When the big guards came down, it sounded like a tree splitting.

I held my breath, waiting for whoever it was to make themselves known. You couldn't see shit down here. You could make out the silhouette of a person, but that was about it. It was another kind of torture, being in complete darkness all the time.

I pushed myself up into a sitting position and bit back the scream that wanted to tear out of me. I was in so much pain. Clenching my teeth, I scooted back along the ground until my back was against the wall and waited to see what was coming next. After a beat, a shadowy figure appeared in front of my cell.

"Well, well, how the mighty have fallen." I flinched at the cold, malicious tone. "Being beaten and bloody suits you, sister." I counted to three in my head before answering.

"I'm glad you are enjoying this, Stevie. I had thought I would see you sooner. I guess Randall has you on a tight leash," I wheezed out. I may not be able to see her properly, as there were no lights down here, but I swear, I saw her body stiffen, and I smiled a bit. I had hit my mark.

"You think Randall runs the show?" Stevie sneered. Clearly I was missing something here. A feeling of dread washed over me.

"Oh dear sister, you really are fucking stupid."

"Don't speak to her like that!" *Oh no, Lucian shut up.* I saw my sister's dark figure turn away. She must be in front of Lucian's cell. If I said or did anything in his defense, she would use him against me, like she did the others.

"Oh, so you can speak, mutt?"

"Fuck you, leave Smurfy alone." My heart swelled at Lucian's protectiveness; he has never seen me or met me properly, but he was loyal to me. Call me dumb, but that made me trust him more, than anyone.

"Oh, so you think you can save my dear sister? Why would you want to save a murderer?" I felt a pang in my chest at the mention of what I had done. Stevie knew what she was doing; she was trying to turn my only friend here against me. I never told Lucian about what happened on my wedding day. I couldn't. I pushed thoughts of that night so far out of my brain they were probably in my toes. I was in denial and I planned to stay that way, until I had a private place to sort through my emotions.

Lucian responded. "Because she is a good person! You, however, seem like a royal bitch!"

"You will watch your mouth, you vile mutt" How dare she? I had to distract her without letting her think I cared for Lucian.

"What are you doing down here, Stevie?" A minute passed before Stevie's shadow came into view again. It looked like she was leaning on the bars. I guess she wanted to keep both Lucian and I in her eyesight now.

"I came to gloat, of course, sister."

"Gloat about what, Stevie?"

"Well, you see, it's a bit of a long story, but a good one, I swear. Anyway, since I took you from your sham of a wedding, your vile cunt of a husband has been trying to get you back." My heart skipped a beat or two. I thought he gave up on me.

"It is delaying our plans, with the fucking elders now involved. Randall is to fucking gutless and won't go against his elders like I did. Now we have the fucking fae elders and the shifter elders wanting to make a trade."

My mind was reeling; Nico has been trying to save me! He didn't abandon me, nor did the others. This new piece of information gave me a renewed sense of hope and determination.

I could keep doing this, with the knowledge that one day, it would end.

"What kind of trade?" I was scared to hear her answer, but I had to know.

"Melakai Cane, for you." My heart stopped and bile rose in my throat. I was working hard to swallow it back down. Kai can't do this; they will kill him this time. Why did they want Kai though?

"Why, Melakai?"

"We know the spell you used made him Randall's blood heir. Randall wants to make an example out of him and obviously can't risk Melakai having a claim to his throne. This time, I promise you, he will die at our hands. Plus, the bonus is that his death will hurt you all over again."

"You're not taking her anywhere!" Lucian yelled. Stevie chuckled, and the sound put me on edge. I was missing something.

"Of course she's not, we're trading her cunt of a mother for Kai. Randall doesn't know that though, so shhhhh. It can be our little secret." What the fuck was Stevie up to?

"Why, Stevie?"

"Because you still need to seal the fae realm. I'm going to make Kai pay for your betrayal, and you'll watch every moment of his suffering. Then I will kill you. You will never be free again, sister."

CHAPTER 2
Ryan

Stevie left after she dropped the bomb that Kai would be traded. I couldn't let him go through with this! Kai wouldn't die for me.

I had to figure out a way to get the fuck out of here. Kai and the others had no idea it was all a trick; Nina was to be traded not me.

I knew I didn't have long before someone came down here and took my blood, injected me, and then beat me.

I had to think while I had the chance—what the hell was I going to do? I can't access my magic, and I don't know why. I thought it might be because of the cell I am in, but it won't even work when I'm taken to Randall's office. Lucian said he doesn't even know if he has any magic, he doesn't even know what type of supernatural he is, but Stevie's comments about him being a mutt certainly were a hint.

Soon after I got here, I had tried screaming, reasoning with guards, and I even tried bribing them. Nothing worked.

I don't know where Nina is, but she was here somewhere in this mansion.

Stevie is so far gone now that I don't think there is any coming back for her. As the days dragged on, I have grown to resent my sister even more. I estimate that I have been here for roughly six weeks now. I smell like I have been here for years.

"Psssst, Smurfy." I smiled at Lucian's attempt to whisper; that boy is louder than a fog horn.

"If you're trying to whisper, you're doing a shit job." We both chuckled, and I winced. Laughing was out of the question while my ribs were broken. It was silent for a moment before she spoke again.

"Who's Melakai, Smurf?" I sighed; I regretted sighing straight away when a searing pain hit me in the side. Clutching my ribs to try easing the pain, I took some slow and shallow breaths.

When I finally got my pain under control, I answered Lucian.

"Melakai is a friend of mine."

"Okay?" I could hear how reluctant Lucian sounded; he knew I had a chance at being rescued and couldn't understand why I wouldn't take it.

"Kai and I have a complicated history; just know that I will not leave here without you. And if there is a way for me to stop Kai from exchanging positions with me, I will do it." I heard his sharp intake of breath; he must think I'm crazy.

"Why would you do that?"

"Because I owe Melakai, and he deserves to have his life. He nearly gave his life for me once; I won't allow my sister to trick him. If they do make an exchange then it would be for nothing, Nina would be free, not me. And of everyone involved, Nina is least deserving of freedom."

We sat in silence for a long time. Something was wrong. No guards have come to inject me, and Randall hasn't come to draw my blood.

"Lucian, something's wrong."

"I didn't want to be the one to say it, but you're right. The guards are always here by now."

"Do you think it's that big elder meeting you were telling me about?"

"Maybe?" We didn't get to finish speculating. The door opened and banged, the stairs started creaking and groaning, but there were so many footsteps pounding down the steps that my alarm only escalated.

A moment later a shadow appeared in front of my cell, but I didn't move from my position. If they were here to beat me, it was better to remain still and just get it over with. The more I fought back, the more they enjoyed it.

"Get up, you're coming with us." This can't be good.

"Where?" I know it was stupid to ask questions; it usually just pissed them off.

"You don't get to ask questions, bitch, now move." I wouldn't leave here without Lucian, I promised him.

"I won't leave without Lucian."

"Smurf, no! I'll be okay. Do what you need to do."

"Quiet! You're both coming. Now get the fuck up!" I didn't argue any further. I used the wall to help me stand and forced myself not to make a sound. My ribs were killing me and my arm hurt like a bitch. I wouldn't give these bastards the satisfaction of seeing me crumble.

Once I was on my feet, the cell door opened, and shadowy figures entered. They gripped both my arms and pulled them behind my back, I couldn't hold my scream back. The pain was crippling and my knees buckled. I remained standing because of the grip the two guards had on me.

"If you fucking hurt her again, I swear to God, I will fucking kill you!" I heard the sickening sound of a crunch come from Lucian's cell. "Is that all you got? What a fucking pussy!" I heard more sounds and a scuffle, then a moment later dark figures passed by me.

Cuffs were placed on my wrists, and I was dragged from my cell. Tears were streaming down my face from the pain. I had to block the pain out; something big was happening. I hadn't seen Lucian leave his cell the whole time I had been here.

I was dragged up the stairs and stumbled more than a few times. I couldn't fucking see anything. As we neared the top of the stairs I closed my eyes knowing that the light was going to hurt like a bitch after being in the dark for so long. They yanked me through the door, and I screamed out in pain, but the guards didn't give a fuck. After being dragged for a while, I braved the light and slowly started to open my eyes. It stung at first, and my eyes started to water. Once I got my vision under control, I started to look around, but nothing was familiar.

"Smurf!" Oh God, where is Lucian? I couldn't see him anywhere. Where the fuck have they taken him?

"Lucian!" I was swiftly punched in the face by the guard on my left, but I didn't black out, thankfully. My face was now throbbing and felt like it had a pulse; I slumped in the guards' hold, letting them drag me to wherever we were going. We rounded a corner and then the front doors of Randall's mansion came into view. What the fuck was going on? I saw a group of six guards standing by the front door holding a man who was slumped forward, unconscious.

That wasn't just any man—it was Lucian. With a new sense of purpose, which was to make sure Lucian was alive, I started to struggle in the guards' hold; I got my feet under me finally and started to pull away, the pain in my arm, ribs and face forgotten for the moment.

"Cut it out before you get knocked the fuck out!" Left guard snapped at me. I turned and glared at the ugly bastard.

"Fuck you!" Lefty cocked his arm back, ready to hit me again, when

a hand appeared out of nowhere and stopped him from landing the blow to my face.

"Touch her again and I will rip your fucking head off, feel me?" I leaned forward so I could see around Lefty and was shocked; the last person I ever thought would save my ass just did.

"Tyler?"

"Don't look so shocked, Ryan." Tyler had changed in the weeks since I had last seen him. His ginger beard was gone and his rust-colored hair was cut short on top and shaved on the sides now. His brown eyes were dull, and he had dark circles under his eyes. Tyler looked like shit.

"What's going on, Tyler?"

"Shut the fuck up!" Oh, so now Righty wanted to speak up. Great.

"Bring her to the car out front, and bring the boy as well."

"You don't tell us what to do, dog!" Righty had grown some balls in the space of a few seconds.

"When Randall and my mate are not here, I am in charge! Now do as I fucking say and hurry the fuck up!" What the hell was going on? Why was Tyler acting weird?

Tyler's eyes kept darting around the room like he was watching for something or someone. We were dragged outside, and Lucian and I were placed in a blacked-out SUV after the guard removed our cuffs. No guards were in the SUV with us, and Lucian was still out cold.

Tyler jumped behind the wheel of the SUV and sped away from Randall's mansion.

"Tyler, what the fuck is going on?"

"Well, I believe I just saved your life and ensured my own painful death at the hands of my mate. Any other questions?"

It had been weeks since our wedding—since the day everything went wrong. She was taken from me, and there was not a fucking thing I could do about it.

I was banished back to Farrarie the night of our wedding. The fae elders called a mandatory meeting that night which led to me being banished from Earth.

The vampire elders made sure to declare that I cannot go back to the Earth realm until the trial. They say I can't be trusted, because Ryan is my wife. They're right. I won't stop trying to get her back; the look on her face that night has haunted me every time I close my eyes. She was begging me with those beautiful, strange eyes to save her, and I couldn't. Something was going on with the elders; I could feel it. Lachlan was being shady, and Victor was having council meetings without me present. The witches had no choice but to listen to Stevie. The shifter elders were the only ones who were being open and honest with us.

"Your majesty?"

"What is it, Cyrus?" I snapped.

"The alpha and Dom are here." I sighed, I had a feeling they weren't coming here to give me good news.

"Send them in, Cyrus." With a nod of his head, Cyrus left my study.

I started pacing, too anxious to sit still while I waited for the guys. After what felt like hours but was more like ten minutes, Jax and Dom strolled through the door.

"Nico." I walked right over to them and embraced each of my brothers. "It's good to see you, too, brother." Dom seemed taken aback by my embrace.

"How's everything going? Is there any news on Ryan?" Jax dropped his gaze to the floor, and Dom gestured for us to take a seat on one of the couches. I reluctantly followed them and sat down. Neither of them would make eye contact, and an uneasy feeling settled in my gut. What the fuck has happened?

"One of you two need to start talking!" I ground out through clenched teeth. Releasing a breath, Jax finally spoke.

"The shifter elders have been trying to get a trial date set since Ryan was taken. Ian has been pushing them to hurry but—
"

"But what?" I snapped, and Jax flinched at my tone. I know this wasn't his fault, but I needed him to hurry the fuck up and get to the point.

"But they say there is no rush, as Ryan left willingly."

I couldn't sit still anymore; I stood and started pacing my study, again. I needed to release my pent-up anger. If I didn't, I was going to blow this whole room apart with the magic raging inside me. Having Ryan's magic inside of me was making my own magic slightly unstable.

I needed to save Ryan. She probably thought I had given up on her.

"Nico?" I turned to face Dom, who wouldn't meet my eyes.

The somber tone in his voice had me on edge. I released the breath I didn't know I was holding and took a seat, again.

"Dominic, in all the years we have known each other, you have never avoided eye contact. Why are you starting now?" Dom and Jax exchange a look that I couldn't decipher. "Seriously, start fucking talking!"

"Okay, let me get this all out before you go bat shit crazy, okay?" I took four calming breaths before agreeing to Dom's terms. Dom shook out his arms out and started cracking his neck from side to side, like he was gearing up for a fight. Dear God, what is he about to say?

"My dad managed to convince Lachlan to have a meeting, just the two of them. When dad got back, he said that the vampires' terms for Ryan return were simple—"

I cut Dom off, needing to know what we had to do in order to get my wife back. "What are the terms? What are you waiting for?"

"Randall wants Kai in exchange for Ryan."

Fuck me!

"Melakai is prepared to make the exchange." I snapped my gaze to Jackson in shock. *What the actual fuck?*

"Why, why would Kai do that?"

"Because he loves her, and he knows what she means to you." I couldn't ask this of my friend. No—not friend. Melakai was my brother. I couldn't trade his life for another; he had nearly given his life for Ryan before. What the fuck am I going to do?

"The elders need to lift the fucking ban on me not returning to the Earth realm. I need to see Kai."

Jax glared at me. "Kai wanted to come with us today and tell you himself, but the fucking portal blocked him." *Oh, shit.*

"What Jax is trying to say is why the fuck have you blocked our brother—our best friend—from returning to his home, Nico?

Are you that caught up in your own jealousy? He is trying to fucking help you and Ryan—" I cut Dom off before he could finish his rant. They had a right to know why Kai could never return to his home. They weren't going to like it, but they had to know.

"If he comes back here he will die!" Both of my brothers reeled back in shock.

"The spell Ryan used to bring Kai back wasn't the spell Kai told her to use."

"What the fuck are you saying, Nico?" Jax growled.

"Ryan has been having daydreams of her father, and he told her the spell Kai was going to use wouldn't work. She used the spell her father gave her, and that spell cancelled out his fae blood." Both of my brothers looked confused.

"So?"

"So, Jax what that means is—"

Dom cut in before I could finish. "Melakai is full vampire now."

"So? You and the elders cast the spell on Farrarie to burn any vamp aside from Kai." Jax wasn't getting what I was saying.

"The spell cancelled out his fae side, which meant the only blood that remained was vampire blood. Kai was turned by Randall Cane. I blocked Kai from entering Farrarie so he wouldn't die." Jax still looked confused, but Dom got it, and by the look on his face he was fucking livid.

One second I was sitting on the couch, next thing I knew I was sailing across the room and pinned to the wall behind my desk. Dom was glowing; his eyes changed to the color of his wolf, gray eyes that were glaring daggers at me. Jax sat there in shock.

"Your fucking wife tricked him! You fucking bastard! Do you have any idea what this news is going to do to him?" Dom raised his arm, and with a flick of his wrist, I was sent sailing into the corner of the room and hit the wall with enough force to rattle my bones. This is an old castle, so the wall I hit was three-foot-thick stone. Fuck, it hurt.

I didn't get a chance to recover because Dom used his magic to lift me from the ground and pinned me against the wall. I was done taking his shit. *My turn to play, brother.* I let my magic build and felt the heat of it in my veins. With a roar, I released a blast of my magic, the hold Dom had on me broke, and the blast sent everything in the room sailing. Dom was fast to act and quickly erected a shield around him and Jackson so they weren't hit by anything in the blast.

I wasn't done yet. I gathered more magic in my hand, making a purple energy ball, and threw it straight at Dom's shield, shattering it. I didn't give him a chance to retaliate, immediately lobbing another energy ball at him and sending him sailing through the window.

Hearing the glass shatter and seeing him fly through the window made me feel better. The next time that bastard wanted to fight, he better be prepared.

"Are you fucking crazy? He could be seriously hurt, Nico." I didn't give a fuck about Jackson's anger. That asshole insulted my wife and tried to best me.

"He needs to learn that this is my fucking realm. He may not have been born here, but as a fae himself, he should know better than to ever challenge the fucking king!" As soon as I finished putting Jackson in his place, a huge yellow orb appeared through the shattered window. The yellow orb stopped a few feet away from me then popped, and Dom stood before me.

Well, fuck me. That was a neat trick. I had never seen him do that before. Dom scowled at me. He was vibrating with anger, fists clenched at his sides.

"The next fucking time you throw me out a window, dick

face, I will fucking end you! I won't hold back next time, Nico. You may be the fucking king of this realm, but you are not my fucking king!" Maybe I did go a bit far by throwing him out of the window.

"Don't ever fucking talk about my *wife* like that again, and I won't throw you out a fucking window."

"Take it down a notch, boys." We spun toward the door to see my sister strolling into the room. She was dressed the same way she did before she was taken: jeans and a crop top, with Chucks. She surveyed the damage and turned to the three of us, glaring.

"I had nothing to do with this, Soph." Fucking Jax, the brown nose kiss-ass, was nudging his head to Dom and me.

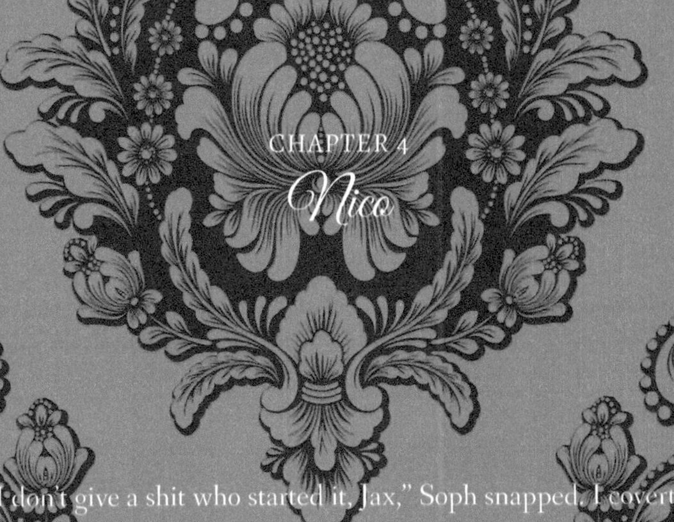

CHAPTER 4
Nico

"I don't give a shit who started it, Jax," Soph snapped. I covertly gave Jax a smirk.

Sophia walked further into the room and started whispering under her breath.

A moment later, everything in the study was returned to how it was before the incident—even the window was fixed!

I stared at my sister in shock.

"Little dove, how did you just do that?" Dom took the words right out of my mouth.

"Wouldn't you like to know? I don't have time for this shit. I just received word from Larick; he is escorting Aurora to the castle now." *What the hell is she doing here?*

I wasn't the only one in the dark. "Why is Aurora here, Soph?"

"I have no idea, Jax, but she should be here shortly."

Sure enough, twenty minutes later there was a knock on my study door and both Larick and Aurora walked in. Aurora's gaze landed on Jax straight away, and he immediately started scenting the air. *Fuck, the spell is wearing off way too soon, and Jax was going to lose his shit and claim her if I don't get a new one laid down immediately.*

Dom went for the proactive approach. "Jax, are you going to be okay?" Jax turned to Dom and started growling, and Dom immediately backed away from Jax with his hands in the air.

Jax viewed Dom as a threat because he was a wolf.

Aurora quickly made her way over to Jax and placed her hand on his chest.

"I'm right here with you, Jax. Look at me." Jax reluctantly pulled his gaze from Dom back to Aurora. After a beat, he started to calm.

"Right, well, that shit is starting to get awkward as fuck. Soon as this shit is over, you both need to either except the mate bond or fuck it out of your system." *Fucking Dominic, that bastard needed to learn how to filter his fucking thoughts.*

Soph apparently agreed. "Dear God, you really need help with that mouth of yours." Dom turned his gaze to my sister.

"Are you volunteering to teach me, little dove?" Sophia sneered at Dom but didn't answer him. *I was going to get to the bottom of this shit between Soph and Dom one day very soon.*

"Could we all have a seat, please? I need to tell you all something."

We all did as we were instructed and sat down. "Melakai went to make the exchange..." My stomach dropped. *Kai, you fucking idiot!*

"We have to get him back!"

"Let me finish, Dom. When Kai got there, he could tell something wasn't right. They brought Ryan in with a bag over her head." My anger skyrocketed. *How fucking dare they do that to her!*

"Dom's dad halted the exchange. He said that the scent of the prisoner the vampires brought didn't match Ryan's."

"Who was it?" I had a feeling I knew the answer to this question.

"It was Ryan's mother, Jax." *I fucking knew it.*

"What happened after that?"

"Mr. Silver demanded that Nina Knox be released into the care of the shifter elders. Randall tried to play it off like it was a mistake. Kai was supposed to make the exchange alone, but Dom's dad wouldn't allow it, thank God. The elders granted the shifters care of Nina."

"I don't give a fuck about Nina Knox. Where is Ryan, Aurora?"

"I don't know, Nico."

"You're a fucking seer, how can you not know?" Aurora flinched at my harsh tone.

"Calm the fuck down, Nico!" Jax was right, I shouldn't be taking my anger out on her; she has been trying for weeks to pinpoint Ryan's location. Everyone has been trying their best to find my girl since she was taken. I was going out of my mind with worry. I detested not having control.

"We'll get her back, brother." Sophia's words didn't reassure me. She couldn't know that for certain, and God knows we hadn't made a bit of progress in these long weeks.

"There's something else." I looked to Aurora and could see she was torn about whether or not she should tell me.

"Please, Aurora, I need to know everything." I begged. She took a deep breath and sat up straight.

"I did have a vision just before I got here. I saw my brother." Jax started growling at the mention of his former beta. Aurora's brother had mated with Ryan's sister, poor bastard.

"What else did you see, love?" Dom asked.

"I saw Tyler making plans to break Ryan out while Randall and Stevie were distracted with the elders. I don't think they ever planned to trade Ryan; I think it was always going to be Nina. I also saw that Randall and Stevie can't locate the main portal to Farrarie to seal off this realm." I was shocked, hearing Aurora's confession. I never expected Tyler to go against his mate; I just hoped that he succeeded in his plans to get Ryan out.

Now I knew why they haven't made Ryan close the portal that stabilizes my world—they couldn't find it. I congratulated myself for my foresight on this; I had set up many decoy portals across the world over the years. The real portal was hidden in Alaska and very few knew of its location.

"That's good news; if your brother succeeds, then Ryan will be free. Better still, those fuckers have no idea where the real portal is." Dom's excitement was contagious. The others were smiling, and for the first time in weeks, I had hope.

"We still need to keep guards stationed at the portal; I won't rest until Ryan is returned and the threat against my realm has been eliminated." Since being back in my realm, I have been training each morning with my men, and Larick and Maverick have been meeting with me each afternoon to go over battle strategies. We have also been planning for worst case scenarios, in case they did find the portal.

"I need you guys to help me convince the elders to remove

the ban on me returning to the Earth realm." Dom started grinning from ear to ear. "Why are you smiling like that Dominic?"

"Did we forget to mention that when we got here?" I started growling low in my throat. "My dad got the elders to remove the ban on you returning to the Earth realm. There are terms, though, Nico." *Aren't there always?*

"What are the terms, Dom?" I snapped.

"You are to be confined to Jackson's compound, and you cannot, under any circumstances, go after Randall or Stevie." I didn't like the terms, but I agreed all the same. I would agree to anything as long as it got me closer to my wife.

"There is one other thing." I looked to Jax, waiting for him to elaborate. "Ryan's cousins are gone."

"Where the hell have they gone?"

"I don't know, Nico. They were at the compound two days ago and then they vanished." *What the actual fuck? Where the hell could they have gone? And why?*

We have been driving for hours, the daylight fading to darkness. My ass is numb from sitting for so long. Lucian has slept the entire time. I have no idea where we are going, or if Tyler is even telling the truth. Why would he help me? That's the one question that has been burning a hole in my mind the whole time we have been in the car. "Are you hungry?" It's the first time Tyler's spoken since we left Randall's mansion. My stomach grumbles before I can even answer. "I'll take that as a yes. We're nearly there."

"Nearly where?" I noticed that the pain from my arm and ribs has subsided a little bit, which is a bit alarming. "Why am I not hurting so much now?"

"To the airfield. While you were unconscious this morning, I came down and injected you with vampire blood." What the actual fuck? How did he get vampire blood, and why were we going to an airfield?

"If you're planning on killing me, at least let Lucian go. He's innocent and hasn't done anything wrong." Tyler's gaze met mine in the rearview mirror, a look of remorse on his face. I won't be fooled into trusting him; he betrayed us before. I am grateful for him giving me the blood, though; my arm and ribs were killing me this morning,

"I'm not going to kill you Ryan; I'm trying to help you. If I was going to kill you I wouldn't have given you the blood to help you heal." Smug prick, I still needed to know why he was helping us.

"Help me how?"

Tyler let out a long sigh before answering.

"By taking you to someone who can help you control your magic. My sister's visions are not always correct." Wait, what? As far as I knew, Aurora's visions were always accurate.

A short time later, Tyler turned down a dark, uneven road, and I started to question whether he was telling the truth about not wanting to kill me.

Lucian was leaning against the door, with his head resting against the window. I hadn't been able to see Lucian's features before, as we were held captive in complete darkness. Looking at him now, I could see he was painfully thin and dirty. I don't even know if he had ever showered; I know I smelled like I hadn't showered in years. Lucian had his hair piled on top of his head, from what I could see in the dim light of the car, it looked silver, with black streaks running through it.

Lucian sat up so fast I jumped back and bumped into the door. It's a strange feeling—he was my comfort when we were locked up, but now, I felt....unsure. We didn't really know each other. Was I being stupid by trusting him?

He whipped his head from side to side. Seeing how tense and unsure he was, I remembered he'd spent all but a few moments inside that dungeon, and knew immediately that Lucian needed me.

"Shhhh, it's okay Luce." He stopped whipping his head from side to side and turned toward me. I still couldn't see his facial features in the car's dim lighting.

"Smurfy, where the hell are we? Why are we moving like this?" Oh my God, Lucian was freaking out because we were in a car! I reached across blindly, feeling for his hand, and as soon as I touched his hand, he gripped onto mine for dear life.

"We're heading to an airfield, we're in a car. A car is something people use to get them somewhere faster." I felt like an idiot explaining what a car was, but Lucian was like a toddler. Everything was new to him.

"Okay...what's an airfield? Tyler saved me from answering Lucian's question.

"It's a place where planes land and take off; a plane is something that lets you fly through the air. You're about to see for yourself, we just arrived."

I looked out my window, and sure enough, there was a small plane sitting in the middle of a vacant field. The only lighting was the lights on board the small plane.

Tyler drove us right up to the steps that descended from the aircraft. I gripped Lucian's hand tighter; I was scared of the unknown, and where the hell was Tyler taking us?

"Tyler, I don't want to get on that plane." I could hear the fear in my own voice.

"I figured you would say something like that, that's why I brought them." I looked out my window again toward where Tyler was pointing, and that's when I saw them. I released Lucian's hand and threw my door open, leaping from the car like it was on fire and running up the stairs. I was lifted off my feet and embraced in the best hug ever.

"God, it is so good to see you, squirt." Being in Alex's arms never felt better; I was almost immediately tugged away from Alex to be bear-hugged by Chase.

"You have no idea how worried we have been."

Tears leaked out of my eyes; once they started, I couldn't

stop them. Horrible sobs wrecked my body, and I clung to Chase, afraid if I let go, he would disappear.

"I...I...missed...you, I thou-thought y-you l-left m-me." Chase squeezed me tighter.

"We would never leave you, Ry; we have been trying to get you back for weeks." Hearing that they didn't give up on me meant more than they would ever know. A throat clearing behind us interrupted my sob fest; I quickly pulled away from Chase and wiped away my tears as best as I could. Once I had myself under control, I turned around on the stairs and faced Tyler, who had a scared-looking Lucian standing next to him.

I made my way down to them and stood directly in front of Lucian. The lighting still wasn't good, so I couldn't see the color of his eyes, but I could tell Lucian was at least six feet tall. He stood there, tense and staring down at me; he needed me to help him find his way in this new world.

"Thank you for keeping me alive. I owe you my life, Lucian." I heard my cousins gasp behind me. "I promise you, I will never leave you. I will help you find your way in this world and make sure you are cared for and loved."

Lucian placed both his hands on my shoulders. He may only be sixteen, but his next words were those of a grown man.

"I pledge my allegiance and life to you, Smurf. I was giving up hope when you arrived. You have my loyalty from now and until the end of my days." I couldn't talk past the lump in my throat, so I pulled him in for the most awkward hug ever. Lucian clearly had no idea what a hug was or how to even return the gesture, so he stood there, arms raised, until I started to giggle.

We were all seated on the plane with our belts fastened; Lucian was sitting next to me, gripping my hand. I turned to look at him and gasped. Now that we were able to see, thanks to the lights in the cabin, I finally got to look upon his handsome face and saw his unusual eyes. They're violet, with a gray ring around the pupils. He had a ring just like mine! He had the sculpted cheek-bones of a magazine model and a perfect straight nose. He appeared to have a similar skin tone as Dom, but I couldn't be sure with the amount of dirt caked on him. Lucian looked down at me and smiled. His teeth were beautiful and straight, and even more strange was the fact that they were gleaming white, I am quite sure he didn't brush his teeth every day.

"We're about to take off. Captain is just loading the last of the bags." I turned away from Lucian to look at Tyler, who had just taken the seat opposite us. He looked so tired and thin. What he did for me today, I could never repay. He went against his own mate to save *me*.

"Thank you, Tyler." He turned to look at me but quickly turned away, staring out the plane window. I knew why he couldn't stand to look at me.

"Thank you for helping me when you didn't have to." I heard Tyler snort from beside me; I turned to glare at him.

"Was something Lucian said funny, Tyler?" Without turning to look at me, he answered.

"Yeah, actually. I knew there was no way in hell you would leave willingly without the trifecta."

"What is a tri-trifecta?" I turned back to Lucian, I had no idea what the hell a trifecta even is. I was saved from answering when the plane started to move.

Lucian gasped and yelled, "What's happening? Why are we moving?"

"It's okay, mate. The plane needs to move in order for us to gain enough speed on the ground so we can launch into the air to fly." My heart swelled at how kind Alex was being toward Lucian. He didn't talk to him like he was a stupid kid but rather with respect . I looked at Chase, who had a look of pure fury on his face.

"Chase, what's wrong?" I asked.

"I swear to fucking God, we are going to kill that fucking leech king for what he has done to you, Ryan. We are also going to fucking torture him first for what he has done to Lucian. I swear to you, bro, Alex and I will make sure you know everything you need to know about the world, we will also make it our mission to help you find out what kind of supernatural you are."

I loved my cousins so much. I told them briefly about how Lucian grew up when we first boarded the plane, they were pissed to hear how he has been a prisoner his whole life. I knew Alex and Chase would help Lucian as much as they could.

"Can I ask you something, Lucian?"

"Yes, Master Chase." Chase glared at Lucian; to Lucian's credit, he didn't flinch.

"Don't ever call me master! You are not a fucking slave!

You're free now, Lucian, don't ever submit to anyone again." I smiled at my cousin. I was so proud of his protectiveness. Lucian nodded his head.

"Okay. thank you, Chase." Chase smiled at Lucian in return.

"So, my question was, why do you call Ryan 'Smurfy?'" I groaned. They are going to fucking mock me about this.

"Because she told me her powers are blue. The lady who raised me told me stories about the blue people called Smurfs." Chase and Alex started laughing so hard that they were both clutching their stomachs; I even saw Tyler's shoulders shaking from the corner of my eye.

Fuck. My. Life.

After a few hours of catching up with my cousins and hearing what they and the *others* had been planning, yes—I was calling them the "others" because I was still salty as fuck that they hadn't come to my rescue.

I was shocked to learn that Nico had been banished back to Farrarie and wasn't allowed back to the Earth realm until the council deemed it was okay.

"We're about to land."

"Land where, exactly, Tyler?" Tyler still wouldn't look at me, and my heart hurt for him. I wish I could comfort him but my appearance just made everything worse.

"Look, I wish I could tell you, but I can't." What the actual fu—. Alex cut off my thought.

"We have been spelled, squirt. We literally cannot tell you. All we can say is that where we are going is the best place for you." I was too exhausted to fight them or try to pry information from them.

After we landed, we all disembarked the aircraft and collected our bags. My cousins took my bags from Jax's compound for me. We didn't go through any security or customs, which I found strange but didn't comment on.

We walked along the tarmac for a few minutes and toward an aircraft hanger, and entered through a side door. Waiting inside was a big SUV. Tyler clicked the key fob in his hand and the car beeped. We loaded our bags in the back and then climbed inside. I was in the backseat, sitting between Chase and Lucian, while Alex rode shotgun and Tyler drove.

After being in the car for roughly four hours, Tyler pulled off the highway and took us to a McDonalds drive-thru. Lucian's eyes lit up at seeing the fast food restaurant. I had to explain to him how it all worked and how to order food from the menu. Lucian couldn't decide what to order, so Chase ordered for him, and after collecting our food, Tyler continued to drive us onto our destination.

"Oh my God, this is so good." I chuckled at Lucian's facial expressions. He was biting from random items and moaning and exclaiming in delight in between. Chase ordered him two Big Mac combos, four cheeseburgers, twenty-four nuggets, and three different flavors of thick shakes. Lucian was in food heaven.

After eating the best food I have had in weeks, and finally feeling full, I relaxed back into my seat. My eyes kept drifting shut, and I didn't fight the pull of sleep anymore; I let it lull me into a dreamless slumber.

CHAPTER 7
Nico

Jackson's compound felt cold and empty without Ryan here. I stood in the room she had been staying in, and noticed all her belongings were gone. Did Jackson move them? Did some low life steal her stuff?

A knock on the door pulled me from my thoughts; I turned around to see Melakai standing in the open doorway.

Kai looked the same physically, but I could see in his gray-blue eyes that a war was going on inside him. He ran his hand through his blond hair, making it stick up haphazardly. We stood there staring at each other for a long while, neither of us saying anything. We used to be so fucking close; he was my right hand man growing up, but now it felt like we were worlds apart.

Kai entered the room and closed the door behind him; I sat on the single chair by the window while Kai leaned against the far wall with his arms crossed over his chest.

"Are you going to tell me why I'm blocked from entering the portal?" I could hear the hurt lacing his tone, and I felt a flash of anger at Ryan for leaving me to explain this to Kai. He is going to go ape-shit, and I don't blame him.

"I did it to protect you." He scoffed and rolled his eyes.

"Don't fucking bullshit me, Nico, am I banned because you're angry at me?"

"No." I said, shaking my head.

"Because you're pissed that I'm still a vamp?"

"No."

"Okay, is it because I fucked your wife?" Son of a fucking bitch, I jumped to my feet, shocked to find that Kai and I were nearly nose to nose, I didn't hear him move. "Why am I fucking locked out of my home, Nico?" Kai was yelling in my face.

"I can't—"

"You fucking spineless prick, answer me!"

"I...I..." How do I tell him that my wife betrayed him in the worst possible way?

"Fucking tell him!" Both Kai and I turned our heads toward the doorway to see both Dom and Jax standing there. Taking a deep breath and steeling my spine, I looked Melakai in the eyes and the truth spilled out.

"Ryan changed the spell that brought you back. She wiped all your fae blood out so you would be full vamp. Which means only Randall's blood remains inside you, so if I let you into Farrarie, you will die."

Kai's face changed. There was no look of anger or sadness... just acceptance. My heart broke; I would have rather him be angry and lash out than just accept what was done to him. I loved Ryan and missed her so much, but right now I was so pissed at her for doing this to my brother.

"Why?"

"Why what, Kai?"

"Why did she change the spell?" he gritted out through clenched teeth, his tone was flat and emotionless.

"Because the spell you wanted her to use wouldn't have worked. Her father told her to change the spell in a dream; he said that you needed to be king of the vampires, and this way, being Randall's blood heir, no one can contest your claim to the throne." Jax and Dom haven't said a word—the one time Dom chooses to stay quiet is the one time I wish he wouldn't. I see the moment it all sinks in: his eyes mist and I have never seen such a broken look grace Kai's face before, not even when he was turned into a vampire. I place my hand on his shoulder to try and comfort him, but he shucked it off and retreated back to the other side of the room, sliding down the wall, cupping his face between his hands.

I have never felt like a worthless piece of shit more than I do now; I have not only shattered his dream of returning home but also taking away any hope he had of ever being returned to his true form.

"Melakai, brother we are all here with you, no matter what." Dom was trying to comfort Kai.

"You will always have a home here, with me and the wolves." Dom glared at Jax. The last thing Kai wanted was to be told he could live here when all he wanted for decades was to return to the fae realm and be among his people again instead of being the "day walking leech."

"I will find a way to fix this brother, I swear. I will not return to Farrarie until you are able to as well."

What the fuck is Dom saying? He couldn't make that kind of promise. "Dominic..."

Dom turned to glare at me, his eyes flashing to the gray of his wolf's.

"You do not get to speak right now. You may not have been the one to do this to him, but you will still bear some of the blame." I hung my head in shame. He was right. If I hadn't skirted around the truth so much with Ryan, she might have come to me and asked for help.

"Lift the spell on Farrarie, Nico, so he can go back."

I wish it was that simple. "I can't Jackson. I wish I could."

"What the fuck does that mean?" Jax snapped.

"It means that when he cast the spell he drew on the power of the elders and the power of the harvest moon. The elders may be the strongest of our kinds, but that spell cost the elders a great deal of power. It took them years to recover."

"Can Ryan do it? She is supposed to be the most powerful supe." That was an intriguing thought; Jackson might be onto something.

"She could. She would need someone to balance her, though." Ryan would need someone to stabilize her power in order for her to remove the spell. If she were to do it on her own, it could kill her.

"Why can't you do it?"

"I can't do it, Jax; the power inside me that is linked to Ryan has to be returned so she is at full strength. I hate to admit it, but I'm not strong enough on my own to stabilize her." I was ashamed to admit that out loud, even to my brothers.

"I'll do it." I turned to look at Dom, shocked. He wasn't strong enough either, to hold that amount of power back from consuming Ryan.

Before we could debate more, there was a knock on the open door, and Lucas, one of Jackson's pack members, stood there.

"What is it, Lucas?" Jax asked.

"The elders have requested your presence in the mess hall, Alpha. All of you. The vampire and witch elders are here, as well."

What the fuck was going on? Why were the elders here?

CHAPTER 8

When I woke from a dreamless sleep sometime later, the sun was up and it was a glorious day. I looked either side of me and saw that Lucian and Chase were both still asleep. Looking to the front of the car, I saw that Alex was now driving and Tyler was sleeping soundly in the passenger seat. Yawning and stretching my arms over my head as best I could in the cramped space, I cringed. I really needed to pee. I always had to go as soon as I awoke.

"Alex, I really need to pee," I whined. I met his eyes in the rearview mirror, and he looked exhausted. How long had he been driving?

"Okay, Squirt, I'll stop at the next gas station." I hoped that wasn't to far, because my bladder was about to burst.

Twenty minutes later, I was bouncing my knee and gritting my teeth.

"Alex just pull over, I need to go now!" Alex grumbled about tiny bladders, but did as I asked and pulled over near some bushes and trees. It feels like we're in the middle of nowhere, no other cars or housing to be seen. Alex hopped out of the car so I could crawl over the center console, not wanting to wake Chase or Lucian to get out.

As soon as my feet hit the pavement, I ran behind the bushes and quickly went about my business, sighing at the instant relief.

After finishing, I made my way back to the car, only to notice the others were awake and standing outside the car, stretching.

"You are such a lady, peeing in a bush and all," Chase said, chuckling.

"She's probably the first queen to ever pop a squat in the bush." At Tyler's comment, all four of the guys started laughing, and my cheeks flamed red. I was going to beat the shit out of Tyler one day—very soon, hopefully.

"Well, some of us can't turn into a wolf and cock our leg to pee!" I snapped at Tyler, which only made them laugh harder. Gritting my teeth, I stomped back to the SUV, shoulder checking Tyler on my way past. The fucker just laughed.

We drove a couple more hours before we stopped at a local convenience store to grab some junk food for our breakfast. Tyler had a fast metabolism due to being a wolf, so he had to eat often. My left butt cheek was numb, and I was getting restless sitting in the car for so long. The confined space of the vehicle only emphasized how bad Lucian and I reeked from not showering. The smell had to be worse for Tyler, with his enhanced senses, but he didn't comment on it. He just kept his window down so he got fresh air.

"How much further, Alex?" I whined.

"Squirt, you have asked me that like ten times in the past three hours. It's a nineteen hour drive from Toronto to where we are going. We had to take the long way in case your husband and his band of misfits tried to follow us." Hearing Alex call the others misfits stung a bit; I was pissed at them, but they were good people. They were my only friends, and I cared about them.

"Just so you will shut up, we have like two more hours and then we'll be there!" I poked my tongue out at Tyler, but I was glad to have a time frame. He still didn't need to be a dick about it.

Upon entering the mess hall with my three brothers, we stopped in the entryway. I haven't seen all the elders together like this since my crowning as king.

"Boy's come join us." Looking to Mr. Silver, who was nodding toward four vacant chairs that were front and center. I released the breath I was holding and made my way over. We sat down and looked to the elders, waiting.

They all wore their traditional black cloaks, most of them with their hoods up except for the main elders. Mr. Silver was the main elder for the shifters. Jax, Kai, and I were all on the elder council but we weren't the leaders; we were given a seat among them but the truth was our votes didn't mean shit. Dom wasn't on the elder council because he wouldn't choose which race he wanted to represent. Dom may be a shifter and fae, but his powers were a cross between warlock and fae. Dom was an anomaly, just like Ryan. I have no idea how he is able to cast and wield magic like a warlock but still open portals and manipulate the elements like a fae.

Lachlan stood in front of the vampire elders with his hood

down, Standing in front of the witches was Ryan's Uncle David, Chase and Alex's father.

I felt a pang in my chest when I turned my gaze to the fae elders, knowing that Gabriel wouldn't be among them.

He died in the blast at the chapel the night of my wedding. Victor now led the fae elders, and he was a power-hungry son-of-a-bitch. I noticed the witches weren't wearing the moon stones they had on the night of my wedding. Interesting.

"Why aren't Stevie Knox and Randall Cane here?" Jax asked the elders.

"We'll explain that shortly, son. We need to ask you boys a few things first." All four of us nodded our heads at Mr. Silver. "Lachlan, did you want to fill the boys in or should I?" I still found it comical how Mr. Silver called us boys; I am 104 years old. Kai and Dom are both 102 and Jax is the youngest at age 98. We weren't boys anymore.

"I will tell them," Lachlan said, nodding his head to Mr. Silver. "The reason we are here without the queen of the Knox coven and the king of the vampires is because we believe there is more to this story than they have shared. As you can see, the number of elders here are less than normal. Some died at your wedding and some cannot be trusted." I looked over the number of elders and was shocked that Lachlan was right—over half were missing. The elder council was made up of thirteen members for each clan, the vamps had six, the witches had nine, the shifters had ten and the fae had eight elders present.

"What do you mean *can't be trusted?*"

"What we have to say, young alpha, could cost us our lives. The queen and king believe we are here to bargain with you." What the fuck? I saw Kai tense next to me.

"We are not trading our brother!" Dom growled.

"Son!" Mr. Silver snapped at Dom.

"Nah, Dad, fuck that! We are not trading Kai for Ryan.

Has he not suffered enough for her? We were lucky they tried to screw us over with Nina; if not, Kai would be dead, or worse!"

"Watch your language Dominic!" To Dom's credit, he didn't shy away or flinch at his father's alpha tone; he just sat there glaring at his father. I had to break the tension in the room—the way Dom was looking at his father and holding eye contact for so long would be seen as a challenge for the alpha of the New York pack.

"Okay, let us speak like grown folk. Dom, calm down, we are not trading Kai." I looked directly at Lachlan when I spoke.

"Correct, we do not plan to take Randall's heir from you. We told them we had come here to try and convince you to trade the location of the portal for your wife." Kai growled low in his throat at the mention of being Randall's heir.

The only elder that knew of the real portal's location was Gabriel. Something felt off with Victor and Lachlan. I couldn't explain the feeling, but I just knew in my gut I couldn't trust them with the location.

"We have come to try and help you."

"Help us how?" Jax asked the vampire elder. I noticed Jax kept scenting the air; he was trying to pick up on any lies.

"To help you stop the coven queen and vampire king. We, as elder members, have sat back too long and let them get away with too much. We learned a lot about our king recently. We still do not have proof that he is indeed trying to seal the portal to your realm. We also have no proof as of yet that Stevie Knox is trying to help him do it, either."

"Well, if you have no fucking proof, why the hell are you here, then? We gave you all the proof we had! They openly admitted it to us; Stevie Knox has even said herself that she wants all fae dead and blames them for her father's death, when in fact she killed Ralph Knox!" Jackson was vibrating with anger. He was right—we had told all the elders this before and none of them believed us.

"How the hell do you know she killed my brother?" David Knox was glowing purple; I forgot we only told the shifter, fae, and vampire elders about Stevie killing her father.

"She told us. Well, she told Ryan, but we were all there and heard it."

"What exactly did she say, boy?" David snapped at Jax, who started growling.

"Ian Silver may get away with calling us boys, but you will not! I am the fucking alpha of all alphas, and you will show me some fucking respect while you are on my land!" Holy shit, I have never seen Jackson so alpha-ed out before. David Knox bowed his head.

"Forgive me, alpha. As you can imagine, I was told that the fae had murdered my brother, and now I find out it was my niece." David hung his head in sorrow. Ralph Knox was his only sibling, and he had known Stevie her entire life.

"I can assure you, Mr. Knox, my people and I had nothing to do with your brother's death. Ralph Knox was a good man. I would never have hurt him in any way." David nodded his head but didn't comment.

"We don't have time for this, I'm sorry—" Dom cut Lachlan off.

"Where are your sons, Mr. Knox?" I hadn't even thought to ask the coven elder that, go Dom for being on point. David tensed at the mention of his sons.

"I-I don't know." I didn't believe him for one second.

"Lie!" Jackson growled, and David snapped his gaze to Jax. "I can hear your heartbeat. It skips a beat when you lie. I can also scent a lie, so do you wanna try that answer again?"

"He can't tell you, Alpha. He has been spelled to secrecy. We are here because we believe that David being spelled and not able to disclose his son's location is because they are with Ryan." *What the actual fuck?*

"What do you mean?" I ground out.

"I'm sorry to have to be the one to tell you, your majesty, but your wife is no longer in the care of the vampire elders."

"Oh, shit!" Yeah, you could say that again Dominic.

CHAPTER 10

Ryan

Finally, after so many hours traveling, we arrived at our destination. We drove down a long gravel driveway, lined with huge pine trees on either side. After a few minutes, we came around another bend and a massive—I mean *massive*—log cabin came into view. It was at least three stories and looked well-tended. It had huge log pillars and broad windows that would allow you to see the beautiful view, with an A-frame roof that allowed for plenty of shade.

If this house looked this good on the outside, I couldn't wait to see the inside.

"Where are we?" I whispered.

"Welcome to the Yukon, Ry." I had no idea where Yukon is, but I would live here if I could have this cabin.

Alex finally stopped the SUV in front of the stairs that lead up to the porch, and we all shuffled out of the car. I looked to the side and noticed a six-car garage situated behind the house. Who the hell needed six cars?

I turned to look back the way we came and all I could see was trees and mountains. This place was freaking beautiful; the air was so crisp and clean, the sun was shining down on us, and even though there was a chill in the air, I was just grateful to be outside and free.

I heard a throat clearing behind me and turned. Standing on the top of the steps was an elderly man and woman. When the woman's gaze landed on me, her hand came up and covered her mouth. She was shocked? Who the hell are these people?

Alex and Chase both dashed up the stairs and embraced the man and woman, happy sounds coming from both pairs.

The old man looked familiar. He was tall, but not as tall as my cousins. He had salt and pepper hair that was slicked back, with high cheekbones and a straight but narrow nose. He wore a flannel shirt with dark blue jeans that matched his eyes.

The woman next to him was petite; she only came up to the man's chest. She had gray curly hair that came down to her shoulders, and she wore a sweater and black leggings with knee-high boots. She had good style for an old lady. I lifted my gaze to her face. She had plump red lips and a small button nose. My gaze met hers and I gasped—they were a deep green. I stumbled back and smacked into something or someone. I turned to peer over my shoulder and saw it was Lucian I stumbled into. I quickly turned back toward the porch to see both my cousins standing behind the man and lady, the man and woman were both staring straight at me. The woman had tears trailing down her face, but the man looked unfazed.

"Smurfy, are you okay?"

"I-I think so," I answered Lucian.

"Who are they, Smurf?" I didn't know how to answer that. I am pretty sure I know who the man and woman are, but I didn't want to say it out loud and be wrong.

"Come here, child," the old man said.

Lucian came around beside me and gripped my hand, leading me to the bottom of the steps. I craned my neck back and looked up.

"She looks just like him, Marcus," the old lady said with a warble in her voice. As soon as she said his name, I knew I was right. I steeled my spine and looked at the man.

"Hi, I'm Ryan. I believe you are Marcus and Bethany Knox, my grandparents, who I thought were dead."

Bethany dropped her hand from her mouth and made her way down to me. She cupped my face between both her hands and leaned forward till she was resting her forehead against mine.

"I have been waiting a long time to finally meet you, my dear. I am so sorry for all of the secrecy, but we couldn't afford for anyone to find out that I am alive."

"What do you mean?" I asked.

"We had to run and hide so you would live. I am a seer, Ryan, and so was your father."

I clenched and unclenched my fist so many times to try and quiet the anger inside of me. Where the fuck was Ryan?

"What happened?" I growled.

"The day that Randall and Stevie went to trade Nina for Melakai was the day Ryan escaped." That was nearly three days ago. "Randall and Stevie have been trying to find her ever since."

"How did she escape, Lachlan?" Dom asked.

"We believe Tyler Evans helped her escape." I clutched my head between my hands. Where is she? Why didn't she come back to me?

"Why do I feel like we are missing something?"

I turned and looked at Kai. This is the first time he has spoken since we began this meeting. Lachlan sighed, and David, Victor, and Mr. Silver all shared a look with each other before Victor answered.

"Stevie and Randall found all the decoy portals. They are closing in on the location of the real one."

"That doesn't matter, though, if they don't have Ryan, right? They can't close it without her."

"We don't know. With the new power the Knox witch now wields, we are unsure. If she does find the portal, she may not have the power to close it, but she does have the power to poison our world." Victor was right; Stevie didn't need to enter my world to kill it. She could stand on this side of the portal and rain hell on my kingdom.

"Shit, okay. If Stevie does find the portal, how long do we have before our world is beyond saving?" I asked Victor.

"I estimate they will find the location of the portal in the next two or three months, sire. They have been relentless in their search. She could kill our world within a month or two of finding it."

"Okay so what you're saying, Vic, is that we have about five to six months, tops, to try stop these fuckers and then find Ryan and train her to kill her sister. Is there anything else?"

The way Dom put it made it sound so fucked up. We didn't have much time at all. I need to try and find a way to stop Randall; if we can take Randall out, then Kai will rule the vamps, and that would leave Stevie on her own. All Ryan would need to do is take the coven back and then get rid of her sister. I wouldn't let my world die no matter what.

"Maybe if you could tell us where the portal is we could help you?" I gazed up at Victor, who wore an unreadable expression. I turned to look at my brother's; each of them had a look in their eyes telling me not to do it.

"If the time comes for you to need to know the location, then I will tell you." Victor seemed annoyed at my response but quickly masked the look on his face.

"Why aren't you wearing the moonstones?" Jax asked David.

"The moonstones have been returned to where they belong. There is no need to worry about them, Alpha." David's answer felt like it had a double meaning.

The four of us and the elders sat for hours, making plans. Get Ryan back, kill Randall, and then destroy Stevie.

I thought it was a bloody good plan, but the hardest part was trying to find Ryan.

The witches had tried doing a location spell already; it was like she had fallen off the face of the Earth. My stomach sunk; what if Tyler killed her? My stomach was in knots with worry. She was finally mine, and now I may have lost her forever.

Ryan

After my grandma dropped her bomb, we all made our way inside the cabin. Tyler had yet to say a word but simply trailed inside behind the rest of us. As soon as we entered the cabin, I gasped. I was right, it was just as beautiful inside as it was outside. There were antlers and huge timber beams, and gorgeous indigenous blankets hanging on the wall. I saw a sitting room to the left and stairs that led upstairs, but we didn't get a chance to stop or look at any of the other rooms.

My grandpa led us straight into the kitchen, which was freaking huge. I mean, this is the type of kitchen Gordon Ramsey would have in his house. I stopped looking around and followed the others over to a massive rectangular table that could seat twelve. It looked like someone had carved it from a tree trunk. The chairs were handmade, and no two were the same. The backs of the chairs were tree branches, all interlaced. I took a seat on the opposite side of Chase and Alex, and Lucian sat on my left and Tyler took the seat on my right. I was shocked he would even sit next to me. Grandma and Grandpa sat at each end of the table.

I looked from my grandparents and then to the others and

cringed. Lucian and I were filthy and covered in so much dirt and blood. The blood Tyler had given me may have healed my broken bones, but residual pain remained.

I schooled my features so the others wouldn't know I felt weak; when I had a moment to myself I would inspect my injuries properly.

My Grandpa cleared his throat and then spoke, looking directly at me.

"I know this is all a shock, but we don't have the luxury of time to sit here and hold your hand. Your grandmother has seen what needs to be done in order to save your husband's world. I will train you and so will she—"

I cut Grandpa off, which earned me a scary as fuck glare from the old man. Whoops. "I thought Dom, Aurora and Nico were the only ones who could help me?" Grandpa shook his head.

"No dear, the young seer let you believe that," said Grandma. I turned to Tyler, and the look on his face told me all I needed to know. He knew.

"I don't understand why Aurora would do that," I stated.

"She did what needed to be done. My sister is a powerful seer and knows she cannot *ever* interfere with her visions. She had to lead you to believe that she, Dom, and Nico would train you, when all along she knew you would need to be trained by your grandparents. Dom and Nico are not equipped to help you." It was the first time Tyler had spoken since we arrived. My mind was reeling with this new information.

"She knew Stevie would take me, didn't she?" I looked from Tyler to both my grandparents. They all nodded. I felt so betrayed; she knew what would happen to me at the hands of Randall and Stevie and still let it happen.

"The young seer has much to learn, dear. She was only doing what she thought was best, do not blame her." I looked to my grandmother and got lost in her eyes for a moment. My father got his eyes from her. I felt my tears building, I took a few deep breaths to stop the tears from falling. Lucian clasped my hand under the table and gave me a reassuring squeeze, letting me know he was there for me.

"Did you even go?" Both my grandparents wore looks of confusion.

"Go where, dear?" my grandmother asked.

"To my father's funeral, or did you both hide here?" My grandmother gasped, and my grandfather pounded his fist on the table and leaned forward, scowling at me, I glared back at the old man. Tyler growled low in his throat as a warning to my grandfather. Why the hell was Tyler trying to defend me?

"You may be blood of my blood, but you will not disrespect me or my wife in our home! You have no idea what sacrifices we had to make in order to keep your father alive as long as we did!" I sighed and gave a short nod. He was right, just because I was hurting didn't give me the right to lash out.

"Grandpa, she's been through a lot." I appreciated Chase trying to stick up for me.

"She doesn't need you all handling her with kid gloves. The more you coddle her, the weaker you make her. She needs to fight her own battles; she cannot win this war if you all try and fight it for her."

I got what he was trying to say. I have never been on my own. After Mom disappeared, I went straight to my sister. When I ran from Stevie, I had my cousins and the guys with me.

"She doesn't need to be on her own, sir. I refuse to let her fight on her own. She is not weak! She is so strong. I don't know any of you, but I do know Smurf, and she is stronger than you all think." Tears trailed down my cheeks, and Lucian's sweet words had warmth spreading through my chest. I squeezed his hand in silent thanks for having my back. I saw Grandpa's sly grin out of the corner of my eye. He lifted his gaze to my grandmother.

"You were right once again, Bethy, the boy will balance her." Huh?

"What do you mean, Grandpa?" Alex took the question right out of my mouth.

"Lucian is the *real* key to helping Ryan stay alive in this war."

CHAPTER 13

After Grandpa dropped his cryptic as fuck bomb, he insisted we were all shown to our rooms. On the second floor, there were five rooms. Grandma and Grandpa occupied the third level by themselves. My room was at the end of the hall. Alex and Chase had the rooms on the left, and Tyler and Lucian had the two rooms on the right side of the hallway. My room was stunning, with a king-sized bed in the middle of the room. It wasn't as big as the one I was staying in at Jax's, but this one felt more homey.

There were side drawers on either side of the bed, topped with lamps. My bags sat at the foot of the bed, and I walked past them to peer out the window. The view was gorgeous. All you could see were mountains and trees covered in snow. Yukon was a stunning place.

I moved away from the window to inspect the rest of the room. There are two doors on the other side of the room, I found that one led to a walk-in closet and the other led to my own private bathroom.

I could not wait another second to clean the filth off my body. The tub looked so inviting, but a glance down at myself told me it was best to shower rather than sitting in my own muck. Quickly, I shucked off my clothes and turned to the mirror over the sink.

Underneath the filth that covered my body, I could see countless bruises and cuts. It looked like I had gone five rounds with Mike Tyson. I had two black eyes, my upper lip was split, and I had dried blood on the side of my temple. Vampire blood will keep you from dying but it isn't like traveling back in time. And it definitely doesn't remove the memories.

I shook off the encroaching memories and worked on figuring out the faucet.

Once the steam was billowing inside the shower stall, I finally stepped in and sighed. The water felt amazing cascading down my body; the shower had the perfect amount of pressure.

After a few moments of standing under the spray, my joints and muscles started to relax. After standing there for a solid five minutes, just letting the hot water wash over me, I decided it was time to wash away the grime covering my body. I shampooed my hair twice and conditioned it a couple times. I used the bar soap to scrub my body, then I used the pump soap for one final wash. I found a razor in the shower that looked new, so I used it.

By the time I stepped out of the shower, my hands were prunes and my skin was an angry red, but I was truly clean.

I quickly dried myself then wrapped one towel around my body and used another to wrap my hair.

In my suitcase I found a comfy pair of sweats and my brush. God, did my hair need a good brushing. I couldn't find an acceptably comfortable shirt in my suitcase, so I switched over to the duffel bag. I pulled out the first shirt I found, but I saw what shirt it was, I dropped it to the wooden floor like it burned me.

I stood there staring at the damn shirt like it was going to talk to me or something. It was the black shirt Nico had worn the night he stayed with me in my room, after our dream together.

Taking a deep breath and giving myself a mental pep talk, I quickly bent down and plucked the shirt off the floor. My brain was telling me to chuck the shirt out the window, but my heart was telling me to sniff it and see if it still smelled like him. My heart won, and the shirt still held Nico's faint scent.

My eyes began to water, and then a second later, tears fell in a rush. I crumpled into a heap on the floor, clutching my husband's shirt to chest, wishing he was here with me.

Nico would hold me and tell me everything is going to be okay. He would stand by my side. I missed him so fucking much. I even missed Dom, Jax, and Kai. I missed the girls as well. I wanted to go *home*.

I snapped out of my thoughts when I felt two strong arms come around me and lift me off the floor, I quickly blinked away the tears so I could see who it is, and was surprised at my rescuer.

"W-what a-are y-you doing, Ty?"

"If you're gonna break down, at least do it somewhere comfortable." Tyler placed me on top of my bed then made his way over to my bags. Within a second, a shirt hit me square in the face.

"Put that on, would you." Oh my God, I was practically naked in front of Tyler. I quickly pulled the shirt over my head, while Tyler's back was to me, I slipped the sweat pants on next. I can feel the blush heating my cheeks. Not trusting my voice, I clear my throat to indicate that I am decent.

Ty doesn't face me, but instead he makes his way over to the window and stands there staring out. I see he has showered and changed as well. He looks better than when I first saw him at Randall's.

"You know, when I first met you, I didn't like you." I wish I could say I was shocked. "But as time went on and I got to know you through your sister, I realized that Stevie was the bad twin, not you." Ty hung his head. He still wouldn't turn and face me.

"I betrayed my mate by saving you."

"Why did you do that? Why did you save me?"

"Because I have known from the start about my sister's vision. I had a part to play in making sure that you would live and escape Randall's mansion. I just didn't bank on falling in love with my mate. It hurts so much to be away from her. My wolf is trying to break free and run back to her. It is taking everything in me to not shift right now."

My heart hurt for Tyler. He gave up his pack, his sister, his friends, and his mate to help save me. I stood from the bed and made my way over to him, wrapping my arms around his waist and resting my head on his back. He stiffened at the contact, but after a minute relaxed.

"I am so sorry for everything you have gone through, Ty. I wish I could change it, but I can't. Thank you for saving me and for everything that you have done to make sure you were where you needed to be in order to save me."

CHAPTER 14

Ryan

After Tyler left, I quickly brushed my hair and then stuffed Nico's shirt under my pillow to cuddle tonight when I slept. I exited my room and quickly went to the first door on my right and knocked.

"Come in!"

I opened the door and then stopped in my tracks. Holy fucking shitballs! Lucian was H.O.T. He wore a pair of jeans that hung low on his hips and a white T-shirt that clung to him. Lucian was thin from years of starvation, but fuck me, if that shirt was tight now, wait a few months and it would be bursting at the seams.

I continued my appraisal of my friend and saw that he didn't have as many bruises and cuts as I did, which I was glad for. It was still so weird seeing him face to face. Lucian's hair was washed and back up in its man bun, and his silver black hair was gorgeous. His eyes were so captivating, too—violet with a gray ring around the pupil. I'm not totally certain, but I have a feeling that he is fae or part fae.

"How did you like the shower?"

Lucian grins like a kid in a candy store. "It was the best

thing I have ever done in my life. The water never fills! It just keeps going down the hole. I was dirty before, and then after washing with some liquid stuff, I am now clean. I even saw what I looked like in the mirror." He sounded so happy, and it warmed my heart. I made my way over to the big guy and wrapped him in a hug, which he returned this time. A throat clearing had us pulling apart. I turned to see who was at the door and groaned. Both my cousins stood there with shit-eating grins on their faces.

"How fucking cool would it be if our cousin divorced the king of the fairies?" Alex and Chased both laughed and I groaned, and Lucian just frowned.

"Your husband is from Farrarie?" How did Lucian know about Farrarie?

"Uh...yeah. He's the king of the fae." Lucian's face lit up like a Christmas tree. He gripped me by my shoulders and leaned down so we were eye to eye.

"The lady that raised me told me that my mom and dad came from that place. Maybe your husband could help me find out who my parents were." Oh my goodness, I was right. Lucian is a fae!

"You have my word, buddy. I will make it my mission to help you find your parents."

We were all sitting around the dining room table in the same seats we sat in this morning, having the most awkward dinner of my life. No one said a word except for me explaining to Lucian how to use a knife and fork. The only sound in the room was cutlery scraping across plates. My eyes kept darting between my grandparents, waiting to see which one of them would break the awkward silence.

"Oh, for heaven's sake, Marcus! Stop acting like a child." I snapped my gaze to my freaking badass grandmother. She was awesome, standing up to Gramps like that.

"What would you have me say, Bethany?" Grams continued to glare at her husband; I saw his eyes flicker from side to side to see if anyone was going to jump to his defense. Chase and Alex kept staring at their plates like they were watching a movie in them. Lucian continued to inhale his food, totally oblivious to the tension, and Tyler and I both stared openly at my grandparents.

"Speak to her Marcus! She is your granddaughter for God sake. Stop blaming her!" What the hell was Gramps blaming me for? What did I do?

"I can't! She is the reason my son is dead!" Oh God, Gramps blamed me for my father's death. I felt five pairs of eyes on me, and I was struggling to hold myself together. I cleared my throat and pushed back from the table.

"Thank you very much for the delicious dinner, Grams" My grandmother smiled at my nickname for her, but her eyes radiated sadness. "I think I'm just going to go take a walk."

I rushed from the room and headed for the door we entered through today, snagging a random jacket off the coat rack and slipping into my shoes that I left there earlier. I ran as fast and as far as I could, tears falling freely down my face. My grandfather hated me; he blamed me for my father's death. Gramps was right, if my dad had just killed me, he would still be alive today.

I've been sitting next to this stream for hours; the only lighting out here was from the moon. I refused to go back to that cabin. I would make Tyler take me back to Nico. I tried screaming Nico, Kai, and Dom's names when I first found this stream. I thought maybe Nico would feel me through our *hugacko* bond. I was so upset and angry earlier, and I thought my magic might spark back to life.

I haven't felt or even had access to my magic since the night of my wedding. The only person who knows this is Lucian. I couldn't save or destroy a world if I didn't have any magic, and at this point, I was counting that as a win.

I heard a branch snap behind, but I didn't turn. I didn't need to. I just knew it was him.

"Your father would come out here as a child. It was his favorite spot to think." I heard Gramps sigh behind me, but I didn't move. "Ryan, I'm sorry. It isn't your fault my son lost his life."

"You're right, though; he did die because of me." My father lost his life because he wouldn't kill me. If he had killed me,

Stevie wouldn't have had any darkness inside her and the fae realm wouldn't be at risk.

"He died *for* you. Your father knew his end was coming, and he made sure he was ready for it. Your father died a warrior and a king. Do not dishonor his memory by quitting."

I balled my hands into fists and jumped to my feet, glaring at my grandfather. How fucking dare he!

"You have no idea what I have been through, or what I have had to live through. I gave my word that I wouldn't quit, and I never break my word. I will end my sister for what she did to my dad, and I will save the fae realm. Now you can either help me or step aside." Wait, could he even help me? I still didn't even know why the hell we were here, honestly. A small smile graced Gramps's face.

"There's that Knox fire! That attitude right there is what is going to win you the war. I will help you wield your power, and your grandmother will teach you spells. I will not coddle you or hold your hand. You will train from sun up to sun down every day. We have three to four months to get you ready and back to Alaska to save *your* realm and end that sister of yours." Holy shit, Grams and Gramps were going to train me? I had a few terms of my own to list first before I agreed.

"I have some conditions." Gramps raised his brows, but I continued. "You have to help train Lucian as well. I'll agree to your four-month training but no longer. And when we leave for Alaska, you and Grams have to come too." I saw Gramps tense. "Please, if I am to lead the Knox coven, I need your help, Grandpa." Gramps chuckled and started shaking his head.

"You truly are your father's daughter. He could always get me to agree to anything. I agree to train the boy. If your grandmother agrees, then we will return to Wonder Lake. We will remain there for three months to help you, then we will return. This is our home now, and this is the house where we brought our sons for vacations. The memories here are precious to us." I didn't know that. There was so much I didn't know about my family, and it was starting to fucking annoy me. I stuck my hand out and Grandpa shook it, sealing the deal.

"Uh, Grandpa? I forgot to mention that I can't access my powers. I haven't been able to access them since the night of my wedding." Gramps smiled down at me and winked. He fucking *winked*.

"That's what happens when you have a neutralizer for a cellmate."

CHAPTER 16

Ryan

The next morning, Gramps woke us at dawn, as promised, banging on our bedroom doors. Groaning, I rolled over and slid my legs over the side of the bed. I moved to stand but tripped over something on the floor and face-planted.

This was not my morning!

Groaning, I sat up and reached for the object that I had tripped on. My bad mood evaporated when I saw Lucian sleeping on the floor next to my bed. I had tripped over *him*.

He looked so peaceful. He didn't deserve the life he had lived. Lucian was sweet and kind. I heard Gramps shouting that we had better move our asses, so I leaned forward and shook Lucian till he woke. When his eyes opened, I smiled.

"Morning, sunshine. We have to get up and start our training today." Lucian didn't complain or comment on why he slept on the floor next to me. He got up, took his blanket and pillow, and left. I quickly got dressed, brushed my teeth and then made my way downstairs.

I met Gramps, Tyler, Lucian, and my cousins in the huge sitting room. I dropped down next to Lucian on one of the couches and waited for Gramps to speak.

"You will be up and ready at this time every morning and that includes feeding yourself." It was *five-thirty in the morning!* That means I would have to get up at five each day just to get fed and dressed before it was training time.

"Today we are going to work on basic hand-to-hand combat. If for some reason you can't access your magic or you have depleted your power for a short time, you will need to be able to defend yourself in combat." This made perfect sense. My magic was so unpredictable that I definitely needed to learn hand-to-hand combat stat.

"You will all train and help each other. Ryan, Chase, and Alex—you three will work together on combat training. Lucian, you and I will work together to try to figure out how your power will work."

"Ah, sorry, sir. I don't even know what I am or who I am." Lucian hung his head in shame, and my heart broke for my friend. I felt so protective of Lucian, and right now I needed to help him by taking the attention off him.

"So how about you all tell me how Tyler knew about you and Grams, and why Alex and Chase couldn't tell me about you?" Gramps looked to the other three males, who wouldn't meet his gaze.

"I'm not one to mince words, so I'll get right to it. Tyler has known from the start because of his sister. Why he kept quiet is a mystery to even me. Alex and Chase have been spelled from a young age to never mention us. We left the Knox coven after your grandmother had a vision; the only way for you to be born and for your father to live as long as he did was because we left." Okay, straight to the point and no mucking around, noted.

Gramps led us all outside and sent the four of us to train while he and Lucian made their way into the woods. Anxiety churned in my stomach. I didn't like Lucian being away from me. Ever since we escaped Randall's, I have felt this need to keep Lucian close to me. I trusted that Gramps would keep him safe, but my anxiety wouldn't let up until Lucian was beside me again.

I followed the three guys over to the huge garage, where Alex pushed a button on the remote and one of the six roller doors lifted, revealing a home gym set up inside. Alex turned the lights on, and with a clearer view, I saw that there was only one car parked inside—the rest of the space was used as a gym.

There was so much gym equipment in here: weight benches, treadmills, exercise bikes, and more. We bypassed all of the machines and moved over to the gym mats that were set up on the floor, which took up two of the parking bays. The three boys started removing their shoes and socks, so I followed their lead and did the same. Tyler made his way to the middle of the mats, and Chase followed. Alex led me over to a couple of plastic chairs. I sat down and turned to ask Alex what the hell was happening but Tyler spoke.

"Okay, Ryan, Chase and I are going to spar, and we'll show you a few self-defense moves. When you can master these moves, we will then progress to attack training." I had nothing to say to that, so I just nodded and settled back into my seat to watch them go at it.

Tyler and Chase began to circle each other, hands raised in front of their faces.

Alex told me to watch their foot work and to keep an eye on how they kept their guard up constantly and never lowered their hands. Tyler was circling Chase like he was hunting, and Tyler watched Chase with keen eyes, just waiting for Chase to make a move or drop his guard so he could attack. Chase stepped toward Tyler with his fist out, ready to strike, but Tyler was so quick on his feet that he spun in a circle and ended up behind Chase.

Tyler didn't stop there; he landed three blows to Chase's back. Chase spun and threw his left arm out to clock Tyler on the side of his head, and Tyler grabbed Chase's arm and spun him so his back was facing Chase and then used Chase's own momentum to throw him over his back. Chase landed on the mat with a loud thud.

I gasped. Tyler was a badass!

"You did good. Next time keep your guard up and your elbows closer to your chest," Tyler said while offering Chase his hand to help him up. "Alex you're up."

Alex and Chase swapped places. Alex wasn't even on the mat for two minutes before Tyler had him on his back.

"Stop dropping your hands! I could have knocked you out five times in the first minute. You need to move your feet and not stand there waiting for the attack. Every time you try to attack you tense, it's your tell," Tyler snapped at Alex while helping him to his feet.

"Ryan, your turn." Oh dear Lord, help me.

I traded places with Alex and stood in the center of the mats facing Tyler.

"Okay, put your hands up like they did." I tried to mimic my cousin's position, but clearly Tyler didn't like that. He sighed and then showed me how to hold my fist properly.

"Don't tuck your thumb into your fist. If you hit someone like that you'll break your thumb." Oh, okay, didn't know that. "Stand with your legs shoulder-width apart, knees slightly bent, left foot turned to point toward your opponent. Make loose fists, to point and hold your right hand by your chin, left hand in front of your face. Chin down, eyes up." Holy shit, it's a lot to take in, and I haven't even done anything yet. I tried to do as he instructed, and after watching me on Struggle Street, Tyler finally took pity on me and positioned my body the way he wanted.

"Okay, you saw how I flipped Chase and Alex?" I nodded.

"That is the first move you are going to learn. It's going to be a lot to take in. You need to create muscle memory, so that your body will automatically assume that stance when a fight breaks out." I nodded again. "You're going to attack me and then I'm going to throw you on your back." Uh—what?

Tyler circled around me; I did the same, so my back wasn't turned to him. I was smart enough to know that you never turn your back on your enemy. Tyler told me to try to hit him. I listened and then before my fist could even connect, I squealed as I was thrown onto my back. It happened so freaking fast. I laid there and groaned. These mats didn't soften your fall much, and my body was still sore from the beatings it had taken.

Tyler offered me his hand, which I accepted, and once on my feet, he said, "Channel your pain, don't let it limit you. I know you're still hurting, but you need to push through it. Pain can be your enemy or it can be your savior. The choice is yours, Ryan."

Tyler's words stuck with me for the rest of the day. My body ached, but I pushed the pain out of my mind. Tyler set us all up on the equipment and told us what to do and for how long. The treadmill sucked balls; I was lazy and I hated that I had to walk on this stupid freaking machine until Tyler said stop. While two of us were using the equipment, Tyler would spar with the other; we had no down time. The only break we got was when Grams brought us some drinks and food for lunch.

Gramps and Lucian still hadn't shown back up when Tyler finally told us we could call it quits for the day. I dragged myself out of the shed and was making my way over to the woods where I saw Gramps and Lucian disappear this morning. A hand clamped on my arm, pulling me back. I spun to see who the hell it was and was met with Tyler's fierce gaze.

"He can help the boy, Ryan. You need to let him. There is more to that boy than even he knows. He is the *trifecta*" Fuck *that*.

"I won't leave him, Tyler. He needs me."

"No, Ryan, *you* need him." What the hell did that mean? I

pulled my arm from Tyler's grasp and turned away. Relief flooded through me as I saw Lucian and Gramps making their way to us. He was okay. I waited at the bottom of the porch steps for them, but when they got to me, Lucian walked straight past without a word and went inside.

"What the hell did you say to him?" Gramps spun around and glared down at me from the top of the stairs.

"Do not question my motives, granddaughter. The boy had to be told some harsh truths. Stop babying him like everyone babies you, and maybe he just might live."

After showering and changing, I thought about going to see Lucian but I stopped myself. What if Tyler and Gramps were right? Did I baby him? Did I need him? Of course I needed him —he was my friend—but I didn't want him to feel like he *had* to stay with me. He wasn't bound to me, he had his freedom now and he could leave anytime he wanted. The thought of Lucian leaving me hurt more than I wanted to admit. I shook myself out of my thoughts. I would not throw myself a pity party.

I joined the others for another silent dinner. After last time, I wasn't going to say a word. Quiet was better than Gramps being a douche.

We all helped clean up and then made our way back to our rooms. It was only six at night, but I was ready to crash. I changed into my sleep shorts and pulled Nico's shirt on. Pulling the collar of the shirt over my nose, I inhaled his scent. It calmed me.

I missed Nico so much. I haven't ever gone this long without seeing him, one way or another. I wanted him to hold me and tell me everything was going to be okay.

I knew I needed to woman up and learn how to fight and to control my magic. I only had a few months to learn all of this, and when I did master my combat skills and my magic, I was going straight for my sister and then Randall. Stevie would fucking pay for what she did to my dad and for everything she has done since. Randall, the ugly piece of shit, would die slowly, if I had any say in it. I went to bed that night with a smile on my face and more determined than ever to train and master my craft.

CHAPTER 18

I awoke the next morning to Grandpa banging on all our doors again. Groaning, I rolled over and sat up. Out of the corner of my eye I saw something on the floor and leaned over. It was Lucian, sleeping on the floor, again.

I hopped out of bed and gently woke him. He didn't say anything; he just grabbed his stuff and left the room. What the hell is going on with him? I fretted about it while I got changed then pushed it out of my mind and went downstairs for food.

I ate quickly with the others, then Lucian and Gramps went to the woods again and the rest of us went to the gym. We went through the same motions as yesterday.

Tyler told us we would keep doing this every day until we could master the simple move of flipping him over. Apparently that was a standard self-defense move. It made me feel better that Chase and Alex hadn't been able to flip Tyler either.

The day dragged on, switching between the machines and sparring with Tyler. The only break we got was for lunch when my sweet Grams would bring us our sandwiches and muffins.

I wished I had some time alone with her, to get to know her better. I didn't know shit about my grandparents. I tried to ask

Stevie about them when we first arrived in Alaska, but she didn't know about them either.

They were a mystery. I needed to get some time alone with my cousins and pump them for some info. A thought struck me while we were eating lunch.

"Where do your mom and dad think you two are?" I asked Chase and Alex.

"I think dad knows where we are; he would never tell anyone, though."

"Why do you sound so sad about it?"

"We have never been able to discuss our grandparents, Ry. Alex and I have only met them twice. We are spelled to never speak of them; they are both very strong. This is our first time here as well. Grandpa is the most powerful living warlock known."

"I thought Dom and Nico were?" I asked. Both Alex and Chase chuckled.

"They are the strongest fae, Ry. They are not warlocks." Now I got what Chase meant, but before I could ask more questions Tyler barked that lunch was over and back to training. Great, it was my turn to train with Tyler now. Yippee.

Sparring with Tyler sucked; I have been flipped on my back more times than I can count. He keeps barking at me to hold my hands this way, strike this way, look for an opening, stop rushing, move your feet. All his fucking orders were giving me a headache! I was exhausted and sore as fuck, but he just kept pushing and pushing.

I know he was trying to help us, but fuck me, it's harder than it looks to flip someone twice your size! All the guys were bigger than me. I don't understand how he thought I could do a move like that. Sighing, I walked to the center of the mats again and got into the position Tyler had been grilling me to remember, which apparently still wasn't good enough, as he adjusted my stance and hands.

By the end of the day, I was still no closer to flipping Tyler. I made my way upstairs, showered, and changed into my sleep-wear, scenting Nico's shirt as soon as I put it on.

Lucian didn't look at me or even acknowledge my presence during dinner or even when we were cleaning up. I was starting to get annoyed at the silent treatment. I decided that once we were upstairs, I would go and speak to him.

After doing dish duty, I made my way back to my room and lay in bed, waiting for when Lucian would sneak in and sleep on my floor.

I was fighting to keep my eyes open, and just as I was drifting off to sleep, I heard my door open and then close. I closed my eyes, feigning sleep, so Lucian wouldn't bolt back out the door. I was shocked when he sat on the side of my bed. I remained still. Opening my eyes slightly, I could see how tense he was.

"I'm sorry, Smurf. If I don't figure this shit out, I could lose you," he whispered. The sadness in his voice was nearly my undoing. I sat up. Lucian didn't flinch. He knew I was awake.

"What does that mean, Lucian?"

"I am your neutralizer." What the hell is a *neutralizer?*

"I don't even know what that is."

"Your Grandpa is helping me understand what I am and how to access my power. I know why they left and hid for so many years; if they didn't, you and your father would have veered off the path fate had intended for you, and you and I would never have met."

"Don't get me wrong—I am so glad I met you, but I'm still not following, Lucian." He took a deep breath and then sighed before speaking.

"I have to access my magic, and fast. I still don't know what I am, and your grandfather won't tell me, as it will alter your grandmother's vision. I need to control my magic in order to help you stabilize Farrarie so it doesn't need a portal to survive." Holy shit!

"I-I don't even know what to say to that. Why are you so sad, though?"

"Because if I don't learn to control my magic and learn how to neutralize your power, you will die! The reason you have no access to your magic is because I am blocking you, somehow. I am your shield, Ryan; I am the one who has to help stabilize your magic so it doesn't consume you."

CHAPTER 19

I was up and ready before Gramps knocked on my door this morning. My grandfather owed me an explanation. I quietly snuck out of my room and went down to the kitchen and waited for Gramps to get up and have his coffee before waking the others. I sat at my usual chair at the dining table and waited. Five minutes later Gramps strolled into the kitchen and froze.

"I'm going to need coffee before getting into this conversation."

Gramps poured us both some coffee and told me to follow him out onto the back patio. We sat on the back steps, staring out at the forest. The air was chilly this morning, which made me glad I wore leggings and a sweatshirt. I turned to look at my grandfather; he looked tired and stressed. Seeing this big strong man look like he had the weight of the world on his shoulders worried me.

"Gramps, what's going on?" He exhaled loudly and slumped forward slightly before answering me.

"Lucian told you he is your neutralizer?"

"Yes, not that I know what that means."

"I knew that boy wouldn't keep his mouth shut." I smiled, Lucian and I had a bond that I couldn't describe.

"You need him, Ryan. Without him, you will die. The power you hold is too much for just one person." Okay, then. Don't sugarcoat anything, Gramps.

"I need you to explain it to me. Lucian is all in knots. I will not ask him to put himself in harm's way for me."

"You don't have a choice. Your grandmother had a vision years ago, before you and your sister were born. If we stayed in Wonder Lake, Ralph would never have been king and wouldn't have had the time with you or your sister that he needed. It was the hardest decision for your grandmother and me to make. We left both our sons and grandsons behind. I haven't seen David in years; it kills your grandmother to be away from her only living child. I know you have had a hard life, Ryan, but the finish line is in front of you now. End this fight and save your people, then you can be free."

Gramps had me stumped; I had no idea what to say. The sacrifice he and Grams made for me and my dad was so selfless. I could never repay them for what they had done. I don't think I could ever give up my children, especially for a granddaughter that didn't even exist at the time they left. I respected my grandparents so much more now that I knew why they left.

"Gramps, what happens if I don't want Lucian to be my shield?"

"You will die. Stevie has the power to kill off the fae realm; she doesn't need to close the portal. The only way to stop the fae from dying is if you stabilize their realm and make it so they don't need a portal on Earth to sustain their world."

"I don't even know if I am capable of doing that, Gramps." I didn't want to lie to him and say I could do it when I didn't even know how to make an energy ball on demand. The fate of the fae realm was resting on the shoulders of a novice hybrid.

"I will train you and help you. You have to do it, or the fae realm will die, and so will you." Well, when he put it like that, I really didn't have a choice, did I?

"There is one other thing."

Seriously? "What's that, Gramps?"

"You need to end your sister, Ryan. No prison can hold her, and she will not stop. The Knox coven will demand her demise. Blood must have blood. That is our way."

I knew it had to be done, but hearing it out loud was a harder pill to swallow than I thought. I knew my sister was so far gone that she couldn't be saved, and she had done so many unspeakable things. I was the only one who had enough power to destroy her, and I had to find the strength inside myself to end her reign of terror.

"You have my word, Grandpa. I will set Stevie's soul free."

"You need to help Lucian understand that *you* need him. You need him to shield you from your power. If it's unleashed at full capacity, you won't be able to call it back to you without his help. Everyone in life has a destiny, and his is to help you. Finish your combat training with Tyler and then you and Lucian will train with me."

"What about Alex, Chase, and Tyler?"

"Your grandmother will train your cousins, and Tyler isn't a warlock. Tyler will continue to work on his control over his wolf. The mate bond is strong for him; he needs to fight it or he will lose control of his wolf when he scents your sister." A thought struck me; Tyler had once said that he would lose control of his wolf if Stevie died.

"Tyler's training to control his wolf so he doesn't go mad when Stevie dies, isn't he?" Gramps turned to look at me with a sad smile on his face.

"Yes, when a wolf loses their mate, they go mad." Oh my God.

"Gramps, what happens if Tyler doesn't control his wolf?"

"Then I will need to be taken out." I jumped to my feet and spun around at the sound of Tyler's voice. He didn't look scared or worried; he just seemed to accept his fate. But I couldn't let Tyler die, not after everything he had done for me.

We may not have always gotten along, but I could tell he was a good guy and he didn't choose her as his mate. I walked over to Tyler and grasped his hand, giving it a small squeeze.

"I will not let you die, Ty. I will do whatever I can to help you." Tyler looked down at me, shocked.

"Why would you help me? I betrayed you and my pack, for my mate. I helped them take your coven elders and their loved ones. I am not worth saving, Ryan."

"The fact that you don't believe you are worth saving is the very reason why you are worth saving. You did all of those things because of the bond you have with my sister. You will not be judged by your actions any longer; you will only be judged on what you do to make up for your mistakes."

We trained harder today than we did the previous days. I learned a few moves that were easier to pick up, including how to do a groin kick effectively against the guys. I also learned how to do a hammer strike, though if you have car keys on you, it helps.

The next day I mastered a heel-palm strike. It took me a few attempts to get that move right, but it proved effective when I sparred with Chase and got him in the nose. He crumpled to the mat after that hit and I dropped with him, feeling so guilty. Tyler just rolled his eyes and told us to do it again.

CHAPTER 20

As the days turned into weeks, I made progress with my hand-to-hand combat. My body had its own internal alarm now, and I woke without needing Gramps banging on my door. Lucian slept on the floor next to my bed every night. We didn't speak about why he did it, it just became a routine. He didn't sneak in anymore – he would come with me to my room after dinner with a stack of books.

Grams has been teaching him how to read, and Lucian was like a sponge; he absorbed any and all information. I was learning new things too. I had learned a lot about where my family came from and that my Gramps was the strongest warlock until my dad came into his powers.

Grams is a seer, and her gift passed onto my dad. No one in the coven knew about Dad or Grams's gift of being a seer. Gramps told me that it would have made them a target; seers are desperately sought by all the clans. That explained why Jax always made sure Aurora's identity was kept a secret, and no one out of the pack really knew she existed.

Grams had shown me photos of my dad as a kid, and she let me keep one of the albums.

Dinner time wasn't awkward and quiet now. We had settled into a routine and I looked forward to it every evening, the sharing of stories and our shared history. Lucian had gained weight and was starting to fill out; he would go with Gramps in the morning and then come to the gym in the afternoon to learn some combat moves. I'm embarrassed to say he picked the self-defense moves up quicker than the rest of us.

I was the last one left to master the flipping move, and Gramps said once I did that I could move on to magic training.

By week seven I noticed that I was starting to develop some muscle definition, and my fighting position was automatic.

Tyler was right; the more I did it, the more my body would remember it.

I now know how to do an elbow strike, alternative elbow strike, I know how to escape a bear hug, my hands being trapped, and a headlock. I had given myself a deadline: I had to master this flip before the end of week eight.

Eight weeks of training, and I was on my last day for my personal deadline. I was standing in the middle of the mats with Tyler.

Gramps and Grams were in here; they had started coming to the gym more often now to check on our progress. I had to block out the fact that I had five sets of eyes on me. Everyone knew I had set a deadline for myself and today was D-day.

"Okay, you have trained your ass off for weeks, Ryan. You need to master this so you can move onto magic training. You have smashed everything else, you just need to master this move." I nodded. Tyler was right; we were running out of time. We had been working on attack training as well, because apparently, I was holding everyone else up with my lack of being unable to flip Tyler.

"Okay, let's begin."

I took a deep breath and blocked everything out. I just focused on Tyler. I watched how his body shifted and how his left hand would twitch. Tyler had been telling me for weeks that everyone had a tell; if you found it then you would know when they would make their move.

I haven't been able to find Tyler's yet.

We circled each other. Both our guards were up. Tyler struck out his left fist, I spun right to dodge, and I lashed out with my fist and made contact with his ribs.

I didn't celebrate; Tyler was a wolf and he could take a lot of hits. We kept doing the same dance for five minutes.

I knew Tyler was getting annoyed and just wanted to end this sparring match, but I kept evading his attacks. He had nearly got me when he had me in a headlock, but I used my training to get out of it.

Tyler threw his right fist out, and I was too overwhelmed with the fact I just found Tyler's tell to move out of striking distance. His fist connected with my face, but I blocked the pain out. I would deal with that later. Tyler thought he had the upper hand, and I encouraged his mistaken belief, lowering my hands, faking that I was hurt.

As soon as Tyler moved forward and placed both his hands on my shoulders, that's when I saw it again: his left eye twitched. He was going to attack! I quickly placed my hands on his shoulders, turned around while maintaining my grip. I took a step forward and pulled Tyler in to my side and bent at the knees. Using his own momentum against him, I rolled him over my hip.

Tyler landed on the mat with a thud. I looked down at him, shocked it actually worked. Even Tyler looked surprised. I did it! I just fucking flipped Tyler! I was elated.

A strong pair of arms wrapped around me and spun me around in a circle. "You did it, Smurf! You fucking did it!" Lucian placed me back on my feet and gave me a side hug while we watched Tyler climb to his feet. I moved out of Lucian's hold and went to stand in front of Tyler with my hand extended; he shook it with a smile on his face. He looked so proud of me, and that warmed my heart.

"Thank you, Tyler, for everything." I owed Tyler so much. No one would ever have the chance to hurt me again, thanks to him.

"Don't mention it, little hybrid." Tyler had given me that nickname a few weeks ago; he still called Lucian *trifecta*. The only other person who knew what *trifecta* meant was gramps and he refused to tell us. He said knowing the meaning behind the name would alter Lucian's path.

Gramps gave us the rest of the day off. It was our first free afternoon in two months.

It was snowing outside, so there wasn't much we could really do. We all made our way back inside the house, where the fireplace was lit and the cabin was so freaking toasty.

I remembered something I had been wanting to do—try out the tub in my room. I haven't had time to even consider using it. I raced up the stairs to my room and slammed the door shut behind me, turning on the faucets while I stripped out of my clothes. As soon as the tub was full, I hopped in and sighed.

I leaned my head back and closed my eyes, trying to clear my mind.

My thoughts drifted to Nico, as they always did. I haven't seen Nico in over three months and wouldn't get to see him for at least another two. What would he think when he saw me again? Would he still want me the way I want him? Did he hate me now?

My heart started to ache. I still slept in his shirt every night, but his scent no longer lingered. Wearing the shirt to bed every night made me feel like he was wrapped around me. I missed my husband so fucking much. We have been married for months, and I haven't even been able to call him my husband to his face. I haven't had any dreams, which worries me daily. Did he use me? Was any of it real?

CHAPTER 21

We were two weeks into our magic training and fuck me—I thought Tyler was a hard-ass, but Gramps is ten times worse!

We were gathered outside in the freezing snow, standing in a circle. Alex, Chase, Lucian, and I had been doing this dance for two weeks now; my cousins could access their power, but I couldn't access mine until Lucian learned how to release his shield. Apparently Lucian's fear of losing me was causing his magic to block mine.

Gramps had told us that Lucian's and my path would have always crossed; he was my savior. He was the only one who could help me control my magic. If he had been there the night of my wedding then no one would have died. He would have been able to neutralize my magic. I still felt sick about that night and all the lives I had taken. I would be held accountable for what I had done after this war, and I should be.

"Lucian! Release it now!" Gramps shouted.

"I can't, sir! I'm trying, I swear!" Lucian shouted back. He was frustrated. We all were. I couldn't do shit until Lucian released his hold on my magic. I didn't blame him, but we were running out of time, and I needed to train.

Alex and Chase were both holding purple energy balls in their hands. Lucian was, as well, except his energy was yellow. Gramps was trying to get him to focus on his own magic so he could release mine.

"If you don't learn how to release her magic, she will die!" I saw Lucian tense; this was a lot for him, and I felt terrible. I had to do something.

"Luce, I'm right here. No one here is going to hurt me. I need you to trust me." I was pleading with him.

"Alex, you and Chase are to train with your grandmother for the rest of the day," Gramps snapped. Both my cousins strode out of the forest as fast as they could without breaking into a sprint. Lucky assholes got to train with the *nice* grandparent.

"Smurf, I am trying, I swear." I saw Gramps look out into the forest and then back to us. He had a sly smirk on his face.

"Let's see if we can scare the control out of you." In the next second, Lucian was lifted off his feet and pinned to the closest tree with his arms stretched out wide.

"Gramps what the hell are y—"

I didn't get a chance to finish yelling at Gramps. Something slammed into me from behind, and I landed face-first on the hard-packed snow. I quickly rolled and jumped to my feet, getting straight into my fighting stance. Tyler was right; muscle memory was the shit.

I gasped when I saw what had knocked me down: in front of me stood a huge, rusty-colored wolf, with bright yellow eyes.

"Tyler?" I asked the wolf, and the wolf growled in response. I was taking that growl as a *yes*. The wolf jumped at me again, and I quickly stepped out of the way.

"Gramps what the hell?" I didn't take my eyes off the wolf; I didn't trust Tyler not to attack me while my focus was elsewhere.

"Release her magic, boy; she doesn't stand a chance against a shifter without her power." Gramps was fucking nuts. "You can't stop her from becoming what she was meant to be! She needs to learn to control it now! When she gets back to Alaska, the other half her husband holds will return to her." Lucian didn't get a chance to answer Gramps. Tyler lunged for me again, and this time, I wasn't fast enough to move.

His sharp teeth sunk into my arm and I screamed as I felt his teeth pierce through my skin. I tried to pull my arm away, but Tyler kept his jaws clamped.

"Let her fucking go!" Lucian yelled.

"NO! Release her magic now!" I turned to Lucian and saw the fear on his face. Tears were flowing down my cheeks freely, my arm was burning like it was on fire.

I pulled my focus back to the wolf and started punching it in the head as hard as I could, trying to get it to release my arm; I saw blood—my blood—trickling out of its mouth.

"Tyler, stop!" I begged. I saw a hint of recognition in the wolf's eyes. I knew Tyler could have ripped my arm off if he wanted to. He kept his jaws clamped on my arm, but didn't bite any harder than he had already.

Tyler released my arm, and my bloody limb dropped to my side. The wolf backed up, and I knew he was gearing up to attack again. My right arm was useless; I had to block the pain out or I would never make it out of this forest in one piece. I resumed my fighting stance again, but I only had one arm up.

"Look at her, boy! She only has one arm to defend herself. She will die if you don't let her go!"

Tyler launched himself at me. I quickly spun and used my leg to kick him in the side. He skidded on the snow-covered ground and came straight back at me. I was screwed. Tyler wouldn't stop coming for me until Lucian let my powers go. If this was the only way, then so be it. I dropped my good arm to my side and stood up straight. I looked the wolf in its eyes and nodded my head. I knelt down on the cold, icy ground and exposed my neck to the wolf.

"Smurf, No!" I saw Tyler run toward me and closed my eyes, praying that this was the incentive Lucian needed. If it wasn't, then I would be dead in the next minute.

I felt a whoosh of air and knew Tyler was in front of me, about to end my life. Before his jaws could connect with my neck, I felt heat in my toes. My body started to warm, and then the warmth turned into liquid lava in my veins.

My magic was back!

I snapped my eyes open just as Tyler was about to bite my exposed neck. I channeled enough power into my good arm to throw him; I didn't want to hurt him, but I needed him away from me.

I swung my good arm toward his chest, and a blue light burst into him, sending him sailing through the air into a nearby tree. Tyler yelped when he hit the tree and landed on the snow-covered ground with a thud.

Oh my God, what the fuck did I do?

I rushed over to the wolf, knelt down beside him and started to stroke his face with my good arm.

"Ty, I am so sorry." He was still breathing, so I took that as a good sign, I watched as the wolf shifted back to a very naked Tyler. I sagged in relief as Tyler looked at me with a huge grin on his face. "Next time, when you throw your enemy into a tree, don't run over and make sure they're okay, little hybrid." I smiled at my friend. We stood and I made sure to avert my eyes so I didn't see little Tyler flopping in the wind. Just as I turned back to face the others, I saw a fist connect with Tyler's face and shrieked.

"You ever fucking do that to her again, wolf, and I will kill you!" I grabbed Lucian with my good arm to stop him from hitting Tyler again.

"Luce, stop, please!"

"It's okay, Ry. I deserved the hit."

"No you didn't, Tyler!"

"Look at your fucking arm, Smurf. It's bleeding." I looked down at my arm and saw that my jacket sleeve was torn to shreds and blood was dripping from the tips of my fingers onto the snow. The pain started to register then, and I cradled my bleeding arm to my chest.

"That's it for today. Go get your arm cleaned up. Grams will help you dress it." I turned to glare at Gramps. He didn't even look remorseful; he looked like a smug asshole.

"Don't look at me like that, Ryan. I tried it the nice way and it didn't work. You should be thanking your dear old Gramps." I scowled at him as I walked past heading back to the cabin, but the old fool just chuckled as he followed us back.

It's been nearly four months since I have seen Ryan. I have tried every night to enter our dreamland, but I can't find her. I am so desperate I even asked Kai to try and access her in her dreams. He can't find her either. It's like she's blocked from us. I thought she might be dead, but Mr. Silver told me that if she was I would have felt it through our *hugacko* bond.

For weeks all I have done is travel back and forth from Farrarie and Earth for elder meetings and training my army for the war. There were tents up all over Jax's land; many of my soldiers have come to Earth in case our timeline is off when the war will start.

I have been asking Aurora for weeks if she has had a vision of Ryan. All she has said is that we need Ryan back or we will never win. Stevie is stronger than five thousand fae soldiers. We found out from the vampire elders that Randall's strength has grown. He ingested the blood of Jackson's father, Ryan's father, and now he has ingested Ryan's blood.

Lachlan told us that he was collecting Ryan's blood and injecting his men so they could all now walk in the daylight. There is nothing worse than having thousands of vampires walking around all hours of the day and night. Randall was now stronger then we could have ever imagined.

Jax, Dom, Kai, Sophia, Aurora, Mya, and I were all sitting in Jax's office with somber looks on our faces. We all knew we were fighting a losing battle. Without Ryan, we have no chance of winning this war and saving my people.

I failed as king. I failed as a leader. My world was going to die because I found my *hugacko*. My soulmate was the reason my world was going to die. I couldn't kill Ryan, and nor could Kai; our love for her weakened us. Even still, I would never regret loving her. She deserved so much more than the life she has had.

I would feel a lot better about death if I knew she was okay, but I couldn't blame her for hiding and staying away. I missed her so fucking much that I physically ached for her. I would give anything just to see her one last time.

"We have just over two months before this war is supposed to break out. Aurora, have you seen anything that would change this timeline?" Jax asked.

"No, as far as I have seen the timeline is still accurate." That was a relief to hear. I have started evacuating those of my people who are too young or too old to fight to other parts of the realm. I know this won't save their lives if Farrarie falls, but at least they can live in peace for now.

"Have you been able to reach Ryan, Nico?" I looked to Dom and saw he was hesitant to ask me about Ryan. Every one of them knew speaking about Ryan was a sore subject for me.

"No, I have been trying every day and still I can't reach her." I lowered my gaze, not wanting to see the resignation on my brother's face. Dom had been spending a lot of time with his father and the New York pack, who came here to help aid us. From the intel we have gathered, we were evenly matched with numbers in this war, but the vamps had Randall and the witches had Stevie. Even with Kai, Jax, Dom, and I going for Stevie, she was still stronger than the four of us.

"Wherever she is, I hope she is happy. She deserves to be free. This was never her fight."

"How can you say that, Soph? Without her, we're all going to be slaughtered." I knew my sister was trying to make me feel better, but of course Jax didn't see it that way. He took Ryan's disappearance hard.

"I know this is hard for all of you, but Ryan has had nothing but misery from the supernatural world. She had eighteen years of misery at the hands of her mother—which we could have prevented—and five months ago she found out she was a hybrid and that she was the only one who could save a world she didn't even know existed. That is a lot for someone so young to deal with," I said.

"She won't abandon you, Nico." I turned to Kai, shocked.

"What makes you say that?"

"I have seen the way she looks at you brother. Even before she knew we were real, she would always talk about you and how you made her feel. It was never a question of whether or not she would choose you, *you* were always her first choice. She will come back for you Nico; you just need to give her time."

Kai's words hit me deep. He has never given up hope that Ryan will return, in spite of her betrayal. She has a lot to make up for with him.

"Thank you, brother."

"Stop it, you're both going to make me cry."

"For the love of God, Dominic, get a fucking filter," Sophia snapped at Dom. Those two have been at each other's throats even more in the past few weeks. I just don't have the energy at the moment to get involved in their shit.

"I've had a vision." We all turned to stare at Mya.

"A vision about what?" Dom asked her.

"I didn't see much—all I saw was Stevie lying in a pool of her own blood."

"Was she dead?"

"Was she breathing?"

"Does that mean we won?"

Everyone was barking questions at Mya; the poor woman couldn't keep up.

"Shut up! Let her fucking answer one question at a time!" Kai shouted. Everyone stopped speaking and sat there quietly. We were all stunned at Kai's outburst.

"Look, all I saw was that she was lying in her own blood, and that's it. I don't know any more than that."

Hearing this gave me a sense of hope. Maybe we weren't all doomed after all. Maybe, just maybe, we might live.

Even with the other half of Ryan's magic inside me, I couldn't use it to help us win the war. It just lay dormant inside of me, waiting for its master to call it back.

"How's her mom doing?" Jax asked me. I had taken Nina back to my realm. I took her there initially to question her and get answers about what had happened at Randall's mansion or if she saw Ryan.

I thought the woman was fucking nuts! She ranted like a mad woman and then was found weeping in the corner. It took weeks to even get a coherent sentence out of her. After weeks of being in my realm, I saw a change in her.

"I don't know how to explain it, but she's changed. The woman doesn't want to drink or do drugs anymore. She swears she can't remember most of her life. The last thing she remembers is Ralph leaving her; she said everything else is blank. I think whatever this curse is was broken the moment she entered my realm."

"How is that even possible, brother?" I looked to Kai; I knew it was hard for him, because he made a promise to save Nina and make sure she was safe, but he couldn't have known that the queen's spell would have backfired.

"I have no idea, Kai. Nina has changed so much. She helps the women with their young children, and so many of the fae love her." I still found it strange; I saw what she was like over the years, and I saw what she was like with Ryan. That woman doesn't exist anymore. Nina is actually kind and caring now.

"Have you told her about her past?"

"I told her some of it, Dom. She broke down and locked herself in her room for days, bawling her eyes out. She doesn't understand why Ryan even tried to look for her; she said Ryan should have killed her." Nina Knox was a changed woman, and I wanted to help her get better. I had to—it was my fault the woman was beaten and starved and missing a finger and toe. The least I could do was try to help her build a better life.

CHAPTER 23

We had two weeks left before we had to leave and head back to Alaska. Gramps was training me and Lucian while Grams helped Alex and Chase hone their power.

Alex and Chase were improving so fast and doing so good! I was so proud of my cousins. I know they were eager to get back and see if their parents were okay.

We were outside in the forest, freezing our asses off. My arm was finally starting to scab over, and I know Tyler felt bad, but without that fear, Lucian might never have released my power. The bite mark was going to scar, but nothing could be done about that now.

"Okay, you both have done great work with accessing your power on demand and throwing energy balls. Your levitation has been amazing, Ryan," Gramps was so proud that I could levitate; no one else here could do that except for me and Lucian. Lucian hadn't quite mastered that skill yet, but he was getting better.

I preened. "Thanks, Grandpa."

"Kiss ass." I turned to glare at Chase, him and Alex were cackling like a pair of school girls.

"Ignore him, Smurf, he's just angry his magic glows a girl's color." Chase stopped laughing and scowled at Lucian. In the time we have spent here, Lucian has come out of his shell and developed a sense of humor and quick wit to rival even Dom's. Chase hated that Lucian had quick comebacks now. He just couldn't seem to best my friend with jokes.

"Enough, you boys go back to your grandmother and train. Lucian, I need you to try pull Ryan's power back when she releases it." Gramps has been making us practice this over and over again to make sure Lucian was prepared for the real deal. Lucian knew it would be harder when the other half of my magic came back to me.

I closed my eyes and focused on pushing my power outside of me. I was better at doing this now; the first time I did it I nearly leveled a part of the forest from the force of my magic. That scared me because I only had half of my magic—imagine what I could do when I got the other back from Nico.

"Okay, Ryan, hold it there." I opened my eyes and saw the blue bubble that surrounded me; it was amazing how I could use my magic at will now. It didn't scare me anymore; Gramps said if I let fear and anger control my power it would always be unpredictable. I needed to embrace it and trust it, so it would listen to me.

"Lucian, I want you to pull it into you and hold it inside as long as you can." Lucian nodded his head and pulled the bubble to him. It disappeared inside of him in a flash.

"Good man, hold it for as long as you can."

Gramps was trying to see how long Lucian could hold my magic in case I needed some time to recover after stabilizing the fae realm and taking care of my sister.

Ten minutes later, my magic was back inside of me. I sighed in relief; I hated not feeling my magic inside. It's become a part of me now, and I couldn't live without it.

"That was great, son. For the rest of the time we have here I want you both and Chase and Alex to spar with your magic." We had been practicing dodging and blocking energy balls, as well as throwing them at each other.

Let me tell you something, those fuckers hurt if they hit you. It was like being electrocuted from the inside and there was nothing you could do to stop the pain. Needless to say we all learned how to block them pretty fucking fast.

CHAPTER 24

Two weeks passed in a blur. It was our last night here in the snowy Yukon. We all gathered in the sitting room, sipping hot chocolate and watching the flames dance in the fireplace.

No one had said a word in ages, each of us lost in our own thoughts. I had something to say to my grandparents and had been working up the courage all day to say it.

Taking a deep breath, I blurted it out.

"Thank you both for everything you have done for us. I love you both so much, and because I love you, I don't want you to come with us tomorrow." Grams's eyes welled with tears, and Gramps was swallowing repeatedly.

Did I just stun Gramps speechless?

"We love you too, sweetheart, and we are so proud of you all." I smiled at Grams. She was such a sweet and kind woman. She has helped me get to know my dad better through the stories she has told me and pictures she shared. She taught me about how witches draw power from the elements. I'm very thankful for the time I have been able to spend with them both.

"Why don't you want us to accompany you, Ry?" Gramps asked.

I took a deep breath and looked around the room. Tyler and my cousins gave me a curt nod and Lucian gave my hand a squeeze; they knew why I didn't want them to come with us.

"I don't want you to come because I couldn't bear to lose either of you. I want you to stay here and be safe. Please, Gramps. Don't follow us back to Wonder Lake. Stay here with Grams and enjoy your life. When this war is over, then come and visit us."

Both my cousins agreed with me, and I could see that having all three grandkids gang up on them wasn't something they were prepared for. Lucian and Tyler voiced the same concerns we had, and five against two is good odds.

"What if you lot need us?"

"Oh Grams, we will always need your love and support, but not if it could cost you your life," I said while wiping tears from my cheeks. Gramps remained stoic in his seat, looking at all of us. He could tell from our expressions that we wouldn't let him come with us; we were just hoping that the stubborn old fool wouldn't follow us as soon as we left.

"I couldn't be more proud of the men you four boys have grown into. Each of you has come into your own and that swells me with pride. Ryan, my sweet granddaughter." Oh my God, the tears were falling faster now. Gramps had never spoken to me or looked at me like this before. "You have overcome so much in your life and still you come back swinging. I see so much of myself in you; you will make an amazing queen to both the fae and the Knox coven. Give them hell, my dear, and take no prisoners."

I jumped up from the couch, hastily put my cup on the side table, and then ran over and hugged my grandfather. He hugged me back, and I whispered in his ear.

"I have never had a father figure in my life, Gramps, but you have been that for me for the past four months. Thank you so, so much." I pulled back and saw Gramps had a stray tear trailing down his cheek, he quickly swiped it away and acted like it never happened.

I smiled at the stubborn old man.

I couldn't sleep. I had been tossing and turning for hours. With a groan, I sat up and tucked my long hair behind my ears so it wasn't in my face. I heard Lucian stir beside me. When the temperature dropped, it was too cold for him to sleep on the floor so I decided to just let him sleep next to me in the king-sized bed.

It felt awkward at the start, but now it just felt normal having him sleep beside me.

"Smurf, I can hear you over thinking from here." I chuckled. Nico had said the same thing to me once.

"I'm nervous about tomorrow, Luce."

"Are you nervous about seeing *him?*"

"Yes! What if his feelings for me have changed? What if he doesn't want to be with me?" Lucian chuckled and I glared at him. I knew he couldn't see my glare in the dark room, but I felt better about doing it anyway.

"So you're not nervous about fighting for your life? You're nervous in case your husband has changed his mind?"

"Yes," I snapped.

"Smurf, he is one lucky man to be able to call you his wife. More than that, you are his soulmate. You don't ever stop wanting or loving your soul mate; you *always* need the other half of your soul." Lucian's words brought tears to my eyes. He was right; I was being silly. I knew deep down that Nico wouldn't have moved on. I also knew he would be worried and wondering where the hell I have been.

Lucian cuddled me and told me everything was going to be okay. After that, I settled back down in bed and finally fell into a dreamless sleep.

CHAPTER 25

Goodbyes sucked! Grams bawled her eyes out when we left, and even Gramps looked a little dewy around the eyes. I was so beyond grateful for everything Grams and Gramps had taught me. For the first time in my life, I had a family. I hated leaving them.

I made a deal with Gramps: when the war was over, he and Grams would come to Alaska and help teach me the ropes of being queen of the Knox coven.

Lucian elbowing me in the ribs pulled me from my thoughts. I turned to him and smiled; my beautiful friend had cut his hair shorter. I was shocked when I saw it this morning. It was just above his shoulders now. Lucian had filled out and bulked up a lot in the four months we were in Yukon. Gone was the skinny boy. The man before me now was broad, clean, and healthy. I loved Lucian like a brother, and I would do anything for him. He was strong, and Gramps had even said he hasn't tapped fully into his own magic yet.

"How are you feeling?" Lucian asked.

"I'm okay. Sad to say goodbye to Grams and Gramps but keen to get back to Alaska." I had butterflies in my stomach about seeing Nico again. I know Tyler was nervous about returning to his pack, too. I just hoped Jax would forgive him.

If Jax didn't let Tyler come back to the compound, I don't think I would be able to stay there. Tyler and I had grown close over our time in Yukon, and he was an amazing guy.

The drive was long. We left at five this morning and arrived at the air strip in Toronto just after midnight. We only stopped twice for food and kept the bathroom breaks minimal, and I was exhausted. I hadn't been able to sleep a wink in the car—my nerves wouldn't let me.

We quickly grabbed our bags and made our way onto the small plane, placing our bags in the overhead compartments and then taking our seats. I sat next to the window so I could stare at the night sky. When the plane took off, I reclined my seat, intending to get some shut eye. I managed to get a few hours in before Lucian woke me.

I rubbed my eyes and quickly excused myself to use the restroom and freshen up. I made my way back to my seat and fastened my belt, hoping my nerves would calm the hell down.

"We land in twenty minutes, guys; it's early in the morning here."

"Thanks, Alex, I can't wait to stretch my legs." I said.

"We're gonna land in the same place we left from; it's safer than the commercial airport." That made sense, but I probably wouldn't have thought of it. I'm glad Alex and Tyler were in charge of our travel plans.

Lucian grasped my hand and interlocked our fingers; I turned and smiled at my sweet friend.

"I'll be with you the whole time, Smurf." Hearing that warmed my heart. I knew Lucian would have my back.

We landed somewhere near Fairbanks in a large open field. I was beyond glad to be able to walk around and stretch my legs.

After twenty minutes of walking around in circles, we all piled into the waiting SUV and began another long-ass drive to Wonder Lake.

"We have just over a month, your majesty. We will be ready."

"Thank you, Maverick. Make sure Larick and Cyrus are briefed about the plan and continue to move all the others to Chicago." Maverick bowed before me and then left the room. I looked at the clock on the wall and cursed; I was late for the elder meeting. I quickly left my room and raced to the mess hall. All eyes turned to me as I burst through the doors. I apologized and quickly took my seat next to Dom.

"Your majesty," Victor said and bowed low. I gave him a nod and told them to continue. "We were just saying that we have received word from Lachlan. The coven elders are being held prisoner on the coven lands. Lachlan and the other elders are being watched, so they won't be able to meet with us anytime soon."

Fuck, this wasn't good news. It sounded like Randall or Stevie knew their elders were betraying them and were making sure to keep them close, but how?

The elders are the strongest of us, and the only reason Stevie can control her elders is because of the power she holds. She doesn't need to take their loved ones from them anymore. I couldn't shake the feeling that Victor was hiding something, but maybe I was just being paranoid.

After the meeting ended, we all made our way back to Jackson's office. I couldn't stop pacing. I was running out of fucking ideas of how to save my realm.

Stevie was too fucking strong, and Lachlan had told us that her power just kept growing. I don't understand why she didn't just attack us now, and then search for the portal. What was she waiting for?

"Brother, sit down before you wear a hole into the floor." I sighed but did as Sophia suggested and plonked down into the single seat.

"I just want to say that no matter how this ends, I'm glad we were all able to be together till the end." Fuck no. Jackson could fuck right off with his goodbye speech.

"Don't do that Jax, this isn't the end."

"How do you know that, Dom?"

"Because I'm too fucking pretty to die." Everyone started laughing at Dom's answer, and it surely did us good. I loved my three brothers and my sister. Aurora and Mya were growing on me, as well.

"I needed that laugh, thank you Dom."

"Anytime Rora—"

Dom's reply was cut off when Jax jumped to his feet and

growled out, "Stevie's here, by the chapel!" I envied the link Jackson had with his pack.

Everyone raced out of the office and toward the chapel. Jax said Stevie had only come with four others. She wasn't here to attack, so what the hell was she here for?

We burst out the back door and ran across the snow-covered ground to where the chapel was. Jackson's pack were scattered throughout the trees in case they were needed. I saw some of my soldiers with their weapons drawn; we were ready if she tried anything. We all stopped running when we saw who three of the guys were; there was a stranger with them, but I couldn't see Stevie anywhere.

I felt like my body was being pulled toward the four men, and I only ever had this feeling when Ryan was around.

"Tyler?" Aurora said, shocked at seeing her brother back on pack lands.

"Hello, little sister." Jax stepped slightly in front of Aurora to shield her from Tyler's view and started growling at his former beta. I saw a look of hurt cross Tyler's face before he quickly masked it.

"What the hell are you doing here, Tyler? And why are Chase and Alex with you?" Jax snapped.

"We're here to help you, Jackson." Alex answered.

"W-who are you?" Sophia said, pointing to the stranger with Tyler and Ryan's cousins. Sophia looked pale, almost like she had seen a ghost. What the hell?

"I am Lucian; I am here to help the queen."

"I'll fucking kill you before that bitch ever wins!" Dom growled at the stranger.

"You will not lay a single finger on him, Dom." Oh my God, that voice. My legs nearly gave out.

Ryan

I pushed between Lucian and Chase and saw all my friends staring at me with looks of shock and confusion.

I turned to Jax's right, and that's when I saw him—his beautiful jet-black hair was a mess and long on top now. He had a five-o'clock shadow, and his piercing violet eyes burned holes into me. He was just as shocked to see me.

Nico took a step forward, and Lucian stepped in front of me to block Nico's path.

"Unless you want me to remove your fucking head, boy, you will move!" Nico growled.

"You can try to move him, *Tink*, but without him she dies." Nico paused his movements and looked to Chase. He tried to peer around Lucian to see me. I gave Lucian a pat on his shoulder, indicating it was okay for him to step aside, and he moved to stand next to me again. Then I was facing Nico, who was closer than before. He smiled, and I swooned a little bit. I didn't know what to do. I darted my eyes around, shocked to see so many people in the trees. It made me uncomfortable.

Lucian grabbed my hand and interlocked our fingers.

"Unless you want to lose that fucking hand you will release my *wife* now!"

"Nico, stop!" I turned my gaze to a tear-stricken Sophia, completely befuddled at her demeanor. Why the hell was she so upset?

"Little dove, what's wrong?" Dom asked her.

"No one is to touch him, do you all understand me?" Sophia was pointing to Lucian. Why the hell was she protecting Luce?

"Everyone calm down. Let's go back to Jackson's office; we have a few things to discuss." Everyone turned to Aurora. I smiled at her, letting her know that I held no anger toward her anymore. The five of us didn't move an inch; we waited for Jackson to say the word and invite us in.

"For God's sake, Jackson, invite them in!" Nico roared.

"The four of them can come, but not the traitor." I felt my magic surge inside of me. I took a step in front of the guys so I could protect them if need be. I heard rustling come from the trees all around us, and I knew the soldiers in the trees were getting ready to attack. I heard bones cracking; some of them had shifted into their wolf form.

"Stand down! No one is to touch her!" Nico yelled. He never took his gaze off me; I let my power run through me and levitated a few feet off the ground until I looked down at my friends. Their eyes were wide.

"If any of you or your men lay a single finger on Tyler, you will have me to answer to. Tyler is my pack, and where I go he goes. Same for Alex, Chase, and Lucian. They stay with me at all times. If you will not welcome him into your home as a courtesy to me, Jackson, we will leave!" I spoke loud enough so those hiding in the trees could hear. Jackson kept opening and shutting his mouth in consternation.

"As the leader of the Shifter elders, I, Ian Silver, grant you, Ryan Knox, and your friends entrance to the compound. No harm will come to you or your friends, you have my word." I turned and saw Dom's dad standing by the trees. I smiled and thanked him. I brought my power back inside me and slowly made my way back down to the ground. Then I turned to Tyler.

"Thank you, little hybrid, you didn't have to do that."

"Ty, you're family now. I told you I wouldn't leave you, and I meant it." Tyler smiled and engulfed me in a hug, and I heard someone growling behind me. I just knew it was Nico.

"Clearly he doesn't like any man touching you," he whispered in my ear.

To say the atmosphere in Jackson's office was awkward would be an understatement. We were all so divided, and I hated it.

Nico stood to one side with Dom, Kai, Jax, Sophia, Mya, and Aurora, while I stood on the other side with my four guys. Kai still hadn't said a word to me. He hadn't even *looked* at me. I knew in my heart that Nico had told him what I had done. I wish I had been the one to tell him the truth, but I couldn't change that now.

"Okay, this is just awkward as shit. Come here, love." Dom opened his arms wide and walked to the middle of the room, and I walked into his embrace without any hesitation. Being wrapped in Dom's arms again felt great.

I missed him and all his smart-ass comments. We stood there hugging each other until Nico pulled him away and stood directly in front of me, looking down into my eyes. We stood there, lost in each other's gazes for a long moment. There was so much emotion swirling in the depths of his eyes.

"Hello, little one." The dam broke, and tears slid down my face. I wrapped my arms around him and buried my face in his chest. His arms came around me and squeezed me so tight. I felt safe, and being in his arms again felt like home.

"I missed you, love." I couldn't talk past the lump in my throat. I clung to him while tears silently leaked from my eyes.

"I don't think she's gonna divorce the king of the fairies, Luce," I heard Chase say with a sigh.

"Did you really have to bring him back with you?" Nico grumbled. I chuckled. Nico clearly hadn't missed my cousins. I pulled away from Nico and wiped my eyes. Being back with him felt so right.

"I think we should all have a seat and talk," I said. Nico nodded but stuck close to me as I said hello to the others. I saved Kai for last.

Standing in front of the giant of a man who had starred in many of my dreams, I saw the mistrust and disappointment on his face and it crushed me. I held his gaze, because I needed to own my shit, and answer for what I had done to him.

"I'm so sorry for what I did to you. I should never have gone behind your back. I have no excuse except inexperience. I know I hurt you, Kai, and I will spend the rest of my life trying to make it up to you, if you will let me." Kai averted his gaze above my head, and what he said next struck so deep I almost fell to my knees.

"You condemned me to hell, Ryan, and took the last hope I had left. I will stay and fight with my brothers, but I will *never* lead the vampires."

CHAPTER 28

I could see the devastation in her eyes as Kai spoke. She chose to sit between Tyler and her new friend, instead of sitting next to *me*.

I could see how her body curved into the new guys' side for comfort. Who the fuck was this guy, and why was my wife so dependent on him?

"Who is he, love?" I asked, pointing to the new guy.

"Oh, this is going to be good," Chase the dickhead said, fist-bumping his brother. Fucking immature dumbasses.

"Lucian is important to me," she said, looking directly into my eyes.

"That didn't answer my question, little one." She looked to Lucian, who nodded his head. *She needs his permission to answer me?*

"Lucian is my neutralizer." Her what? Before I could ask, my sister butted in.

"Where did you two meet?"

"Lucian and I were both prisoners at Randall's mansion," Ryan answered.

"Why were you held there?" Dom asked Lucian. A storm of

emotions passed through Lucian's eyes: remorse, shame, anger. Ryan clasped his hand in hers, and he relaxed at the comfort she offered him. I started taking deep breaths as my fury rose. She wasn't his to touch, she was *mine*.

"I was born at the vampire king's mansion." I saw tears gather in Sophia's eyes. What was up with my sister today? I have never seen Sophia so emotional.

"How old are you?" my sister asked.

"I don't know exactly, I think I'm around sixteen." Sophia gasped and covered her mouth with her hand, her eyes darting to Dom.

"Soph, what the hell is going on?" I asked. She tore her gaze from Dom and stared at me. She looked...scared. She started shaking her head, got up, and raced from the room. I turned to Dom to see he was staring at the closed office, looking befuddled.

"What the hell aren't you telling me, Dom?" I snapped.

"I honestly have no idea what the fuck just happened, Nico. I don't know what is going on with her." Dom turned and glared at Lucian. "Why is she acting so strange toward you?" he snapped at the kid.

"I-I don't know"

"Don't lie to me boy, I have known her most of her life and have only seen her cry twice! Why is she continuously crying when she looks at you?" Dom was seething with anger.

"Don't talk to him like that! Lucian has done nothing wrong. There is no way he knows Sophia!"

"How can you be sure of that, love?" Dom asked Ryan.

"Because I spent my whole life in the mansion until four months ago. I have lived my whole life in a prison cell, in the dark. I didn't even know I was a supernatural until I met Ryan. I have never seen that woman before in my life, I swear." I could hear the truth in Lucian's voice, and I actually felt sorry for the boy. I turned to Jax, who nodded his head, indicating that the boy wasn't lying.

"We didn't come here to talk about Lucian. We came here to help fight. Lucian isn't a threat to any of you." Ryan spoke like a true queen, she sounded so much more confident in herself now. She even dressed differently: she wore tight black jeans, a black shirt that showed off her midriff, and a black leather jacket. She looks badass, and my blood heated as I scanned her tight and toned body.

"First though, I think Aurora has a few things to set straight." Everyone shifted their gaze to Aurora. To her credit, she didn't shrink back. She straightened up in her chair and met our gaze, determination in her eyes.

"I will not apologize for keeping things from you all. I did what I had to in order to ensure everyone, *especially* Ryan, ended up where they needed to be." Aurora's tone left no room for argument.

She turned to Ryan. "I am sorry for all that you have endured. I couldn't help or alter your course. If I interfered in any way, you would never have met Lucian."

Ryan didn't look angry or upset, but rather smiled at the seer. I could see my wife held no ill feelings toward Aurora, but I wasn't too happy that Lucian was the cause of all this lying.

"I understand. I am not mad at you. I would go through it all again if it meant that Luce would be free."

I bit my tongue, knowing if I lashed out because I was jealous it would make me look like a fool.

"Wait, you knew where she was and what was happening this whole time?" Jackson asked. Aurora nodded. "Why didn't you say anything?"

"Because Nico would have gone after her. Ryan needed the time to train, and she couldn't have done that with you four males breathing down her throat. Jax, I know you are angry and hurt about my brother leaving you, but he had a part to play as well." Jax reeled back in his seat like Aurora had just hit him.

"What was his part to play, *mate?*" Jackson snapped at Aurora.

"Okay, I am getting tired of you using the word 'mate' like that. I have never interfered with any of my visions before, *except one.*" Jackson hung his head in shame. "Tyler needed to be on the inside so he could set Ryan and Lucian free, should the opportunity arise."

I looked at Tyler. He betrayed his pack and his best friend just to save my wife's life. I could never repay that debt. I stood and crossed the room to stand in front of him. Ryan looked like she was ready to intervene at any moment if I should try anything. I extended my hand to Tyler.

"Thank you." He looked at me with confusion. "I treated you like shit. What you did for Ryan is something I will never be able to repay. Thank you for saving my wife's life. I, Nicholas Stone, King of Farrarie, am in your debt." I bowed my head to Tyler.

Where I come from that is *the* highest honor, to have a king bow before you. Tyler jumped to his feet and clasped his hand in mine and shook it.

"There is no debt to be repaid; I did what I had to in order to ensure my pack would live. Training Ryan was my honor, Your Majesty." I snapped my gaze to Ryan, shocked that Tyler had been the one to train her.

Dom huffed. "Okay, I am tired of this back and forth. Ryan, start from the beginning, love, and fill in all the missing pieces for us, please."

CHAPTER 29

I watched as Nico returned to his seat, checking his ass out. I'm not even gonna lie or try and deny it; he had a great ass, plus he is my husband, so I should be able to check him out whenever I want.

"Eye-fuck your husband later, love." Dom said in a stage whisper while winking at me. I didn't even blush. I just smiled at him and winked back.

"Okay, here goes. After I was taken from the chapel, I was thrown in a cell at Randall's, I was beaten three times a day." I heard a lot of growls and grunts around the room; the guys clearly didn't like that. "I was given vampire blood to heal my wounds and then injected with something that would knock me out. Randall would come and draw my blood three times a day. I don't know what he did with my blood; maybe he drank it or gave it to his men, who knows. Lucian and I bonded as he was in the cell across from me. When Randall and Stevie left the mansion one day, Tyler set us free and took both Lucian and I to meet up with my cousins."

Sophia re-entered the room, looking more composed now. She sat in the seat she occupied before.

"We chartered a plane. Before we continue, I need you all to swear to me that what I am about to tell you will not leave this room."

After everyone gave a verbal agreement, I continued.

"We flew to Toronto and then drove to the Yukon, to my grandparents, Marcus and Bethany Knox." I heard gasps around the room; they too believed my grandparents were dead.

"Once there, they took us in and cared for us. Gramps trained Luce, while Tyler trained me, Alex, and Chase in hand-to-hand combat and self-defense. After training with Tyler, we then moved on to magic training with Gramps. It was then that we learned that Luce was my shield, or neutralizer. Lucian is the only one that can help me draw my magic back inside of me so I don't die. Lucian and I are bonded and must remain together in order to save—"

"Have you fucked him?" Nico blurted out.

I turned to him and glared. I could tell from the look of shock on his face that he didn't mean to say that out loud. Chase, Alex, Tyler, and Lucian all began to laugh, and Nico jumped up, obviously embarrassed and ready to defend his dignity.

"For the love of all that is holy, Tink. You really are stupid." Nico growled at Chase and I could see his pulse pounding in his forehead.

"Nico, Lucian is very important to me, and I love him dearly."

Nico turned his eyes to me, and the look of heartbreak on his face nearly broke me. He thought I had replaced him.

"Don't look at me like that, big guy."

"Look at you like what, love? I have been here worrying and searching for you, while you've been off fucking some kid! How am I supposed to feel, huh?"

I jumped to my feet and we stood there glaring at each

other, neither of us willing to back down. Lucian stood and tried to step in front of me, but Nico lashed out and blasted Luce with a purple energy ball. Sophia screamed, and I didn't hesitate to launch my own energy ball at my husband and send him sailing into the wall. He crumpled to the ground.

He sprang up and made his way back to me, where I stood waiting, in a fighting stance.

"So, this is how it ends, is it?" Nico sounded so angry and betrayed. I tried to formulate a response but nothing would come out.

"It will never end for you and her." I turned to see Lucian climbing back to his feet with Sophia's help.

"The whole time we were held captive all she wanted was you! When she did manage to get some sleep, it was you she called for. When we were free, she would sleep in *your* shirt every night. She was worried sick that you didn't love her anymore. You are a fool if you think she would ever love another man like she loves you!"

Lucian's words brought tears to my eyes. I didn't know I called out for Nico each night. Lucian really was the best; I loved that guy so much.

"How do you know she called out to him every night?" Fuck, only Dom would pick up on that bit of info. I turned back to Nico and saw a look of hurt cross his beautiful face.

"Because I couldn't bear the thought of sleeping alone again. Plus everything was new and scary. I couldn't sleep without Ryan."

Nico started growling and so did Dom. I quickly cut in to try smooth things over.

"He slept on the floor, Nico. Then as it got colder, we did share a bed." Nico's expression darkened and he looked like he wanted to murder Lucian. "We have never had sex, I swear."

Nico took a menacing step forward. We were so close I

could feel his body heat. My body wanted to lean into him and have him hold me, but I could see we were still at odds.

"Am I just supposed to believe you, little one? You have changed in your time away, you even dress differently now. Wouldn't be the first time you fucked someone else while being with me."

Wow! That was a fucking low blow, and he knew it. I chose to be the bigger person and let his dumb-fuck comment go.

"You should believe me because I am telling you the truth." Nico reached up with his hand and pushed my hair behind my ear. I shivered at the feel of him. He leaned down to whisper in my ear.

"I. Don't. Believe. You."

Nico

I feel her shiver at my touch. As I stand here, staring down at the woman that has stolen my heart, I want nothing more than to believe her words. A part of me doesn't trust that the boy kept his hands to himself. She stands there looking up at me with desire and longing swirling in her eyes. I groan internally. I want her so bad, but I have to know the truth first.

I also want to know what else happened while she was away and why we couldn't locate her. I pull my gaze from hers and look over her head at the boy. My sister is fussing over him, checking for any injuries. What the hell is wrong with her?

"Soph, leave the kid alone, he's fine," Dom snaps.

"Shut your mouth, Dominic." Shit, my sister is in a mood. A hand wraps around my neck and another on my cheek. My face is turned and pulled down, so I'm looking into my wife's eyes again.

"I swear to you, I never betrayed you. Lucian and I have found it difficult to sleep on our own since Randall's. We both have nightmares. That's *all*, Nico. I love Lucian like a brother." Her words had me slumping and the anger draining from my body. I rest my forehead against hers and just breathe her in.

Her eyes flutter shut, and I wrap my arms around her and pull her against me, resting my chin on top of her head. My gaze meets Lucian's, and he smiles and nods his head. I see it in his eyes that he loves Ryan like a big sister.

"Why couldn't I locate you?" I pull away from Ryan and wrap one arm around her waist so she is tucked into my side.

"Luce, do you want to answer that question, buddy?" Huh, why would he answer for her?

"Oh, right. Because I am Smurf's shield or whatever, as long as I am with her, you won't be able to track her or locate her." Well, Lucian might just come in handy after all.

"That's a nifty little trick. I wondered why I couldn't find her. I knew she was alive, but I couldn't pinpoint her location." Mya looked impressed with Lucian's abilities. That reminded me...I turned to look over my shoulder at Lucian.

"What kind of supernatural are you?"

"I think we should all sit down for this one." Tyler sounded ominous, so we all listened and sat. Ryan was tucked into my side. "Okay, so—" Jax cut Tyler off.

"You don't get to speak!"

"Jackson, how many—"

Aurora's scream cut her brother off and shut everyone up. "I have had enough! Jackson, stop behaving like a fucking child. Tyler, make a formal apology, then we can move on. If you two can't sort your shit out there will be no family reunion or no chance of talking about being mates!"

Holy shit, Aurora just went Hurricane Sophie on their asses. Both men looked—or rather glared—at each other, neither moving.

"I swear to God, I will move out of the room next to yours, Jackson, and Tyler, I will not speak to you again."

"Fuck you, Rora!" Tyler yelled. "I did all of this for you! You told me about your fucking vision, and I went along with it because you told me it would *save* the pack. Now look, I'm two minutes away from being pack-less and out on my own, and my wolf is driving me half-mad over my betrayal."

"Tyler, you will never be on your own. I told you this. Where you go, I go," Ryan snapped at Tyler. Tyler turned to her, and the anger in his eyes started to dissipate. "I mean it, Ty. We're in this together, remember?"

Tyler smiled sadly and turned to Jackson. "I'm sorry, Jackson. I never meant to betray you. I thought I would be strong enough to fight the mate bond. I was never meant to fall in love with Stevie Knox. I got sucked in, and when the time came to choose a side, I hesitated, but in the end I kept up my part and set Ryan free. I was always the one meant to train her, and Gramps was always going to be the one to help her train to use her magic. I did what I did to save the pack."

I could hear the truth in Tyler's words, and I saw Jax scent the air to see if he could detect any deceit.

"As alpha of the Alaskan pack, you are forgiven and welcomed home." Aurora and Tyler were both smiling at his words. "As your friend, I can't forgive you....yet. Once more, though, my mate has lied to me, again! Vision or not, Aurora, you need to stop lying to me!" Aurora and Tyler weren't smiling anymore. They both had a lot of work to do in order to win Jackson's trust back.

"Can we get this talk over with? I'm starving." Fucking Dominic needed a muzzle. Ryan giggled beside me, the sound sending warmth coursing through my body. I missed her so much while she was gone.

"I tried to come to you every night, love. I even asked Kai to try." Ryan stiffened at my words and glanced at Kai then quickly back to me. After a long sigh, she finally spoke.

"I tried for weeks to reach you. I even tried to reach Kai." My jealousy surged at the mention of her trying to go to Kai. I took a few deep calming breaths to control my jealousy. "I didn't know what was up until Gramps told me that Lucian cancels out any magic that tries to get near me." That little fucker was blocking me! I snapped my gaze to him and glared.

"Hey, it's not my fault. I don't even know what the hell I am, dude. It wasn't something I did intentionally."

"What do you mean?" Sophia asked Lucian.

"Look, all I know is my parents were fae, that's it." Sophia hung her head and wouldn't meet the kid's gaze. There was something going on with her and I needed to find out what it was, soon.

"Look, this has been a long-ass day, and I'm hungry as shit." Tyler, Lucian, and her cousins started laughing, and she flipped them the bird.

"All I have to say is we're here now, and we're ready to fight. I have learned how to master my magic, and I can fight now. Tomorrow morning I will take the other half of my magic from Nico, and Lucian and Tyler will help me manage the new power."

Like fuck would they be the only ones helping her. Ryan has another thing coming if she thinks I will sit back and let her do this on her own.

After leaving Jackson's office, we all made our way to the mess hall. We all gathered our food from the buffet and sat down to eat. I'm sitting between Lucian and Nico, and Alex and Chase keep sending me sly smirks and winks from across the table. I want to slap both their stupid faces right now. Everyone is talking and catching us up on what we have missed and what the battle plan is. Dom continues to scowl at Lucian, because Sophia can't seem to stop staring at my friend. I have no idea what her fascination is with Lucian, but clearly Dom doesn't like it.

I didn't realize how much I had missed these guys until now. It's been great catching up with them and laughing, but I do miss Grams and Gramps.

"Hey does anyone have a phone?" All eyes turned to me.

"You can use mine, little hybrid. The number is already saved." I thanked Tyler and grabbed his phone.

"Who are you calling?" Nico asked, and before I could answer, Alex cut in.

"You need to get a handle on your trust issues. She spent the past twenty-two weeks trying to figure out a way to get back to you, Tink. To save you and your world. Give her some breathing space, and for the love of fucking God, at least trust her."

Before Nico could go ape-shit on my cousins, I placed my hand on his forearm and said, "I'm going to call my grandparents, big guy."

I didn't wait for a response. I stood from my seat and made my way out of the mess hall. I walked toward my old room, hoping it was still empty. As I opened the bedroom door and stepped inside, a sense of nostalgia hit me. I had missed this room.

"Didn't think you could leave me behind, did you?" I spun around at the sound of Lucian's voice and smiled.

"Sorry, Luce, I didn't even think."

"Don't sweat it, Smurf. Let's call Gramps and Grams." Lucian shut the bedroom door and we made our way over to the bed and sat down. I scrolled through Tyler's contacts until I found Grams and Gramps, saved as "Secret Knoxs." I chuckled at Tyler's silly name for them and hit the green button. It rang four times before someone picked up.

"Hello?"

"Grams, it's Ryan!"

"Marcus, it's Ryan, come here. Hello, my dear, how are you? Did you get there safe?"

"Let her talk, Bethy." I smiled at Gramps telling Grams to slow down on the questions.

"I'm fine, we're all fine. We're here now, Grams, and we're all safe."

"Thank heavens, we have been so worried about you all."

"We're fine, Grams, I swear."

"Is that trickster husband of yours treating you right? If he isn't, send one of those boys to deal with him!" I chuckled at Gramps's overprotectiveness, but I also loved it. This is what I had missed my entire childhood.

"He's been fine, Gramps. He was shocked to see us and to meet Lucian." Gramps laughed, I knew he was laughing at Nico's expense. Alex and Chase had told Gramps how jealous Nico could get. Gramps wanted payback for Nico using a glamour on himself when they first met many years ago.

"Good, serves him right for the shit he put you through. How is the battle planning going?" I filled them in on the plan and how we were going to meet with the elders tomorrow. I was nervous about seeing the elders and how they would react to me after what I had done the night of my wedding. I had taken so many lives, and I knew I had to face the consequences for my actions. But that would happen after the battle and after I saved the fae realm.

"You keep your head held high, you hear me? You are the queen of the Knox coven, and you come from a strong line of witches and warlocks. You are also the queen of the fae. You bow to no one, granddaughter."

Gramps's words made me feel proud. I felt like I could take on the world with them behind me.

"If you need anything, you call us, dear. We will be there as soon as we can." I thanked them both and told them I would call again soon. I missed them so much already, but I had to end this war in order for them to be free. Stevie would use them against me if she found out they were alive.

"It was good to hear their voices."

"Yeah, it was, Luce. I miss them so much already."

"I know you do." Lucian pulled me into a side hug, and I rested my head on his chest. The bedroom door burst open and Nico stalked in with a vile look on his face.

"Get the fuck out, *boy!*"

CHAPTER 32
Nico

As soon as she left, her lap dog jumped to his feet and followed her out. I scowled at his retreating form then sat there quietly seething. How fucking dare he go after her? *I'm* her husband.

"Calm the fuck down, Tink, it's not even like that with them." I snapped my gaze to Chase and glared at the bastard.

"Nico, he is a child, and lost. He needs Ryan to help him, they care for each other like siblings." Tyler's words did nothing to ease my jealousy. She was eighteen, and he's sixteen. They were close in age and probably had more in common than she and I did. I'm over a century old and had lived a life full of adventure while she was just starting hers.

"Brother, he is of no threat to you, I swear it." I turned and looked at my sister with brows raised.

"How would you know that, little dove?"

"I just do, Dominic. He cares for her, but she loves you. I told you I saw that you and she would be together."

"I never saw him coming! I didn't even know he would play a part in her life," Mya said to Sophia.

"Fuck this." I stood from my seat and marched out of the mess hall, the guys' laughter following me out. I could feel through our bond where she was. I stopped in front of her bedroom and tried to calm down. I heard them talking, and then it went quiet, and I couldn't stop myself. I burst through the door and froze at the sight of her in his arms. I saw red.

"Get the fuck out, *boy!*" I snapped. Ryan pulled away from him and frowned at me. "Tell him to leave now!"

"Don't tell her what to do!" I lashed out and wrapped him in my magic, lifting him from the bed. Ryan jumped to her feet, and her hands started to glow blue.

"Smurf, no!" Ryan looked to Lucian and then her hands stopped glowing. She glared at the boy, who was suspended off the ground, and made a small, angry screaming sound that almost distracted me, it was so cute.

"I got this, trust me." What the fuck was this boy on about?

"Lucian, don't, please. Nico, put him down now before—" She didn't get to finish. The boy let out a deafening roar, and my hold on him snapped.

My magic returned to me, and the boy stood there, glowing yellow, his eyes morphing from gray-violet to pure violet. I underestimated the boy; he was stronger than I thought. I could feel his strength. He was part fae, but there was something else.

He was another hybrid! How could that be?

Besides Ryan, Sophia and Dom were the only two hybrids we knew. Sophia couldn't access her fae side. Dom could access both his sides, but I have never heard of another.

"I have been beaten, starved, and treated like shit my whole life. I will never let another treat me that way again—or anyone I care about." I heard noise behind me and saw the whole gang was here— great. Ryan never took her gaze off the boy.

She moved to stand in front of him, and I took a step forward to stop her when I was blasted by a force so strong it sent me sailing into the others.

We all crashed to the ground, and with a groan I quickly

stood and helped Dom and Jax to their feet. They both looked pissed that they were the ones to break my fall. Whoops, my bad. I glared at Lucian, and watched as my wife stood in front of him.

"He has a force field around them, I-I can't breach it." Dom was the strongest fae I knew, but if he couldn't breach this force field, it meant that this boy was stronger, strong like Ryan.

"He won't let you breach it. Lucian is strong, one of the strongest fae I have ever met. Unless he wants you near him or Ryan, you will never enter his field." I could hear the awe in Alex's voice.

"Luce, look at me, please, buddy." Ryan was trying to calm the boy. "It's okay, Luce, I'm right here. Nico would never hurt me, I swear. He was just being an overbearing jackass. It's kinda his thing." I opened my mouth to protest but Dom pinched me, hard.

"I will not let him treat you that way, Smurf."

"I know, Luce. Thank you. I need you to drop the shield now, buddy. I promise Nico won't hurt me." I would rather die than ever cause Ryan physical harm, and the fact that Lucian thought I would ever harm her made me angry. I loved that girl more than anything.

Lucian started to draw his magic back into himself, and as soon as the last of it disappeared, Ryan engulfed him in a hug.

"He may be her shield, but she is his anchor." I heard the truth in Tyler's words. There was more to this boy, and I had a feeling my sister knew what that was.

"I'm sorry, Smurf."

"Don't be, buddy. I love that you protected me. Nico and I have a lot to sort out, and until we do that, he is going to be an ass."

"You know I can hear you, right? I'm standing right here!" I snapped at my wife, and she and the boy both chuckled.

"Do you think you would be okay to hang with Ty and my cousins for a bit while I talk to Nico?"

"Yeah, Smurf. If you need me, just call out. I won't be far." I growled.

"Boy, you are overstepping your place and need to back the hell off," I snapped.

"I will back off when you can prove you can keep her safe! Until then I will not leave her side, *Tink*" I heard the others snicker behind me at the use of the nickname Ryan's cousins had been calling me.

I was going to lose my shit soon!

"All of you, out!" Everyone started to file out of the room, and I could hear them all giggling like a pack of assholes.

Lucian hugged Ryan one last time before making his way out of the room. I slammed the door as soon as he left and locked it—not that locking it ever stopped any of them from entering before. I took a deep breath before turning around and facing my wife.

"Hello, love." She started laughing, and I couldn't help but laugh with her.

"After all of that macho display, you go with 'hello love?'" I shrugged my shoulders.

"I thought it might be a good ice breaker."

"Touché, big man" I sighed and ran a hand through my hair. I could feel how awkward things were between us, and I wanted to fix that.

"Can we sit down and talk, love, please?" She nodded her head and made her way over to the single seat by the window, and I sat on the edge of the bed. We sat there, staring at each other for a while. I had dreamed of those beautiful, strange eyes every night while she was gone.

"I missed you." Her admission shocked me. "Don't look so shocked, Nico."

"I can't help it, love. I just never thought you would say that out loud. You really have changed. You're not so shy anymore."

"I have changed. I didn't really have a choice, though. I went through a lot; I needed to be stronger and learn to stand on my own. I couldn't reach you or Kai, and I'll be honest, if it wasn't for Lucian, I would have given up while I was stuck at Randall's."

"Don't say that. Don't ever say that, love."

She smiled a sad smile. "It's true, Nico. I gave up hope that you would come for me." I stood and stalked over to her, placing my arms on either side of the chair, caging her in. I leaned down so we were nearly nose to nose and said, "I will never not come for you. I will burn the whole fucking world down for you, Ryan Stone."

CHAPTER 33

Ryan

Him being this close to me was intoxicating, and his words didn't really register until he said *Ryan Stone*. I never thought about my name changing when we got married.

"What's wrong, love? You look scared." I started shaking my head, and Nico clasped my face between both his hands so he could look into my eyes. "What's wrong?"

"M-my name."

Nico smiled a cocky smile; he knew what I was talking about. He loved the fact that he shocked me about the name change. He wanted to mark me as his in every way possible.

"Of course your name has changed, love, we're married." I batted his hands away and pushed to my feet. I needed to pace.

"I know we're married, it's just a shock to hear my name come out of *your* mouth." Nico's arm snaked around my waist, and I was pulled flush against him, my back to his chest.

He kept one arm wrapped around my waist and used his other hand to push my hair away so he could run his nose up and down the side of my neck. I stilled, unsure what was happening.

"Relax, love," he whispered in my ear. He continued to run

his nose up and down my neck, and I gasped when he licked the same trail with his tongue. He stopped licking, only to start sucking the side of my neck. I craned my neck to the side so he had better access.

He stopped sucking, and then started peppering kisses over my neck and then my cheek. I turned my head toward him and captured his lips in a searing kiss.

He spun me around without breaking our kiss and ran his hands down my body, gripping the back of my thighs and lifting me. My legs wrapped around his waist, and I locked my arms around his neck. Being here like this with Nico felt right. I've missed him so much. He walked us toward the bed and laid me down gently.

He pulled back and looked at me, so much love and desire swirling in his eyes.

"I have missed you every day, little one. I couldn't think straight without you, and it killed me when I couldn't reach you in your dreams. It hurt more and more each day when I couldn't find you. Now that you're back, I won't ever let you go, love...I can't." I could see from the hard lines in his face it was hard for him to admit this to me.

"I'm sorry I didn't call you when I got to the Yukon. We had to be so careful not to tip anyone off as to where we were, not just for us, but for my grandparents, too. I tried to reach you in my dreams every night. I didn't know Lucian was subconsciously blocking my dreams. Please don't be mad at him."

"Can we not talk about him while I'm standing between your legs with a fucking boner, love?" I gasped, and as if my eyes had a mind of their own, they trailed down Nico's body and landed on the hard bulge straining against his jeans. Nico started chuckling, and I quickly jerked my eyes up. I was busted! I felt the blush creeping up my neck. I don't know why I was embarrassed. It's not like I haven't seen it before—I just haven't seen it in real life.

"Why do you look sad, love?"

"I'm not sad, I-I'm just nervous, I guess." The smile dropped from Nico's face.

"Nervous about what?"

"You and me and you know?" I said, gesturing between us with my hands. He started laughing again and I groaned; I was beyond embarrassed now. I used both my hands to cover my face. I was inexperienced, and he had nearly a century of practice.

What if I wasn't good enough?

Nico pulled my hands away from my face and leaned down so he was hovering above me, resting his hands on either side of my face.

"Don't hide from me, love. Tell me what's going through your mind right now." I knew I needed to be honest with him. I took a deep breath and then said.

"Nico, you know I have never done this before. I mean, I have, but—"

"What the fuck do you mean *you have?*" I could see the anger brewing in his eyes. Dear God this guy and jumping to conclusions was like a moth to a flame.

"Stop interrupting! I meant you know I have only done this in my dreams. I've never done this while I was *awake.*" I saw the moment Nico registered what I was saying. He leaned down and captured my lips, and I opened for him as I always did. He slipped his tongue inside my mouth and started exploring.

I relaxed into the bed and started to run my hands down his back and under his shirt, scraping my nails along his spine. He moaned into my mouth and started to rock his pelvis into mine. The friction of him grinding into me, and my jeans rubbing me in the right place, had me writhing beneath him. I needed more.

I wanted him inside me *now*. I bunched his shirt in my hands and pulled it up, and Nico helped me pull it off and chucked it to the side. I shrugged my jacket off and lobbed it across the room. Nico immediately slid his hands under my black crop top and peeled it right off my body. I lay there beneath him in my jeans and my red lacy bra, chest heaving.

His gaze turned dark as he looked down at me, lust swimming in the depths of his eyes. That look bolstered my confidence, knowing I was the one who put that look on his face and caused that bulge in his pants.

"I want you, love." I could tell from the raw huskiness of his voice that his restraint was about to snap. I wanted him; I have *always* wanted him to be my first. He said he didn't want to have sex until we were married, and now that we are, and we're finally together again, there is nothing stopping us from making love. I looked him in the eyes and ran my hand down his cheek.

"I want this. I want you." He kissed me while he undid my jeans, only breaking the hold on my lips to pull my jeans off. His hungry gaze rakes over my tiny red thong and I shiver. He's looking at me like I am a feast after a long fast. The anticipation of what is to come is killing me.

"You're so fucking beautiful, love...I can't wait to taste you." Goosebumps break out over my skin as Nico runs his hands up my legs and over my stomach. When he reaches my breast, he pulls the cups of my bra down and exposes both the girls.

My nipples are rock hard already, and I can feel the liquid pooling between my legs.

Nico leans down and captures one of my nipples between his teeth and starts to suck, hard. I moan loud and arch up off the bed so I can force my breast further into his mouth. His other hand comes up, and he begins to twist and pull my nipple. I buck beneath him, desperate for him to touch me elsewhere.

"Nico, please." He releases my nipple with a pop and peers up at me through his long lashes.

"Please what, love?" He loved doing this shit to me in my dreams. He got off on me begging.

"I need you to touch me." He began to tweak both my nipples between his fingers.

"I am touching you, love." I groaned. He knew what I meant but he wanted me to say it.

"I want you to touch me down there." The smug bastard smirked at me.

"Touch down where, love?"

I growled. "I want you to touch my pussy, Nico, and make me fucking come!"

"Well you don't need to shout, love." I wanted to slap that smug look off his face. Before I could reply with a smart remark, he began to make his way down my body, trailing kisses across my stomach and then down my thighs.

He was torturing me with how slow he was moving. He kissed all the way down my leg and back up, then started nibbling on my inner thigh and slowly making his way to the apex of my thighs. He leaned in and inhaled.

"I can smell your arousal, love." I couldn't find it within me to be embarrassed.

CHAPTER 34

Nico

It turned me on, scenting her arousal. I pulled her thong down her legs and discarded it to the side. I had seen her sweet pussy so many times, but seeing it for the first time while not dreaming was something else. I couldn't hold back any longer. I wanted to draw this moment out, but my restraint was about to snap. I dove in and started to feast on her sweet pussy, swirling my tongue around her enlarged nub. She cried out, and I licked and sucked her even more vigorously.

"I-I need more, Nico!" I didn't make her beg like I normally would, I wanted her first time to be different. I slowed down and licked her while I slid a finger inside her wet pussy. Fuck, she was so tight. I groaned; my dick was straining against my jeans, painfully.

I started pumping my finger in and out of her, and she moaned loudly, her moans spurring me on. On the next push in, I added another finger so I could get her ready for me. I wasn't small, so I needed to stretch her as much as I could to make this first time easier for her.

I picked up the pace and ate her like she was my last meal,

all the while pumping my fingers in and out of her. She was thrashing beneath me and grinding her pussy against my mouth.

"Nico, I-I'm gonna come."

"Come all over my fingers, baby." I sucked her enlarged nub into my mouth and pumped my fingers inside her pussy faster. Within a minute she was screaming my name, her tight channel pulsing, squeezing my fingers.

I slowed my movements to let her come down from her climax gently. Aftershocks wracked her body. I pulled my fingers out of her and kissed her inner thigh before making my way up her body. I pulled her up so I could unclasp her bra, chucking the garment to the side. I laid her down gently and began running my hands down her body. I was mesmerized by her beauty. She's a goddess. Looking down at her beautiful face and seeing how flushed her cheeks are from her orgasm made my dick twitch. Her long brown hair is fanned out around her, her eyes are staring at me with wonder, excitement, and fear. I want to make this special for her.

CHAPTER 35

I can see the torment on his beautiful face. I reach down and unclasp his jeans pushing them and his briefs down, I don't break eye contact with him. I'm trying to tell him with my eyes that I'm ready and I want him.

He helps me by removing his jeans and then settles between my thighs. I lie there, looking up at him, and I see so much love and devotion in his eyes. I reach up with my hand and run it through his hair, pulling it lightly so he'll bend down to me. When he's halfway, I sit up and capture his mouth in a kiss. He starts grinding his hips and I moan, feeling my center once again warming at his touch.

I pull back and smile at my husband. He is so beautiful, with his jet-black hair, violet eyes, and a body to kill for. I am one lucky woman to be able to call this man my husband. He steals my breath away every time. I never thought I would ever be lucky enough to ever find someone like Nico. He literally is the man of my dreams.

"I love you, Nico." His eyes soften at my words.

"I love you too, Ryan." He lines himself up at my opening.

"Are you sure you're ready? We have the rest of our lives together to do this. We can wait."

I pull his face down to mine and look him straight in the eyes as I say, "I want this, Nico. I am absolutely ready."

He nods his head and slowly, he starts to push inside of me. I feel a slight sting and I tense and try to take deep breaths. He stops pushing and I can see the strain on his face. It's taking everything inside of him to not slam inside of me.

"Relax, baby, I'm halfway there." I nod my head and try to relax, but if he was trying to reassure me, that wasn't the right thing to say. Only halfway! It's never felt like this in my dreams. He waits for me to adjust to his size, and after a few moments, I give him another nod.

"Keep going." This time he doesn't go slowly; he slams the rest of the way inside me, and I feel the moment he snaps my innocence. I feel so full, yet complete, like my final puzzle piece has been put into place.

"Are you okay, love?" I can hear the strain in his voice, and I see sweat dotting his brow. I know it's hard for him to be still and let me adjust to him being inside me, but I just need a minute to breathe through the pain.

I nod my head after the stinging starts to abate, and he begins to move, the pain giving way to pleasure. I moan loudly and rake my nails down his naked back.

"You're so fucking tight love," he pants, picking up the pace and pounding into me. I can feel a storm brewing inside me... I'm so close to coming.

"Nico, I-I...oh, God. That feels so good, gonna come." I couldn't form a proper sentence. He slams into me so hard, I start to see stars, then I shatter beneath him, screaming his name. He continues his relentless assault on my body, tipping over the edge himself just moments later.

He collapses next to me, both of us panting. That was the most incredible experience of my life. Nico pulls me against him, both of us lying on our sides, staring at each other. I open my mouth to talk to Nico, but before I could say anything, Nico jumps off the bed and saunters into the bathroom. Holy shit, he just left me here. Before I could continue to spiral down my rabbit hole, Nico returns with a washcloth in his hand and his boxers back on.

"What's the cloth for?"

"To clean you up, my love. You didn't think I just left you did you?" I want to shake my head and tell him no, but I don't want to lie, so I nod my head instead. He looks hurt that I would think so little of him. He opens my legs, and I blush immediately, I know he was just inside me, and his face was down there, but come on.

Nico gently wipes me then takes the cloth back to the bathroom before rejoining me on the bed again.

He reaches over and gathers me in his arms, then tugs the comforter over the both of us and places a gentle kiss on the top of my head.

I sigh in contentment and snuggle into him.

"I know you still don't trust me fully, love. One day I hope that you will, though." I hate to admit it, but he's right. I may be in love with him, but I don't trust him fully. Things between us moved very quickly, and we have a history that has not helped develop that mutual trust.

"I don't want there to be any secrets between us, love."

Holy shit, does he know? I push the thought out of my mind; there is no way he could know.

"Why do I feel like there's a *but* coming?" I mumble into his chest. He takes a deep breath and starts rubbing my naked back. I hope what he has to say doesn't ruin this moment. I want this to be a happy memory, one I can hold onto.

"Your mother is in Farrarie," he blurts out. I tense, and he stops rubbing my back. We're both as stiff as boards, waiting for the other to say something or do something.

If I'm honest, I was more worried he knew about *my* secret. Here I am, letting him think he needs to earn my trust back, when in reality whatever progress we make I will shatter when the time comes. I don't want him to know the truth; I want to enjoy these last moments we have together before everything blows up in our faces. I know he will be hurt and angry, but I have to pay the price for the sins I have committed.

"Why is my mother in the fae realm?" I whisper. I feel Nico deflate; he was waiting for me to go off and lose my shit. Glad I could surprise you, big man.

"After you went missing, I had her sent to my realm so I could question her. The elders had me banned from this realm, because they knew I would come for you. The only way the fae elders could ensure peace was to lock me in Farrarie."

Holy crap, that's why Nico didn't come for me? He was literally a world away. I felt guilty for thinking less of him. I thought he had given up on me but the whole time he was trying to get back here so he could come for me. I held him tighter and kissed his chest. This man never ceased to amaze me.

"Did my mother tell you anything?"

"No, love, her memory is blank. She doesn't remember much about raising you. I filled her in on some of it, and she was devastated. She hates herself for what she has done to you. I believe being in my realm is helping her and taking away the curse that was placed on her years ago. She is...well, a very different person."

"I...I don't know what to say. I mean, as a child, I always wished my mother would change, but now I don't know if I could view her as anything but the star of my nightmares."

CHAPTER 36

Nico

Ryan finally drifted off to sleep. We laid there talking for hours. She told me about her training and how close she had gotten to her grandparents. I filled her in on what she had missed out on here. We spoke about other mundane things, and I felt like we were becoming closer. We used to talk like this all the time, before she knew I was real. I missed these talks. I would never let her go again, not after what we had just done. She willingly gave me a part of herself that no other man would ever have.

My love for this woman just keeps amplifying. I don't know how I stayed away from her for so long. My cock starts to stir inside my boxers at the thought of how amazing it felt to be inside of her.

Having sex in her dreams was nothing compared to the real thing. She fit me like a glove, and watching her come apart beneath me while we were both awake was the most beautiful thing. She is my beautiful dream, come true.

A knock at the door pulled me from my thoughts. I looked down at her to make sure she was covered properly under the blanket before telling whoever it was to come in. I groaned at the sight of Lucian entering the room. He scanned the room, his gaze landing on my wife's sleeping form. I cleared my throat to draw his attention to me; I didn't like him looking at her, especially because she was naked under the covers.

"What do you want, boy?" Lucian smirked at me and made his way over to the window to gaze out at the scenery.

"You know, if you weren't such a dick, I might actually like you." I smiled at his back; the kid had balls, I give him that.

"You do know I am a king and can have you punished for speaking to me like that." He chuckled quietly and then turned to face me; his eyes were downcast and his shoulders tense.

"I actually came to ask you a favor."

"Oh, this should be good. Give me a minute and I'll meet you outside?" Lucian nodded and left the room. I untangled myself from Ryan and quickly dressed, dropping a light kiss on her shoulder before leaving the room. I closed the door quietly behind me, finding Lucian was leaning against the wall in the hallway.

"What's the favor, Lucian?"

"So you do know my name." he said with a smirk. I narrowed my eyes at him. He straightened and steeled his spine. I respected him more in this moment; he met my gaze and never wavered. "I was told my parents were from your realm; I want to find out about them."

"What exactly are you asking me?"

"I want your permission to enter your realm after the war. I want to search for answers and find out what my mother did to become a prisoner of Randall Cane's." Well, well. The boy wanted to do some digging and find out where he came from. If I denied him, my wife would be pissed, if I granted him entry, he would be close by when Ryan moved to my realm. Having him there with her might help her settle in better, though.

"I don't want Smurf to know about this, though."

"Why don't you want her to know?"

He averted his gaze from mine and mumbled, "I need to do this by myself. She needs to live her life. If I tell her, she will want to help me." He's not wrong—Ryan would want to help and wouldn't rest until she got answers for her friend, but I also wouldn't lie to her again.

"You have my permission, but I won't lie to my wife, Lucian." Our conversation was cut short when the bedroom door opened behind us and Ryan walked out, back in the clothes she arrived in. She glared at Lucian.

"All you had to do was say that to me, Luce, and I would have left you be. Asking Nico to hide shit from me is low." She shouldered past Lucian but didn't get far before he gripped her arm and pulled her back. I growled. I was ready to put this bastard down if she said the word.

"Don't, Luce, let me go now!"

"Smurf, please—I'm sorry, but I don't want you to put your life on hold for me. You deserve to be happy and live a life with your husband, not chase ghosts with me." I saw her eyes soften and her body deflate at his words.

"Luce, you are family to me. I would chase ghosts for the rest of my life if it meant you were happy. Please don't ever shut me out again, or ask Nico to hide things from me, just talk to me." They embraced each other in a quick hug, Lucian whispering a promise to never hide anything from her again. I nearly puked at how mushy they were being.

Fuck, I really needed to get a handle on my jealousy.

CHAPTER 37

Ryan

Lucian, Nico, and I made our way to the mess hall to grab some dinner. After the workout Nico and I had just completed, I needed some fuel for my body—and a shower.

We entered the mess hall, and I must say for the first time it was actually refreshing to see and hear all the hustle and bustle in here. We made our way over to the food station and loaded our plates full of delicious food before getting a table toward the back of the room.

We ate in comfortable silence. Halfway through our meal, I looked up to see Dom, Jax, Aurora, Mya, Sophia, Tyler, and my cousins join our table. Kai was nowhere in sight. My heart sank; he was so angry with me. I knew he would be pissed off and hurt, but I didn't think he would cut me off completely.

"The mosquitoes must be bad around here," Dom said, laughing. I looked around the table, confused. The only people not laughing were Nico, Lucian, and I.

"Here I thought Kai was the only biter." They all started laughing harder at Jackson's comment.

What the hell are they all on about?

"I don't understand what is so funny?" Sophia's gaze softened as she turned to face Lucian.

"We're laughing because clearly my brother has a thing for biting the hybrid." Sophia was trying hard to not laugh again, I turned to face Nico and saw a frown marring his beautiful face.

"What do they mean?" I asked. He pulled my hair over my shoulder so it covered the side of my neck and leaned down to whisper in my ear.

"I may have *accidentally* marked you." Oh for the love of all that is holy, did he give me a fucking hickey?

"Nico did you....did you give me a fucking hickey?" I gritted out between clenched teeth. The smug fucker just grinned at me. I was going to kill him. Now everyone at the table knew what we had just done. I slouched in my seat and kept my head down while pushing food around my plate, my appetite was long gone now. I was so embarrassed.

"Come on love, don't be mad." I turned and glared at the prick I had to call my husband.

"Your stupid jealousy just had to let everyone know what we were doing. You are a dick, you know that?" I could see he was trying hard not to smile, and I knew I was blushing. I glowered. Jackson cleared his throat and spoke.

"Wolf shifters have great noses, love. Dom and I could smell him on you."

"And. in you," Dom added. I froze. Oh, for the love of mother Mary. They could smell him inside me. Fuck my life. I jumped to my feet and marched out of the room, their laughter following me as I high- tailed it out of there.

I ran all the way to my room, slamming the door shut behind me. My suitcase and duffel were sitting at the foot of my bed, thank you Lord. I quickly pulled out my sleepwear and went straight into the shower.

After the shower warmed, I quickly stripped my clothes off

and stepped under the spray. I scrubbed every inch of my body to try get rid of Nico's scent.

Fucking overbearing asshole knew what he was doing and wanted everyone else to know it as well. I shampooed my hair with the wonderful shampoo Aurora had given me for my wedding day, but quickly shook thoughts of that day out of my head. I would deal with those when the time came. I rinsed the shampoo out and started to lather conditioner in my hair and closed my eyes.

Two hands landed on my waist and I shrieked, ready to attack the bastard with a ball of energy. One hand left my waist and quickly gripped my wrist to stop me.

"Calm down, love. It's only me." Nico stood there, staring down at me, with droplets of water falling down his face. He was naked!

"You're naked." The bastard cracked up laughing while I stood there and glared at him.

"Yeah, babe, I'm naked."

"Why are you in here?" I felt self-conscious all of a sudden. He had seen me naked plenty of times in my dreams, and he saw me naked today, but I couldn't help but feel less than him. He was beautiful, with a body carved by the gods. I was average height and average looking; what he saw in me I don't know. I dropped my gaze to the floor, but he was having none of that. He released my wrist and tipped my chin up so I had to look at him.

"What's wrong, love?"

"Nothing, I just don't think we should shower together," I lied.

"Why shouldn't we shower together?"

"Because I, I thin—I mean, like..."

"Spit it out, love."

"Because you're beautiful, and I'm not, and now that we're

both standing here in our birthday suits, you can see all my flaws —and you might not like what you see. You might think I'm yuck and not want to be married to me anymore." I blurted all that out so fast I was panting, trying to catch my breath.

Nico's face took on a serious look, and he gripped my waist with his hands and pushed me back until my back was against the tiled wall. He glared down at me. Why was he angry?

"Don't ever, I mean ever, fucking say that shit again! I don't ever want to hear you talk about yourself like that. You are not something to be replaced, Ryan! You are my wife, my *hugacko*. I would die without you; you are my reason for living. You are the most beautiful creature I have ever seen in my life." He didn't give me a chance to reply. He slammed his mouth against mine, forcing my lips open and slipping his tongue inside.

CHAPTER 38
Nico

I take my time exploring her mouth, moving my hands and using one to fondle her nipple while I grip her hair with the other. I continue to kiss her like she is the air that I need to live. When I pinch her nipple between my fingers, she groans in pleasure, and the vibrations send a shiver down my spine. I release my grip on her hair and move to cup her sex. She gasps when I run my index finger through her folds, gripping my shoulders for balance as I push my finger inside her. Her sheath tightens around my finger immediately, and this time I'm the one groaning.

I know she is probably still sore, but I need to be inside her again. She's like a drug to me; I can't seem to get enough of her. I break our kiss and look down at her, all hooded eyes and flushed cheeks.

"Are you too sore?" She shakes her head. "I need to hear the words, baby."

"No, I'm okay," she murmurs. I pull my finger out of her and she pouts; I love this look on her. She's looking at me like she needs me inside of her as much as I need to be in her. I drop to my knees in front of her, and she gasps at the sight of me, under-

standing the significance; I'll never kneel before anyone, except her.

I hook one of her legs over my shoulder and dive in, feasting on her. She cries out as I lick up and down her slit, and then I suck her nub into my mouth. She tastes so fucking good.

"Oh my God!"

I pull back and gaze up at her. "How about we try 'Oh my Nico?' God won't ever get to taste this pussy, baby." I don't wait for her response, I dive back in and lap at her folds, swirling my tongue around her clit. I insert two fingers inside her and pump in and out of her while I suck her clit into my mouth.

"Holy fuck, Nico." She grips a handful of my hair and rides my face like there's no tomorrow. A minute later, she screams out my name, and I pull my fingers out and jump to my feet, lifting her up and slamming her down on my hard, waiting cock. She cries out, and I know I should be gentle, but fuck me, I just can't.

I step forward so her back is against the shower wall and start to move inside her.

"Fuck, your pussy is so tight."

"Mmmmhhhh. Don't stop, Nico. I need more, please." Her words shatter any restraint I had left. I slam into her over and over again, using her body weight to keep her firmly against the wall as I pound inside her until we both find our release in one fantastic crescendo. As we come down, I rest my forehead on her shoulder, panting. Not ready to let her go, I turn us so my back is against the wall and slide down until I'm sitting on the floor.

She doesn't attempt to get up, instead wrapping her arms around my neck and snuggling into me. It's in this moment, with her cuddled against me, and straddling my lap with my dick still inside, that I realize she owns me. I am unconditionally in love with Ryan Stone. I grip her long hair in my hand and pull until she stares up at me, looking annoyed that I interrupted her snuggle session. I release her hair and push the stray strands behind her ears as the water continues to beat down on us. She looks breathtaking, rosy cheeks and glassy eyes, rivulets of water pouring down her body.

"I love you," I blurt out. She places a kiss on my lips before leaning back.

"I love you too, Nico."

CHAPTER 39

Ryan

Nico and I made love in the shower once more before getting out. I say made love, because it was slow and passionate and fucking beautiful. I was losing my whole heart to him and no part of me wanted it back. I wanted him to have my heart forever. I was going to miss him so fucking much.

After changing into my PJs, I hopped into bed, waiting for Nico to get back. He needed clean clothes from his room, and he said he would bring all his stuff into my room tomorrow. We were both too tired to even attempt to do that tonight. My bedroom door opens, but it wasn't Nico that walks in—it's Lucian.

Shit, how the fuck could I have forgotten that Luce was my bed buddy?

Lucian must have showered somewhere, because he was in sweats and a shirt now. He made his way over to the empty side of the bed and drew the covers back. I didn't have the heart to tell him Nico would be back soon. He climbed into the bed and rested his head against the pillow. I had to say something, but what could I say?

Hey, Luce, now that Nico is here, you can't be? Or hey, Luce, back to the floor you go so I can snuggle my husband.

"Smurf, I can hear you overthinking from here. What's on your mind?" I released the breath I didn't know I was holding and laid down on my side so I could face Lucian.

"I don't know, Luce...I didn't expect today to go how it did."

"You mean you didn't expect to fuck your husband six ways to Sunday?" I giggled and hid my face for a moment.

"Who the hell taught you that saying?"

Lucian shrugs his shoulders and says, "Chase has been teaching me some slang." We both laugh, knowing Chase was the worst person to teach Lucian slang.

"Don't listen to my cousin, he will lead you astray."

"He's good people, Smurf. Now stop stalling. What's got you so worried?" Lucian reached over and clasped my hand in his. Being here with Lucian like this felt familiar and safe. I knew I could confide in Lucian with anything; well, except one thing.

"I love him, Luce, and that scares the shit out of me."

Lucian's eyes softened. "Why are you scared?"

"Because one day, something might tear us apart." A look of confusion crossed Lucian's face, then understanding.

"What aren't you telling me, Smurf?" Lucian was great at reading me, so I had to steer this conversation in a different direction before he clued in. He had an inkling about what I had planned, but Gramps and I wouldn't confirm his suspicions.

"Nothing, I'm just scared that after the war I have to leave this place behind. I've only ever been to the fae realm once, and soon I'll have to live there. Not only that—I just found out my mother is there too." Lucian sucked in a sharp breath; he knew what happened to me and what my mother had done to me.

"Fuck me, Smu—"

Lucian was cut off when the bedroom door slammed open

with a loud thwack. A seething Nico stood in the doorway, glaring at us and then at our joined hands.

Fuck, could this situation get any worse?

"*Fuck me?* Did you just ask my fucking wife to fuck you, boy?" Well, that answered my question. Nico launched an energy ball at Lucian, who deflected it with the flick of his free hand. Nico stormed over to my side of the bed and ripped my hand out of Lucian's. Lucian jumped to his feet, and they stood on either side of the bed glaring at each other.

"Calm the hell down, Nico!" I snapped.

"Calm down? Calm down? I open the door and see you in bed with another man, and you think I should calm down?" He was blowing this way out of proportion.

"Seriously? Nico, you're being a dick, let go of my arm." He didn't release my arm immediately, until I started slapping his hand that was gripping me. I shifted to the middle of the bed, not wanting to be near Nico right now. He was being an absolute drama queen.

"How would you feel, Ryan, if you walked in on me with another woman?" I flinched at his tone. Nico was past the point of being angry, he was livid. I hate to admit it, but he does have a point.

"Nico, I..."

"No! You don't get to turn this on me, not this time, love." Fuck him, how dare he. Lucian was there for me when he wasn't; Lucian was my savior in the night when I would wake, screaming.

"Fuck you! He was there when you weren't. He kept me alive while they broke me each and every fucking day for *weeks*. He stopped one of the guards from raping me! He took a beating that day just so they wouldn't rape me—*me,* a stranger he didn't even know. You do not get to come in here and compare our situation to you in bed with another woman. This is different, and you know it!"

I needed to calm down; I could feel my magic surging inside of me. I was too angry to do it myself, and I quickly turned to Lucian.

"Luce, help me, please." Lucian leaned across the bed and gripped my face between his hands. He closed his eyes, and I mimicked him.

"Deep breaths, Smurf, and release it to me," Lucian commanded.

"What the fuck are you doing?" Nico snapped at us.

I couldn't see him; I couldn't risk opening my eyes. I had control over my magic, but it seemed like whenever I was around Nico, all my training went out the window.

"I'm saving her from blowing this whole fucking place up. Shut up or get out. You're making it worse." I kept taking deep breaths, blocking Nico out and focusing on matching my breathing to Lucian's. After a few minutes, I felt calm and my magic receded. I let out a deep breath and opened my eyes. Lucian smiled, and I leaned forward and rested my forehead against his.

"Thank you, Luce."

"Don't thank me, Smurf. I'll always be here to help you."

CHAPTER 40
Nico

Standing here, staring at the two of them, I feel out of place. He's kneeling on the bed, cradling her face between his hands, while resting his forehead against hers. I have never felt so unneeded in my life. He's the one she needs. Maybe fate fucked up and chose wrong; maybe he was meant to be her *hugacko* and not me. What if she chooses him?

I thought everything would be okay after the whole Melakai thing. He told her the truth and admitted to using his emotion control on her to make her love him. Now I have to go through it all again. I can't, not again, not after what we had shared today.

"You good now, Smurf?" he asked her. Why the fuck does he even call her that?

"Yeah, I'm good." They didn't break apart, they were still resting their heads together. I can't take it anymore, I turn on my heel and pretty much run out of the room. This is total devastation, not jealousy; this was me being honest with myself. I wasn't what she needed—Lucian is. He is the one who can save her from herself.

I exit the compound and keep walking until I find a creek in the middle of the woods. The moon is the only lighting out here.

I pull my knees up to my chest and wrap my arms around my legs. I peer out into the darkness, listening to the running water in the stream.

What has my life become?

Before her I was a fearless king who ruled his people fairly, now I was a mess. I don't know which way is up or down. I've shirked my duties as king a lot lately; I've spent more time in the Earth realm than need be. I should be in Farrarie. My soldiers should be in Farrarie training, not sleeping in tents on Jackson's land. What the hell is wrong with me?

I'm more angry at myself for letting my feelings over cloud my duty to my people. My world is on the brink of dying, my people are at risk of losing their life—hell, *I'm* at risk of losing my life. All because I fell in love with a hybrid who has the power to kill my world. Imagine that, my *hugacko* is the only person in the world strong enough to seal the portal that grants my world life. I am so fucked.

A branch snapping from behind me pulls me from my thoughts. I didn't need to look to see who it was, I could feel them coming. A second later, Dom, Jax, and Kai appeared. Kai had two bottles of whiskey in his hands, and Jax and Dom both had bottles with them, as well. I smiled at my brothers as they sat beside me.

"So, why the hell are you sitting out here in the dark and not banging your wife?" I couldn't hold my laughter back; Dom was always great at breaking the tension in serious situations.

After I got my laughter under control, I snatched one of the whiskey bottles from Kai's hand, unscrewed the top and raised the bottle in cheers to my brothers. They each opened a bottle and raised theirs. I took a few big gulps and shuddered as the whiskey burned its way down my throat.

"Do you wanna tell us what's going on? Ryan's running around the compound looking for you." I released a long breath and looked up at the night sky. I took a deep breath and then answered Dom's question.

"I don't think we're meant to be." Admitting the truth to my brothers felt like a weight had been lifted off my shoulders.

"Why do you say that?" Jax asked. I filled them in on what just happened and how it made me feel to see my wife with another man, a man who could help her.

"That's fucked up." I couldn't agree with Dom more.

"Have you tried talking to her?"

"Yes, Jackson I have, but she's different now." Jax and Dom agreed. Kai had been quiet this whole time.

"What are you gonna do?"

"I don't know, Jax." Kai released a loud exhale.

"Do you have something to add, Melakai?" I snapped, irritated that he was huffing and puffing next to me. I didn't ask him to be here, so he was free to leave whenever the hell he wanted.

"Actually, yeah I do."

"Oh pray tell, Kai, we're all dying to hear this," Dom remarked dryly.

"Okay, smart-ass." Kai said tartly. "Ryan is different. She has changed a lot since being here in Alaska. She has been through a lot."

"No shit!" I sneered.

"Let me fucking finish before cutting me off, Nico! Before coming here she thought she was human, now she has learned she is a hybrid. She has the power to end a world she didn't even know existed. That is a lot for any one person to deal with. To top it all off, the one person she thought she could rely on is a psycho bitch and wants to kill her. She meets two guys she thought were part of her imagination. Then one of the guys she *thought* she loves nearly dies. She then starts seeing her dead father and then marries the other dream guy she actually loves, only to end fifty or so people's lives *the night of her wedding*. She then gets taken prisoner and is tortured for six weeks. Every day while she is beaten, there is one saving grace. Her cellmate, the one person who was there for her at the hardest time of her life. She then flies to a whole new country and meets her long lost grandparents, whom she thought were dead. She trains for four months, learns to master her magic. Comes back to Alaska to help save a world she doesn't even really know. She was free, Nico—she could have run and left us for dead, but she didn't. She came back to help us...to help you!"

Well, fuck, when he puts it like that, it is a lot. I never really sat back and thought of it like that. Kai was always the best of us at reading people and looking beyond the mask people wore.

I understand what Kai just said, but it doesn't change the fact we are too different. I hadn't realized I had drunk the whole bottle until I went to take another drink, only to find the bottle empty.

Jax offered me his other bottle while he and Dom shared Dom's spare one. I think it was safe to say we were all getting a bit tipsy. We sat in silence for about ten minutes until I spoke; well, slurred is probably a better word.

"I get what you're saying, Kai, and you're right. It just doesn't change the fact that she needs *him* more."

"She doesn't need me more."

What the fuck? I turned my head and saw Lucian standing behind us. Fuck, we must be drunk. I turned to Jax and Dom, and by the looks on their faces, they didn't hear him coming either. I turn to Kai and squint in the low light to see his bottle is still nearly full. The fucker heard Lucian coming and never said a word.

CHAPTER 41

Nico

Lucian walks around to stand in front of us. I glare up at the little bastard. I'm pissed Kai didn't even give us a warning that the shithead was coming. I lean over and snatch the mostly full bottle from Kai's hand and the fucker just laughs as I pass it over to Jax.

"Why are you here, young one?" Kai asks.

"Because my best friend is out of her mind with worry." Fuck him. I don't give a shit that Ryan is looking for me right now. That woman is doing my fucking head in.

"Why don't you go comfort *my* wife then?" Saying those words hurt me more than I wanted to admit. I was drunk and angry, and I didn't mean it, but it was too late. I said it. The little fucker scowled down at me.

"You know what? You can hate me all you want, Nico, but don't take this out on her." If I could have stood without falling over I would have. Instead, I stayed sitting and glared at him as best as I could.

"Fuck you! You don't get to tell me what to do, you little shit. You have fucked everything up!" I snap.

"Nah, man, you're doing a good job of that yourself."

I went to stand so I could attempt to hit the smug prick, but Kai placed his hand on my shoulder and pulled me back down. I landed on my ass with a thud.

"Dude, were having a bro sesh. If you're here to fuck with that, just leave," Dom said to the kid.

"I'm not here to do that, *dude*, I'm here to try help him understand," Lucian said, pointing to me.

"Just say what you have to say and then leave, kid." Jax sounded irritated.

"Look, she doesn't have feelings for me. Smurf and I.."

"Why do you call her Smurf?" I cut in.

He smiled down at me before replying. "Because she glows blue." We all started laughing—a full-on belly laugh. Kai was even laughing, and that the kid managed to get the giant stone statue to laugh was an achievement. After we managed to get ourselves under control, I told Lucian to continue with his story.

"Smurf and I bonded while we were locked up. She wouldn't even speak to me at first—it wasn't till the day one of the guards tried to... you know."

I nodded my head, Jax and Dom growled, and Kai was breathing fast. They knew what Lucian was insinuating.

"Anyway, they never used to beat me, but they came to beat Smurf everyday like clockwork. That one day, I screamed and yelled and did everything I could think of to get his attention off her and on me. Long story short, he beat the shit out of me instead of hurting her. After that day, she talked to me and we bonded. I tried as much as I could to get them to beat me instead of her. A couple times it worked, most of the time it didn't. Once Tyler broke us out, we formed a different bond.

"Look, I know you don't like me, but I love her like a sister— at least I think that's how you say it. All I know is I don't think Smurf is someone I want to kiss." Hearing that made me feel a bit better.

"Why do you insist on sleeping next to her?"

Lucian dropped his gaze and looked at the ground while he answered.

"I don't like to be away from her, because I'm afraid she will leave like my mom and the woman who raised me did. I can't sleep on my own. I have never slept through the night until I slept next to Ryan at her grandparents. I may be able to help her with magic, but her just being near me is helping me heal. I'm not used to people and living outside of a cage, you know? Smurf is helping me deal with this, and so are Tyler, Alex, and Chase. Smurf just helps me on a deeper level; she gets me. Anyway, I just came to say that if my presence is causing you two trouble, I'll stay away and keep my distance until she needs me.

"I've never met you until this morning, but I feel like I know all of you, from how much she has talked about you all. She loves you so much, Nico. Don't let my problem of not wanting to be alone tear you away from her. She won't survive losing you."

"How do you know she won't be better off without me?" I ask. He lifts his gaze to meet mine, and I see sadness in his eyes.

"She told me you were the Yin to her Yang, her better half. She lost her dad, her sister, and she thought she lost her mom— not that it sounds like that was much of a loss. But she said losing you would end her. You are her everything, but she won't tell you that because she has been hurt so much in her life. She would lay down her life for yours."

Maybe this kid wasn't so bad after all. I respected him for being willing to face me and admit his own insecurities, for Ryan's sake. He has had a shit life, and I didn't want him to suffer any more than he already had. Ryan needed him, and he needed her. I was going to have to get used to that.

Because I couldn't let her go.

I managed to climb to my feet after three attempts. By the time I stood on my feet, the others were already standing. Fuck, I was drunk as a skunk. I reached my hand out to Lucian, who stood there staring at my hand like it was going to bite him. After a minute, he placed his hand in mine and shook it.

I held onto his hand and looked directly into his eyes.

"I'm sorry about the life you have had. I will keep my word and help you find your parents after this war. I also won't push you away from her, but don't ever let me catch you in the same bed as my wife again." He shook my hand again and nodded his head. "You sleep on the couch or the floor, you get me?" He smiled at me and nodded. The floor or the couch was the best compromise I had.

"I feel like a proud dad! Nicky boy is all grown up and acting like a big boy now!" We all chuckled at Dom's smart-ass comment and made our way back to the compound. Okay, fine —I stumbled most of the way back.

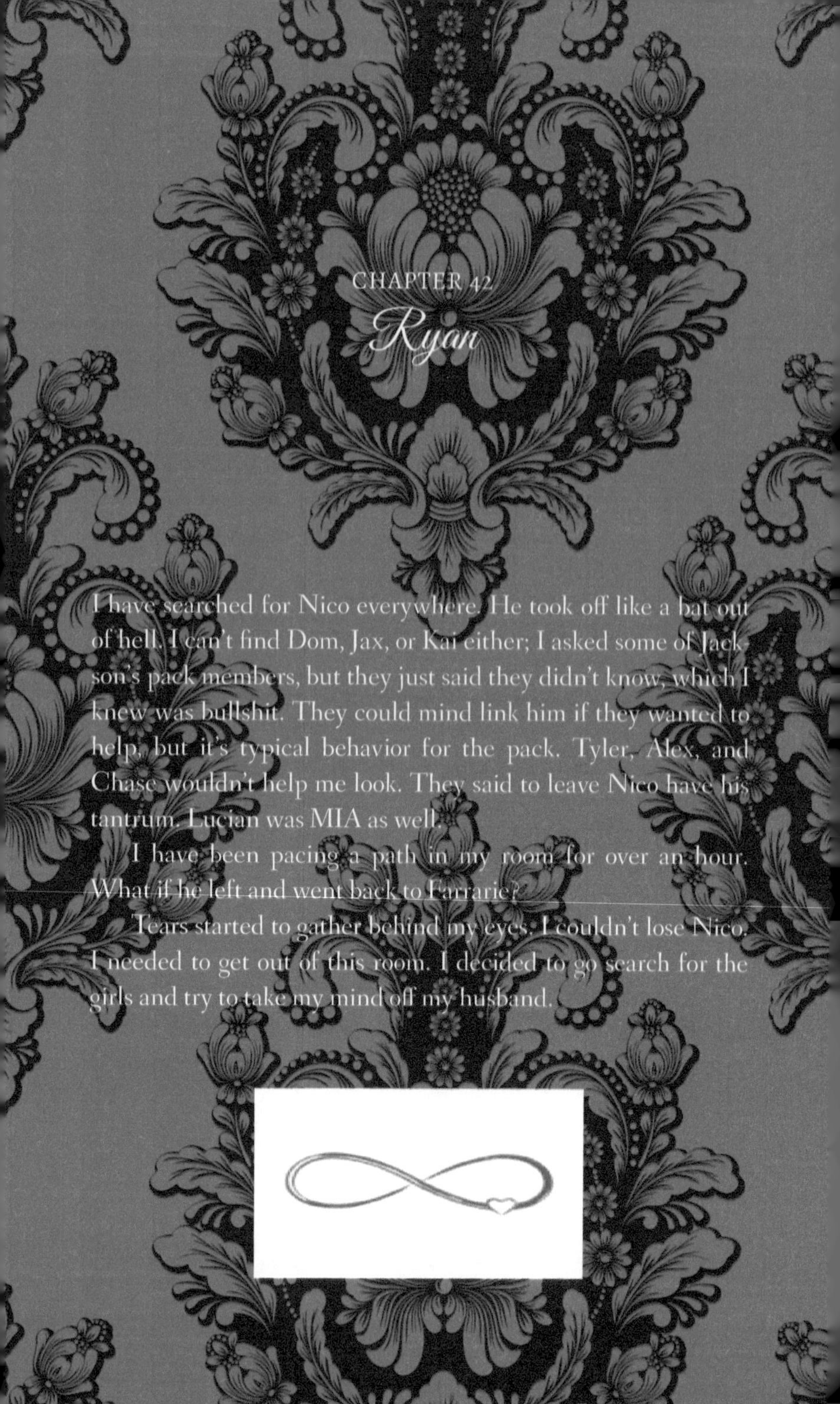

CHAPTER 42
Ryan

I have searched for Nico everywhere. He took off like a bat out of hell. I can't find Dom, Jax, or Kai either; I asked some of Jackson's pack members, but they just said they didn't know, which I knew was bullshit. They could mind link him if they wanted to help, but it's typical behavior for the pack. Tyler, Alex, and Chase wouldn't help me look. They said to leave Nico have his tantrum. Lucian was MIA as well.

I have been pacing a path in my room for over an hour. What if he left and went back to Farrarie?

Tears started to gather behind my eyes. I couldn't lose Nico. I needed to get out of this room. I decided to go search for the girls and try to take my mind off my husband.

I found Sophia, Aurora, and Mya in the game room. I made my way over to them and plopped down on the couch next to Sophia, resting my head on her shoulder. She tensed immediately.

"Soph, what's wrong?" Aurora asked. Sophia shook her head and then turned her gaze to me.

"What's happened between you and my brother?" I reeled back, shocked.

"How do you know something happened?" She smiled sadly.

"I can see peoples love lives, remember?" Oh, that's right, did she have a vision when I touched her?

""Did you just see something?" I asked.

"I can see that Nico's heart is hurting and that so is yours. Why are you both hurting?" I released a loud exhale before answering her.

"Nico's pissed at me. He walked in on me and Luce talking and got the wrong idea. I love your brother more than I love my own life, but I can't give Lucian up." Sophia's eye's softened and began to glaze— was she about to cry? What happened to Sophia while I was away?

"I think I respect you even more now. My brother can be an ass, and Lucian is of no threat to him. Be patient with Nico. He loves you, and I don't need a vision to tell me that. I can see it in the way he looks at you. Nico has never been like this before, with anyone."

Her words warmed my heart. Nico and I could work this out. He was my soul mate, and I wouldn't give him up without a fight.

The girls and I left the game room and headed to the mess hall to get some dessert before heading off to bed. It was late, but I wasn't about to turn down the chance to have some sugar. I knew sleep was going to evade me tonight, so I might as well hang out with the girls to keep my mind busy and off Nico.

We each grabbed a bowl of pie with some ice cream and sat down at one of the tables. We chatted about mundane things and how they had been the past few months. I told them about my time while I was away.

"When will you take your power back?" Mya asked, but I didn't get a chance to answer as Alex, Chase, and Tyler sat down at the table. Tyler answered Mya's question.

"As soon as possible. She needs to learn how to control her whole power before the war." It was like a bucket of ice water had been dropped over me; my good mood evaporated immediately. Here I was, obsessing about my argument with Nico, when his whole world was at stake—*his life*. How fucking petty could I be? I needed to get my head into the game. I guess it is true what people say—sex really does change things. Maybe I should have waited till after the war before losing my V-card to my husband.

Shaking myself out of my thoughts, I spoke to the group. "First thing tomorrow we will begin the exchange. After that I will continue to train daily with Tyler, Alex, and Chase in combat and then train with Lucian in the afternoon to hone my magic skills. We've got to get this show on the road."

I returned to my room ready to fall into bed. I was mentally drained and my coochie was feeling the after effects of losing my V-card. I needed an ice pack for it, but I wasn't about to try find someone and explain why I needed it. Sighing loudly into the empty room, I decided I needed to just go to bed and then deal with Nico tomorrow. I climbed under the covers and switched the bedside light off, staring up at the ceiling and thinking about how shit my first day back in Alaska had been. Of course I was happy to see everyone again and be with them, but I didn't expect to lose my V-card and then fall out with Nico all in the same day.

With a sigh, I forced the fears from my mind. I knew I needed to stop overthinking and try and get some sleep, or tomorrow I would be a bitch-a-saurus.

I didn't bother to shower or change after the guys brought me to my room. I lay down on my bed and closed my eyes, hoping sleep would claim me, but it didn't. I laid there for so long thinking about how the day went from being the best moment of my life to one of the worst. Ryan and I have fought in the past, but this felt different. I don't know how I am supposed to breach the gap between us.

She has changed so much and is a different person now—a person I didn't know. My feelings for her haven't changed in the slightest; she is still the center of my world.

Moving forward, I think it best that I keep my distance and then after this battle is over we can try work on us. My feelings for her are clouding my judgment. I would help her release the power inside of me and then I would return to my realm and take my men with me, so they could train at home and not live in tents.

My soldiers deserved to be home with their loved ones; it might be their last chance to be with them. I fucked up so much these past few months, and I needed to get my head on straight and be the king I have always been instead of this lovesick dog.

Sighing, I turned over and decided to just deal with everything in the morning. I couldn't change how the day went today, but I could change the outcome of tomorrow, hopefully.

I awoke with the worst headache known to man or beast. I showered and changed then made my way to Jackson's office for our morning briefings. I opened the door, but the office was empty. I look to the clock on the wall: seven-thirty, I'm not late. Where the hell are they?

I shut the door and made my way to the mess hall; maybe they decided to grab breakfast first, without me.

The mess hall is bustling with activity this morning, as usual. I scan the room, peering over the top of people's heads, and spot Dom's silver hair. The bastards *were* eating without me.

I grab a plate and load it with all the greasy food available: bacon, eggs, sausages, steak, toast. My stomach growls as I make my way over to the guys.

Just before reaching them I pause. Ryan, Tyler, Alex, Chase, Lucian, and the girls are all at the table with Dom, Kai and Jax. The fuckers ditched me to eat with Ryan and her groupies? I curse under my breath and plonk my ass on the seat between Dom and Kai.

I refuse to utter a single word or make eye contact with any of them. Their conversation quiets down as soon as my ass hits the chair. I can feel the awkward tension in the air, but I refuse to acknowledge it. I'm going to enjoy my breakfast before getting into a verbal sparring match with my wife.

I decided last night that I was going to keep my distance and let her come to me. I haven't told the others yet that I plan to return to Farrarie today.

"Well, this breakfast went from being enjoyable to plain old awkward." Trust Dominic to make a wise-ass comment about the situation.

"I feel like a butter knife could cut through the tension." The table erupts into laughter at Chase's remark. After their laughter subsided, I could feel *her* gaze on me. I continued to eat like I didn't notice the hole she was burning into me.

"Nico, can we talk please?" All conversation around the table stopped. I finished my mouthful and then took a drink of my juice before meeting her gaze. I could see so much remorse and shame in her eyes, but I couldn't let her emotions change my mind. Sitting up straight and clearing my throat, I answer her.

"I think we should go ahead with you taking your power back this morning, straight away." She reels back in shock at my emotionless response. I made sure to keep my face blank.

"W-why?" she stammers out.

"Because I need to return to my realm." Everyone around the table gaped at my confession. I was a king, for fuck's sake, and I needed to run my kingdom. I couldn't shuck off my job for love, that wasn't how it worked.

"Why are you leaving?" Jax asked. I never took my eyes off Ryan while I answered him.

"I have a kingdom to run, and I have spent enough time away from my realm. I need to return with my soldiers and train them back home. They have lived out of tents for months, I owe them more than that. They should be with their families, in their own homes, in case shit goes bad."

Ryan's eyes start to mist with unshed tears, and I can't take it. I stand and tell them I will meet them outside in an hour to begin the transfer of power. I exit the mess hall with Kai hot on my heels.

CHAPTER 44

I swallow past the lump in my throat, blinking my tears away. Nico is leaving. He was really going back to his realm. My chest feels like it's about to break in half. I waited *months* to be with him again. Now, so close to D-day, he wanted to run away.

I couldn't let him leave. I raced out of the mess hall and down the hallway that leads to the back of the compound, hoping and praying this is the way he went. I round the last corner and pause at the sight in front of me.

Kai had Nico by the scruff of his shirt, pushed up against the wall. Nico didn't even try to fight back; they stood there nose to nose glaring at each other.

"Why are you running away?"

"I'm not, Kai."

"Don't fucking lie to me, Nico! We need you here. *She* needs you here."

"Nah, you guys will be fine. I have a kingdom to run! I need to go home. If everything turns to shit, I need to make sure that I have everything in order. She will be fine, won't you, love?" Nico's gaze turns to me, and I gasp. There was no love in his gaze, no warmth. He looked at me like I meant nothing to him. My heart splintered in my chest.

"Don't do this, brother—don't you dare self-sabotage. You deserve this, Nico, let her break down those walls." Kai was pleading with Nico, trying to make him see that he was needed here, that I needed him.

Nico pulls his gaze back to Kai and scowls. "I don't deserve shit, Melakai. You know nothing! I married her, and I did my duty. She has made her choice. She doesn't need me. Now, get your hands off me so I can go and tell my people we are leaving." As soon as Kai releases Nico, he barges out the door.

I stand there stunned and rooted to the floor. *I did my duty, I married her.*

His words keep playing on repeat over and over in my head. Nico only married me out of duty to his people? Did he even really love me?

I was such a fool! I was in love with a man who threw me aside as soon as he got into my pants. I was so lost in my dark thoughts that I didn't even see Kai approach. I craned my head back and looked up at his beautiful blue-gray eyes, full of so much pity.

"He doesn't mean it. He has been through a lot, and seeing you so close to another man hurt him. Give him some time." I felt awkward having this conversation with Kai; he has barely said two words to me since I got here yesterday and now the first real conversation we have is about my love life, great.

"He meant what he said, Kai. I don't know what I have done to make him think I have feelings for someone else." Kai has a sad smile on his face, I didn't want him to pity me.

"You are *everything* to him. He thought he didn't deserve love."

"Why would he think that?"

"When Sophia— the only woman he ever truly loved—was

taken, it destroyed him. He searched everywhere for her. It broke him when he found out Randall had taken her, and no matter what he did, he couldn't get her back. Nico only started to find peace when he began visiting you in your dreams. Nico doesn't know this, but Dom and I kept in contact over the years, and Dom would give me updates on how Nico was coping. He thinks he doesn't deserve happiness or love because he couldn't protect the person he loved most when she needed it. Just like he couldn't protect you from Randall, either."

My heart hurt even more now after hearing that. Nico blamed himself for Sophia being taken...Oh my God.

"Nico isn't really angry at me, is he?" Kai shook his head. "He's angry at himself because I was taken and there was nothing he could do about it." Kai nodded his head. "So this is some kind of trigger for him, his old doubts and feelings are coming back from when Sophia was taken."

Kai nodded again. "He is using sarcasm and jealousy to throw us all off track. I know him too well, though, and he wants you to think he is leaving because of Lucian. He is really leaving because he is afraid of losing you, and there is nothing he can do about it."

Tears dripped down my face, but the tears weren't for me. They were for Nico and all the pain he has suffered. Kai grasped my hand and led me out the door Nico had just left through. I didn't protest or try to fight; I let Kai lead me to wherever we were going.

Kai stopped in front of a large tent pavilion, pushing the flap open and leading me inside. There were eight men and Nico inside. Nico glared at Kai.

"Get out, Melakai, I am meeting with my generals," Nico snapped.

"All of you get the fuck out now." No one moved. "I said NOW!" Kai roared. The men looked to Nico, who hadn't taken his gaze off Kai. Nico gave a stiff nod and they quickly stood and exited. As soon as the flap shut behind the last man, Nico snapped.

"How fucking dare you. You do not get to come in here and tell my men what to fucking do!" I moved out from behind Kai and released his hand. Nico briefly looked at me then averted his gaze. "What is *she* doing here?"

I paused and looked at Nico; his words and derisive attitude hurt. I needed to put my feelings aside and help him. He looked so stressed and tired, and his black shirt was wrinkled and his jeans had grass stains on them, he looked a hot mess.

"She is not Sophia, and you are not the same person anymore. You will keep her safe, and she will remain with you." With that said, Kai turned and left. Nico and I stood rooted in place, avoiding eye contact. I have never felt so out of my element before. I loved Nico, and he was my fucking husband. I needed to bridge this gap between us and fix things.

I took a deep breath and then made my way over to him, stopped directly in front of him. With a loud exhale, I closed the gap between us and wrapped my arms around his waist. He just stood there, stiff as a board.

"I wasn't taken from you. I left. I didn't have a choice, Nico; Stevie was hurting our friends. There is a huge difference. If there was another way, I would never have left you. I love you, and I want to spend my life with you. Don't push me away, please. I couldn't handle losing you. If you have to leave, I understand, just don't run away from me. Let me fix this between us first."

CHAPTER 45

Nico

I stood there with her arms wrapped around me, stunned. Listening to what she was saying didn't make me feel any better. If I was honest with myself, I *am* running away. I'm so scared of losing her like I lost Soph. I couldn't handle her being taken from me, again. I nearly lost my mind when Stevie dragged her out of here. I wrap my arms around her and rest my chin on top of her head and she relaxed in my hold. King or not, I couldn't live without her.

"I love you too."

"Then don't leave me, Nico. We are stronger together, I'm so sorry about yesterday. I will talk to Luce and see if we can work something out with his sleeping arrangements."

I smiled. The boy hadn't told her about our conversation last night. "I don't want to lie to you, Luce did stay in my room last night." I growled. The little prick was going to get it.

"He slept on the floor, I swear." My smile was back in place. The boy would live to see another day.

I knew I owed her an explanation, but I didn't want to talk about it here. I released her and took a step back, and she frowned at the space I put between us.

"Let me just set my guys up and then we'll talk, okay?" She smiled, but it didn't reach her eyes. I placed both my hands on her shoulders and bent down so we were eye to eye. "I'll be back shortly; I promise I'm not running away."

"Okay." I placed a chaste kiss to her forehead and left the tent.

I returned to the tent from giving my generals their orders; they were to return home. Ryan was sitting in one of the high-backed chairs, and I slumped into the twin chair next to her. She was going to be upset that I was still leaving, but I had to put my people first, and they needed their king.

"Ryan, I—"

"I know, Nico, you're still leaving." I was stunned that she knew.

"How?"

"I heard people talking as they walked past. Why are you leaving?" She looked so crestfallen, and the light in her eyes had dimmed. She may look different and act different, but she was still the same on the inside, scared to lose anyone she loved.

"I'm not leaving because of *us*. I need to return home to rule my people. I have let my emotions control my judgment since you arrived here. It's not your fault, it's mine. I moved my men here as soon as the ban was lifted from the elders. I have taken them from their home and their families, because I wanted to be here for you. But you're back and safe, and my people should be able to spend their last weeks in their own world." I see resignation in her features, she knows my mind is made up. I know the timing of my leaving her world isn't ideal, but I needed to rule with my head and not my heart. She leans across and places her small delicate hand on my arm, her eyes meeting mine. I see turmoil shining in her eyes, and I swallow past the lump forming in my throat. I hate that I am the one to put that look on her face. I never want to hurt her, ever.

"I understand. I just wish there was another way. You're right, though, your people need their king. When this battle begins, they need you to have a clear head and not have your judgment clouded by your emotions."

I stood and pulled her to her feet, wrapping my arms around her and holding her tight. For a few minutes we just stood there, holding each other.

"Nico, I need you to tell me that we're okay. I need you to tell me you will never stop fighting for us." I felt her tears on my shirt, and I felt the lump in my throat return. She really had no idea how much she meant to me. I pulled away to look down at her; I can see the uncertainty in her gaze.

"I will never stop fighting for us—for you. I told you before, I would burn this whole fucking world down before I let you go. I thought yesterday that maybe you wanted something else, someone else. I see now how wrong I was. I let my fear of losing you cloud my clarity. You mean everything to me. You, Ryan Stone, are the beginning and ending of my life story."

Tears leaked out of her eyes and slowly trailed down her cheeks. I wiped them away and bent down to kiss her. She tasted so sweet. I groaned. I knew she would be sore from losing her virginity yesterday, so before I lost my self-control and took her, right here, right now, I pulled away from the kiss.

"Why are you stopping?" She looked annoyed; fuck me in the ass for trying to be a gentleman around here.

"I know you're sore, love; I'm trying to be considerate." I smiled down at her, and she glared back.

"Since when have you ever cared about being a gentleman?" I grinned, she had me there. I wasn't known for being sweet or gentle, but for her, I wanted to try.

"Since now, and don't make me fail on my first day of trying, love." She burst out laughing, and I joined her. It felt so good to laugh with her again, and I knew, in this moment, we were going to be okay. We have faced our fair share of downs, but now it was time for us to have our *up* moments.

CHAPTER 46

Ryan

Nico and I made our way through the forest to the same place we had met Stevie and Tyler all those months ago. Being here again brought back mixed emotions. The others were gathered near the fence. I gripped Nico's hand, and he stopped his movements to turn and face me.

"I just need a minute." Nico's eyes softened, he knew why I needed a moment. He wrapped me in his arm and stroked my back, and his embrace helped stop the pounding in my chest. I took some deep breaths and gave myself a mental pep talk before stepping back from Nico. I gave him a nod, and he gripped my hand again, leading us toward the others.

"Took you love birds long enough." I smiled at Dom; he was so good at easing tension and helping people relax with his outlandish comments.

"We had some things to sort out," I told him. I didn't want to lie. They all knew Nico and I weren't on good terms yesterday.

"Oh, so you were doing the horizontal dance while we were all here waiting for you?" I blushed immediately and tried to use my long hair as a curtain to shield me from their gazes.

"Nah, I can't smell him on her. Plus he looks too tense to

have just blown a load." I could hear the laughter in Tyler's voice. I was going to kill him for that comment later.

"Wait, you're more scared of us knowing you had sex than when Tyler bit you?" Lucian remarked; I heard gasps and growls erupt around me. I quickly lifted my gaze and gripped Nico's hand tighter, trying to hold him back.

Dom, Jax, and Kai had murderous looks on their faces. The three girls looked shocked. I had to make a quick decision. I released Nico's hand and quickly stood in front of Tyler. I would not let them hurt him. Alex and Chase moved to stand either side of me, and Lucian stood next to Chase.

It felt like a Mexican standoff, with Nico and the others on one side with me and my crew on the other side.

"Step aside now, love," Nico gritted out between clenched teeth. Oh boy, this wasn't going to end well. Dom was glowing yellow, Jax's eyes had changed, and Kai was snarling with his fangs out. Nico's hands started to glow purple, and their display of power caused a reaction from my side, Alex, Chase, and Lucian had their power on display as well. I wouldn't display my magic unless I had to.

"Step aside, little hybrid. I knew it was wrong when I did it." I turned to look over my shoulder so Tyler could see the look in my eyes. He sighed, clearly accurately reading the expression on my face. I would never let him fight this alone.

"Jackson, please, he's my brother!" Aurora was trying to reason with her mate. Why were they all so uptight about a bite?

"He knew the rules, and he also knows the punishment for what he did." What the hell?

"What the fuck are you all going on about? I'm fine." I even showed them my arm, the one Ty bit. There was a scar, but it didn't bother me. I was proud of my battle wound.

"You don't understand, Ryan; it is forbidden to attack some-one's mate, or in this case, *hugacko*. The punishment is death."

I reeled back at Mya's admission—what the actual fuck! No way in hell was Tyler dying for something my grandfather had told him to do. Jax and Kai took a step forward, and I released my magic and my hands started to glow blue. They both paused at my power display.

"If any of you—yes, Nico, including you—try to harm him in any way, you will need to go through me first!" I growled to the group of men.

"And us!" Chase chimed in.

"He bit you, Ryan! He could have killed you!" Jax shouted.

"He was doing as he was told. If he hadn't done what he did, Lucian would never have released his hold on my power!" I snapped at Jax.

"Who told him to bite you?" Dom asked.

"My grandfather. He had Lucian pinned to a tree and made him watch as I battled Tyler with no magic. The only way Lucian could get over his fear of losing me was to watch me nearly die." I mumbled the last bit out, I didn't want to put Lucian in the hot seat, but I didn't have a choice right now.

"Your grandfather is fucking crazy!" Kai shouted.

"Watch the way you speak about our grandfather, Cane," Alex sneered.

"Why the hell wouldn't you release her power *before* he bit her?" Dom asked Lucian, looking perplexed.

"Because she told me when we were locked up that her power consumed her. When the seal was broken on her power, it took control of her and *that thing* happened that night. I was scared that if I gave it back to her that she would be lost to the power inside of her." The three girls looked touched and awed at Lucian's admission, but the guys looked conflicted. They didn't know whether to be angry with him or shake his hand.

Nico stopped glowing and so did Dom. Kai stopped snarling and retracted his fangs. Jax was the last to calm down, but his eyes finally changed back to chocolate brown after a few moments. As soon as I saw Jax relax, I pulled my power back and so did my three guys.

"I kind of want to find any reason to hate you, but I just can't find one good enough yet," Nico ground out to Lucian. I smiled.

"So, am I still on death row....or?" Jax looked over my head at Tyler, glaring.

"This is your final warning. You step out of line or break any more rules, and your sister being my mate will not save you." Jax pulled his gaze from Ty and looked directly at me. "I am the Alpha of all wolves, Ryan. It is my call on how I punish my shifters, and you will not interfere again." I glared at Jackson. How fucking dare he?

"You may be the Alpha of Alphas, but she is the queen of the Knox coven and the queen of the fae. I think she outranks you, *Alpha*."

I looked at Mya in shock. I never expected her to come to my defense like that.

"Okay, enough of this shit. Nico and I need to leave and go back to our realm soon. We need to do the transfer of power now, we're wasting daylight."

Oh my God, Sophia was going back with Nico. I loved having Soph around and it made me sad to think of her not being here.

"Don't look so shocked, Ryan. I need to help my brother lead *our* people. We will be back before the war, I swear." I nodded my head in understanding. It still sucked that they were both leaving, though.

Nico

Ryan and I walked out to the center of the empty field. I had no idea what I was doing. She looked confident enough for the both of us, so I was taking that as a good sign. The others spread out around us, making a circle.

"So, how do we do this?" I asked, and she smiled.

"Trust me, big guy, I got this." I nodded my head, but I was still a bit nervous.

"Luce, come on, buddy." I opened my mouth to ask what he had to do with it, but she anticipated my question.

"Lucian will help me control the power coming from you. He will filter it to me in doses, so I'm not overwhelmed with it all at once." I nodded my head again. That was actually fucking smart. I didn't trust Lucian as far as I could throw him, but Ryan trusted him, and that had to count for something, right?

"Are you ready, Smurf?" Lucian asked as he approached us in the center.

"As ready as I'll ever be. You got this, Luce." She turned to face him and clasped both his hands in hers. I stood there watching their strange interaction. He seemed to relax at her touch—why?

"I trust you, Lucian. I know you won't let anything bad happen to me." He was looking at her with such intensity, and I could see the war raging inside of him. He was scared to fail her.

"Your Gramps isn't here to coach us this time, Smurf. What if I stuff it up or what—"

"Don't do that, Luce. I believe in you. You need to believe in yourself, you're so much stronger than what you think, buddy." She released his hands and then pulled him in for a quick hug, and he sagged in her arms. His lack of confidence wasn't exactly awe- inspiring for me.

"Can you do it or not?" I didn't mean for it to come out sounding so harsh, but Lucian flinched none the less. Ryan shot me a death glare. Whoops.

"He can do it, I know he can." I looked past Ryan to Lucian, who was nodding his head. He still didn't seem confident, and suddenly I wasn't okay with this plan.

"Little one, maybe we—"

"No, Nico, we are doing this now. I trust Lucian, and I know he can do this." All righty then, I guess we were doing this whether I liked it or not.

Ryan stood in front of me, and Lucian stood to the side between us. He placed one hand on my shoulder and one on Ryan's.

"Okay, Nico, I need you to release your hold on Smurf's power, and I'll pull it into me." I nodded my head, closed my eyes, and concentrated. I reached deep inside of myself to feel for her power; once I located it, I began to push it outward. I didn't know if I was doing this right, but I just had a feeling this was how I was supposed to do it.

I stared at Nico in awe; his whole body was covered in blue light, my color, and it was a beautiful sight to see. Nico opened his eyes and I gasped—his eyes had changed. They were no longer violet; they were now the same color blue as my power. Lucian's shaking pulled me from my thoughts; I turned my head slightly to see sweat had broken out across his brow and upper lip.

That wasn't a good sign at all.

"Luce, start channeling it into me now. It's too much for you to hold onto." Lucian gritted his teeth and nodded his head. I didn't feel anything at first, then suddenly I began to feel warmth spread from my shoulder where Lucian was touching. The warmth spread like wildfire, and within a second my whole body was warm. Once Lucian started funnelling the power back into me, he couldn't stop. The magic wasn't responding to him like Gramps said it would.

It knew who its master was and wanted to be back with me. I wasn't ready for that, my body started to grow hot, I felt sweat drip down my back. I tried to focus on my breathing and remain calm. Magic was ruled by emotions, and if I freaked out now, all hell would break loose.

"Why is she shaking?" Nico snapped. I couldn't answer him. If I did it would break my concentration, and I couldn't risk that. I needed to focus; I closed my eyes to block everything out.

"D-don't t-touch h-her. Y-you need to move back by the others." I could hear the strain in Lucian's voice. I knew this was taking a huge toll on him, but we couldn't stop now.

"I am not leaving her!"

"Y-you need to go, Nico! I can withstand her blast if she loses control. You can't. Leave for her—if she hurts you, she will never forgive herself." Lucian was right, I would never survive hurting someone I cared about. Nico was muttering curses underneath his breath, then I heard him leave. I felt Lucian move from beside me to stand in front of me, and he placed his other hand on my shoulder.

"I can't hold it much longer, Smurf." Lucian's voice was trembling, and I opened my eyes to see him struggling. An idea came to me, quick as a flash.

"DOMINIC!" I screamed out, and not a moment later Dom is standing beside me.

""What is it, love?" He looks between me and Lucian, seeing the struggle on both of our faces.

"You are the strongest magic wielder I know, and Lucian is just as strong." Dom nods his head, but I can see in his eyes he's confused. "Lucian is going to release my power, and I don't know if I can handle it all at once. Can you help him funnel it?"

I don't know if what I am asking is even possible. Dom is my last resort, or I will level this whole forest and kill everyone within the vicinity, and I can't go through that again. Nico is too emotionally attached to me and wouldn't risk my safety; he would try to make Luce and I stop the transfer.

"I-I think I can...I will have to do it through him, though."

Dom turned to look at Lucian. "Will you allow me to do that? I will need to push through your bonds and help you stabilize the power inside of you." Lucian gritted his teeth and nodded. Dom moved to stand behind Lucian and placed both his hands either side of Lucian's head.

"I need you to let me in, don't fight it. If you do it will hurt you." Luce nodded. "Hurry, I can't hold it much longer," he ground out.

"How much power could she really have?" Lucian and I didn't find Dom funny at this moment. Dom shook his head then closed his eyes.

"*Tereso tereso calulu calide, Tereso tereso calulu calide, Tereso tereso calulu calide entaly!*" I had no idea what the hell Dom was saying, but whatever he was doing was helping Lucian. I felt Lucian relax his hold on my shoulders, and his face lost some of the strain he was sporting minutes ago. I even felt warm now and not like I was burning up. At the rate Dom was helping Lucian funnel the magic into me, I would be able to handle this.

It took everything inside of me not to run to her when she called for Dominic. Well, that and my sister pulling me back, telling me to trust Dom. I *do* trust Dom; I just didn't understand why she called for him and not me. I stood on the sidelines and watched as Dom placed his hands on either side of Lucian's head.

The blue light started to dim between Lucian and Ryan. Whatever Dom is doing is working; he's slowing the speed of the transfer.

"He's doing it!" I could hear the awe in my sister's voice. The others started to migrate to where Sophia and I stood by the edge of the forest.

"Well, isn't that a blow to your ego, Tink?" I turned to glare at Chase. I hated that fucking nickname.

"Why would Nico's ego be hurt?" Mya asked, and Chase and Alex chuckled before Chase answered. "Because Ry wanted Dom and not him."

I growled.

"Let's be honest, though, you may be king, but Dom is better at magic than you." Alex was really enjoying this. I was not weak, but even I had to admit Dom was powerful. Dom may only be half fae, but he trained harder than anyone I know to be the best.

He was one powerful son-of-a-bitch. Before Ryan and Stevie came back to Alaska, Dom was the only person who could rival me in the power department. That said, I didn't like having my shortcomings announced in public like Ryan's cousins had just done. Dicks.

My attention was pulled back toward Ryan and the two guys. It seemed like the transfer was taking hours, but in reality only about ten minutes had passed.

I could see the strain on all three of their faces from here. I could tell Ryan was fairing okay with the transfer, but the two guys weren't.

It wasn't often that you saw Dom struggle with magic and seeing it now was not reassuring. Lucian was trembling and gritting his teeth. They needed to hurry before Lucian lost his hold.

"The boy is losing control," I said to the group.

"He'll be fine. He is stronger than even he knows." I looked at my sister from the corner of my eye.

"How do you know that, Soph?"

"I just know, Nico. He will not let any harm come to her." My sister was being cryptic, and I wasn't in the mood for her games.

"Ever since that kid has shown up, you've been acting weird. Why?" My question came out harsher than I intended, but I was sick of never being able to figure her out.

"All of you shut up! I can't fucking concentrate," Dominic screamed at us. I flinched at his tone; I could hear the strain in his voice. Sometimes I forget how good his hearing is, being half shifter. Everyone shut their mouths and watched.

CHAPTER 50

Ryan

I could feel my magic come alive as it came back to me. I didn't realize how incomplete I felt until the other half of me started to come back. My magic felt like a warm caress, almost like the waves of the ocean swaying inside of me. It was a feeling I couldn't explain...euphoria was probably the only word that could best describe this feeling.

"Hold on, kid, we're nearly done," Dom gritted out through clenched teeth. I pulled myself from my inner bliss and focused on the two men in front of me, both wore looks of fatigue. I hadn't realized how much of a toll this was taking on them.

"Luce, I need you to let go of the rest now!" Lucian started shaking his head. "Lucian, listen to me, you're turning gray. If you hold it any longer, it will kill you." I felt tears gather. I couldn't lose Lucian, he was too important to me.

"Do it, kid! I can feel your life force draining." Lucian wasn't listening to Dom, and he started swaying on his feet. I felt his hands start to go slack on my shoulders, and my tears fell without my consent. I could see his eyes starting to dim.

"Luce, please!" I choked out.

"Release it now!" I have never in the months that I have

known Dom ever heard such authority and control in his voice like that. His tone reminded me of Jackson's in alpha mode. Lucian's eyes widened, and his trembling stopped.

Without warning, I felt it all rush in to me, like a tidal wave. I stumbled back a few steps as it crashed against me.

I saw, from the corner of my eye, the others running toward us, and I quickly erected a shield around myself. I needed to calm down and not have everyone in my face or I would explode. I looked to Dom and saw that he had his arm wrapped around Lucian's waist. Lucian's head was hanging down lifelessly.

I snapped my eyes closed and blocked my emotions out. I would deal with the guilt later.

"Ryan, let me in. Let me in, love." I refused to open my eyes and look at Nico; if I let him in I would lose control. I sat down and crossed my legs. Keeping my eyes closed, I began to take deep steadying breaths.

Calm as the trees, calm as the sky. Think of the ocean and how it moves as one with all its different currents.

I kept thinking of the phrase Grams had told me over and over again, until I felt my blood start to cool down and my magic stop warring inside of me. I remained seated for a few more minutes, just to make sure I was in control. When I was certain, I pulled the shield down and brought the magic back into me. Within a second, Nico's arms wrapped around me and lifted me off the ground. I didn't have a chance to protest before he was marching us back toward the forest.

"Nico, I'm fine. You can put me down." He glared down at me. Why the hell was he fucking angry?

"We'll meet you in the mess hall, little hybrid." I leaned my head back over Nico's arm to see Tyler and Dom carrying Lucian and the others following them toward the compound. If the compound was that way, where the hell is Nico taking me?

"Nico, I need to go check on Lucian! Put me down now."
He didn't answer me.

"*Portaly awa wiremu opeinga.*" I know what *portaly* meant; he was opening a portal to somewhere, great. I get to be whisked off to God knows where with the brooding king of the fae. Yay me.

I couldn't look at her right now; she had just shut me out again. Why does she keep doing this? As soon as we passed through the portal to Lake William, I deposited her on her feet. Once I was sure she was steady, I removed my hands from her shoulders.

I moved away from her and walked to the end of the dock. I stood there, staring out over the lake and the mountains, and felt myself relax. This place had a calming effect.

"Nico, why are we here?" I felt her standing behind me, but I refused to turn and face her. I couldn't, not yet, my anger was still burning inside of me. She reached out and touched my arm, and I flinched away from her.

"Why did you bring me here, if you're just going to ignore me?" I wheeled around to face her, and she stumbled back a step. I narrowed my gaze on her; how could she not know?

"You keep blocking me out, why?" She flinched at my tone. I didn't have it in me to care that I had upset her.

"I-I don't intentionally do it," she stammered out.

"Bullshit!" I yelled, and she moved back a couple of steps, a look of hurt crossing her face. "You blocked me out back there, again." She glowered back at me and closed the space between us, craning her neck back so she could look me in the eye.

"You dumbass! I put the shield up in case I couldn't hold the power inside of me. I didn't let you in because I was scared I might hurt you!"

"Stop being scared of hurting me! I want to help you, but you keep shutting me out." She dropped her gaze and moved back a step, and I took deep breaths, trying to control the rage inside of me, but it wasn't working. She released a loud sigh and then spoke.

"I don't mean to do it, I swear. I'm scared, Nico. This is all new to me, and the last time, I hurt so many people." My resolve started to falter; how could I be so dense?

"I didn't think, love. I know you're scared. I just want to help you through this so badly." She reached out and clasped my hand, looking me in the eyes.

"I'm trying to deal with this as best as I can, Nico. I hate that so much of this battle rests on me. I'm not special, yet I am the only one with the power to save a world."

Couldn't she see it? I closed the gap between us and peered down at her.

"You were *born* special, Ryan. You were never meant to be ordinary. You're the most extraordinary being there ever was, embrace what you are." I cupped her cheek with my free hand, and she nuzzled into it.

"Don't fight what you are, love; if you do, it will only make wielding your power harder." Tears started to glisten in her eyes. She released my hand then gripped the back of my neck to pull me down for an earth-shattering kiss.

The taste of her was driving me insane. I wanted inside of her now, but we didn't have time. I pulled away from her reluctantly and gazed down at her. Her strange eyes held so many conflicting emotions.

"We don't have time, love; we need to get back."

She nodded and leaned forward so her forehead was resting against mine and whispered, "I know you have to leave, but I don't want you to go."

I wish I didn't have to return to Farrarie, but my soldiers deserved to spend whatever time they had left in their own homes. And I knew she couldn't come with me; she needed to be here and train.

"And I wish you could come with me, but you must remain here and train with the others. I wish I could be the one to train you, sweetheart, but I could never push you past your limit like the others can. I love you, Ryan Stone." She smiled so wide at the sound of her new last name, and her smile warmed my heart. Before she could reply, I pulled back and clasped her hand in mine and began to walk us back toward the forest, opening a portal that led us back to Jackson's compound.

Shit, I didn't mean for us to arrive at *this part* of the compound. Her gasp said it all—she was devastated at the sight of what remained. I unintentionally opened the portal right by the chapel.

I turned to shield her from the charred remains of the building, but it was too late. Jackson had ordered the chapel to be destroyed; he said it was too hard for everyone to look at.

"Deep breath, love." She looked up at me, and my heart splintered at the look of utter devastation on her face. I cupped her face between my hands. "It wasn't your fault, and the elders aren't pursuing this, love. They know it was an accident."

Ryan

Guilt weighed so heavy on me. I couldn't escape the ghost of my past. Nico had no idea...no one would get over what I had done. Fifty-two people lost their lives that night, all because I came into my powers. No matter what anyone said, I was the one to blame for the events of that night, no one else.

I didn't have the time right now to ease Nico's worries. I would deal with the fallout of my deceit later.

"I'm okay, can we just go inside now? I want to check on Lucian." Nico nodded his head and released his hold on my face. I clasped his hand in mine and led him toward the compound.

We entered the mess hall, searching for the others; I spotted them near the back and was relieved to see Lucian awake and upright.

I made my way over quickly, with Nico following. As soon as we neared the table, I went straight for Lucian. He saw me coming and stood. I wrapped my arms around him and rested my head on his chest, and his arms were like a vice around me. After a moment, he pulled back and looked me in the eye.

"I'm sorry, Smurf, I thought I could handle it." I could see remorse and regret warring in his gaze, and I was having none of that.

"Don't you dare apologize; you did amazing, Luce. I am so proud of you, and I know Gramps would be proud as well." Lucian smiled and we both sat down, and the others resumed their conversation. Tyler was sitting on my other side and nudging me with his elbow. I turned to glare at him.

"Now that I have your attention, I think we should start training tonight." I groaned internally. Tyler liked to train at all hours; he wanted us to be prepared in case Stevie decided to attack at night. I hated night training, and I sucked at it.

"Come on, little hybrid, you have like three weeks max to learn control." I slumped in defeat. He was right, I needed to use every spare moment I had to train. I looked to Luce to see if he was listening to Tyler and me, and he nodded his head. I guess we're doing night training.

"I must be going now. Maverick and Larick are waiting for me." I turned toward Nico, it had slipped my mind for a moment that he was leaving. I took a few deep breaths and told myself to woman up. I wasn't going to sit here and cry. Nico was a king, and he had a job to do. We all stood and followed Nico out of the compound toward the forest where Maverick and Larick were waiting for their king. As soon as we neared the portal, Nico began to bid everyone goodbye, and everyone wished him well.

I waited for him to reach me. I couldn't meet his eyes. I had a lump the size of a boulder in my throat. I tried to swallow past it and not cry, but it was fucking hard. I just got him back, and now we are about to be apart again!

When would we ever get to just be together and not have a threat of imminent death or destruction hanging over us? Nico cupped my face and used his thumbs to wipe away my tears. He lifted my face so I was looking at him.

His violet eyes softened, and he looked over my head to whoever was standing behind me and said, "Look after her. If anything happens to her, you will have me to deal with. Believe me, you may think Dominic is strong, but *I* was the one to train him!"

"You don't need to threaten us, *Tink*. We would die to protect her." I pulled out of Nico's hold to turn around, and Chase, Alex, Tyler, and Lucian all stood behind me, nodding their heads. Out of the corner of my eye, I saw Dom, Kai, Jax, and the three girls nodding their heads as well, and my heart swelled.

"You have our word, brother. We will protect her with our lives." I turned and faced Dom; he wasn't looking at Nico, he was looking at me. I nodded my head and mouthed a silent *thank you*.

Nico turned to me so I was facing him, brushing the pad of his thumb across my lips. I lifted my gaze to his, and I could see he was torn between his duty to his people and staying with me. I had to be a queen in this moment, and not a wife.

"I'll be okay, I promise. It's only a couple weeks, and then you'll be back." I tried to keep my tone light, hoping to ease some of Nico's tension. He tried for a casual smile but it didn't reach his eyes. He dipped his head forward to avoid my gaze, and his jet-black hair fell over his forehead.

No way—he was not going to avoid looking at me. I needed to show him that I could do this. He needed to know that the woman he married was strong enough to last a few weeks without her husband. I wasn't weak anymore; I would be strong for him. I cupped his face and lifted it till his gaze met mine.

"We can do this. You have a world to run, and I need to stay and train with the guys. We're going to be apart now so we can be together forever." Nico's smile was blinding, and I knew had appeased his doubt with my words.

"You are going to be the best queen Farrarie has ever known." It was my turn to smile now.

"I don't think Farrarie is ready for a queen like me." His face turned serious.

"Well, they had better be ready, because I am." His words boosted my confidence. If Nico thought I could do it, then I would. He leaned down and kissed me, sending fire through my body. I kissed him back like it was the last time I would ever touch those lips. A throat clearing had us pulling apart, and Nico grinned down at me while I stood there panting and trying to get my racing heart under control.

"Be safe, love. If you need me, or if anything happens, go to the place you love the most, and you will find your way to me." Cryptic much? What did he mean? Before I could ask, he turned and walked toward the portal. Just before entering, he turned to look over his shoulder and smiled at me. A second later, he was gone. Sophia bid us all goodbye and followed her brother through the portal. Larick and Maverick nodded their heads at me before following their king and Soph through the portal. As soon as Maverick's second foot cleared the threshold, the portal closed with a popping sound.

As we all made our way back to the compound, it hit me—I know what Nico meant. I know where the portal that stabilizes Farrarie is. Was that why I was so drawn there? I always knew that place was magical.

"Put your shield up!"

"I'm fucking trying, Tyler!" I snapped. We have been doing this every day for the last five days. Morning, noon, and night, we trained. I do hand-to-hand combat in the mornings with Alex and Chase. After lunch, I work with Lucian and Dom on magic and control.

Every night I train with Tyler in the clearing of the woods. Jax, Dom, Kai, Aurora, Mya, and Lucian joined us tonight. Alex and Chase have been busy studying up on coven law. I assigned them the task under the pretense that they would teach me how to rule the coven after the war.

"Try harder! Do you think your sister will stop attacking you because you ask her to? Suck it up buttercup and let's go again!" I glared at Tyler. Whenever we trained, my friend Tyler was gone and in his place was a drill sergeant.

"Ty, cut her some –" Tyler turned and glared at his sister.

"If I had gone soft on you, Aurora, you wouldn't be who you are today." What the hell? Tyler trained Aurora? How did I not know that she could fight?

"But Ty, she is—" He cut his sister off once again.

"No, Aurora, I told all of you, if you can't stay out of her training then don't come out here. She can handle it; she just needs to believe she can." I didn't have time to process his words, because within a second, Jax was on his feet and crowding into Tyler's space, growling.

"She may be *your* sister but she is *my* mate! Watch how you speak to her." To Tyler's credit, he didn't flinch or shy away from Jax.

"My sister doesn't need you to fight her battles, *Alpha*. If you pulled your head out of your ass for more than a minute you would see that," Tyler snapped back.

Before they could bash each other's brains out, Kai quickly stood and pushed them apart.

"That's enough, Jackson. We don't have time for this shit. Ryan needs to train, and you are taking up that time." Thank God for Kai, he was the best at diffusing tension-filled situations. Once Jax and Kai were seated again, Tyler turned back to me, a look of determination on his face.

Oh boy, I know that look.

"You will not leave here until you can either shield yourself from me or push me away." I didn't get a chance to prepare. Tyler charged at me, and I tried to build a shield quickly, but I was too late, and Tyler knocked me on my ass—again. He didn't help me up. He just looked down at me, disappointed.

"I'm trying, Ty," I protested.

"Try harder, Ryan. If you can't even push me away in my human form, how do you expect to push a vamp away?" He was right. I don't know why my magic wasn't doing what I wanted.

"We're running out of time. You need to be able to take down your sister and stabilize Farrarie all in the same day."

You know, take down my incredibly powerful twin sister and stabilize an entire world, all before bed. The elders had ordered it all be done in one day; I knew why, but the others didn't.

"Tyler, if I may?" Dom stepped forward and made his way over to us. Tyler looked him up and down and then reluctantly nodded and made his way over to the others.

"Hello, love, you seem like you're in a bit of a pickle."

I chuckled. "Yeah, you could say that."

"What seems to be the trouble, love?" That was the problem; I didn't know what was wrong or why my magic wasn't responding to me.

"I don't know. I had it all figured out before I got the other half back from... you know." I couldn't say his name. I missed him too much. I hadn't seen or heard from him since he left. No dreams, nothing.

"Ahhhhhh, I see what the problem is." I cocked my head to the side— what did he get?

"Our magic is tied to our emotions, love." I nodded. "You miss him. You're blocking your feelings, so your magic is blocked."

"Wait a second, are you saying my magic won't work because I refuse to think about Nico?" Dom nodded his head and smiled at me. Fuck my life.

"You need to let yourself feel, love—all the anger, hurt, everything. The more you suppress it, the more your magic will fight you." That was a lot easier said than done. I didn't want to re-live all the hurt and anger I had been through. Once was bad enough.

"Believe me, love, the more you block yourself off, the more potent the magic becomes and the harder it is to control." Is that why I lost control *that* night? Because I refused to feel and then it all came rushing out when I got my power unlocked? Nico wasn't the only one occupying my thoughts, though.

"Okay, I need you to do me a favor."

"What is it, love?"

"I need you to take me to Nico." Dom looked taken back, and I heard the others murmuring behind us.

"Why, love?"

I sighed. "I need to speak to my mother."

CHAPTER 54

Nico

"Sire, the queen is here." I spun away from the bookshelf and faced Cyrus.

"What do you mean?"

"The queen isn't alone, sire." I rushed out of the room with Larick, Maverick, Cyrus, Sophia, and a few guards taking up the rear and picked up speed as I went.

"Drop the bridge, NOW!" I yelled to the guards at the guard tower. The bridge wasn't all the way down before I was sprinting across it and jumping off the end. As soon as my feet hit the ground, I was running toward the forest, where I saw four figures emerge. I scanned the group for her, catching sight of her long brown hair blowing in the breeze.

My breath caught in my throat. I stood in the middle of the open field, waiting for her to come to me.

She looked gorgeous in her trademark Chucks, dark wash jeans, and a form-fitting plain black shirt. She lifted her gaze, and I saw her scanning my group, looking for me.

When her eyes found mine, a smile so bright and wide graced her beautiful face. She broke away from the others and started running. When she was a couple steps away from me, she launched herself into my arms. I caught her, she wrapped her legs around my waist, and before I could say anything, she leaned down and stole my breath with a kiss.

"I think the queen of the fae wants to bone the king of the fae." Just as I pulled back from Ryan, I heard the distinctive sound of flesh being slapped.

"Why the hell did you hit me, Soph? To think I actually missed you!"

"Because you can be such a dick, Dominic."

I grinned up at my wife, who was smiling down at me. She wiggled in my hold, and I reluctantly set her on her feet. I pulled her into my side as I greeted Dom, Tyler, and Lucian.

"This place is so...unreal." I could hear the awe in Lucian's voice at seeing my home for the first time. "Oh my God, Smurf, he lives in a fucking castle!" I chuckled, the others joined me.

"Yeah, Luce, he does."

"He really is a king." Lucian turned to face me with a look of fear on his face. "You know how I called you a dick and said some dumb shit? I really didn't mean it, so please don't, like, order for my head to be removed or any—"

I cut off his mindless rambling. "It's fine, don't worry about it. Welcome to Farrarie. My home is your home." Lucian grinned, and I felt Ryan snuggle in closer into my side. She was happy to be here. I looked down at her and kissed the top of her head. I missed her so much.

"Okay, this is gross watching you fawn all over her. I'm going to your office; I need a drink." I chuckled at Dominic. Even though it's only been six days, I missed him as well.

We all followed Dom back to my office. Larick and Maverick greeted their queen as she walked passed them, and Ryan blushed then nodded hello. She pulled out of my hold briefly to greet my sister and hug her. She was still finding it hard to accept that she was a queen. What she didn't know was that she was the only one who didn't.

Dom, Soph, Tyler, Lucian, Ryan, and I all stood around my office with drinks in our hands I could feel the tension pouring off Ryan in waves now that we were inside the castle. What the hell was going on with her? She was standing by the window that I had thrown Dom out of. I stood beside her, slipping my hand in hers.

"What's wrong, love?" The others ceased their conversation. I looked around the room, but their faces were unreadable. My gaze landed on my sister, who gave a small nod of encouragement.

I turned my gaze back to my wife and tried again. "Did something happen?"

She took a deep breath and looked me in the eyes. "I can't access my magic fully until I deal with all my emotions."

"I don't quite understand what you're saying, my love." She let out a sigh before steeling her spine and standing taller. I reached out with my free hand and cupped her cheek. She nuzzled into my hand and closed her eyes for a moment, enjoying my touch.

As soon as her eyes opened, I saw determination in them.

"I need to see my mother, Nico." I dropped my hand. I didn't expect her to say that. "In order to control my magic and use it properly, I need to deal with my emotions. I thought I was struggling because of how much I missed you, but it wasn't you. I did fine training with Gramps. My magic has been funny since you told me that my mother was here, and I'm pretty sure she is the cause of the block, and I need to fix it."

I had no words. I nodded my head like an idiot and turned toward my desk to retrieve a key from my desk drawer then motioned for her and the others to follow me.

I had put her mother in the east wing. At the request of Nina herself, after I told her what she had done to Ryan, I had the east wing locked off so no one could enter and she couldn't leave. She was terrified of losing control of her mind and hurting someone again. After a five minute walk, we finally arrived at the double doors that led to Nina's suite. I placed the key in the hole but stopped and turned to look at Ryan.

"Are you sure you're ready for this, love?" She took a steadying breath and nodded her head. I turned back and unlocked the doors, and with a deep breath, I pushed the handles down and opened the doors.

"Nina?" A moment later, Nina popped around the corner from her sitting room with a wide smile on her face.

"Nico, I'm happy to see—" She stopped speaking as soon as she realized who was standing next to me. Nina's hand came up to cover her mouth.

There she was, standing right there. She was right in front of me, but she didn't look the same. She didn't look like a monster anymore.

Her face wasn't hollow, and her eyes weren't sunken into her face. She had put weight on. She looked...healthy. I ran my gaze over her. She was in a beautiful yellow summer dress. Her hair was out and flowing around her, the blonde much more pronounced. Her rich brown eyes were filled with tears.

If I didn't know any better, I would swear this woman wasn't my mother. She was clean and healthy and looked normal. She wasn't drunk or high. I have *never* seen my mother sober. Completely overwhelmed, I turned to leave.

"Please...Ryan." I spun around and glared at her. How fucking dare she!

"Please, you fucking think you have the right to speak to me?"

I felt myself growing warm, and I could feel my magic surging inside of me. Oh, *now* my magic wanted to work. I felt a hand land on my shoulder and turned to glare at the owner of the hand, but stopped when I saw it was Lucian. He was siphoning my magic so I didn't hurt anyone. I pulled my gaze from him to turn back to face the star of my nightmares.

"You're right, I don't have a right to speak to you, but I want to." Tears rolled down her face freely. I shrugged Lucian's hand off my shoulder and moved toward Nina. I felt Nico and Lucian behind me but refused to acknowledge them.

I stopped a foot away from her and looked her right in the face. This woman broke me in so many ways.

"Do you have any idea what you put me through?" I didn't realize I was crying until I felt the tears rolling down my face. I have to give Nina credit; she didn't avert her gaze or look to the others for help.

"No, I don't. I have no idea what I put you through. Nico—"

"You don't get to say *my* husband's name!" I screamed, and she stumbled back a step.

"Dom, why don't you Soph and Tyler go get something to eat?" Nico said.

"Nah, man, I think I want to stay and—" I heard a *thwack* and flinched; someone had just hit Dom across the head, I would bet money on it.

"Fuck, Sophia, are you this frisky in bed now?" Nico growled, a moment later I heard the doors close behind us.

Nico came to my side and clasped my hand. I felt the tension drain from my body at his touch.

"Why don't we go into the sitting room and talk?" Nico suggested. Nina—I refused to call her mother—lead the way to her sitting room.

I sat on one of the two couches, and Nico and Lucian sat on either side of me. Nina sat on the other couch with her hands clasped in her lap, her eyes downcast.

Good. How did she like being the weaker one in the room now? I relished in the feeling of her being inferior and afraid.

"Why are you here, Ryan?" Nina murmured, and I gritted my teeth. How fucking dare she ask me what *I* was doing here.

"You are in *my fucking home*, Nina!"

"Ryan, that's enough." I turned to glare at Nico; he didn't get to tell me what to do with *her*.

"Don't you dare, Nico—"

Nina cut me off. "It's fine, Ni—. It's fine. She has every right to be angry with me."

I turned back to Nina. "You don't know anything about me, let alone how I am feeling! You fucked up my life!"

"Yes, I did! I didn't mean to; I didn't know what I was doing. You want to be mad and treat me how I treated you, then fine, do it. Trust me, it won't make you feel any better. I punish myself every day since being here and having a clear head.

I hate myself for what I did to you, my own daughter! To make it worse, I don't even remember it. You are my daughter, and I hurt you. I will spend the rest of my life trying to make it up to you and trying to fix the wrongs I have done.

I am so, so fucking sorry for what I put you through." Nina burst into gut-wrenching sobs, and all the anger leaked out of my body like a pinhole in a balloon.

What the hell is wrong with me? Nina was sick, and here I am condemning her for something that was out of her control. She was a victim, as well.

I stood and walked round the coffee table and plonked my ass down on it in front of her. She dropped her hands from her face and met my gaze, tears running down her cheeks. I took a deep breath and faced the woman who gave me life. I had to let this anger go. Not for her sake, but for mine.

"You're right, you weren't in control. But I can't forgive you." She dropped her gaze and twiddled her hands in her lap. "Maybe one day I will, but right now, I can't. I would like to sit down with you one day and talk. I don't have the time for that right now, but soon I will, hopefully." Her gaze met mine again, and I saw fear in her eyes.

"You have to fight your sister don't you?" I nodded. "W-will she survive?"

I wouldn't lie to her. "No. I wish there was a different way, but there isn't."

Lucian and I left Ryan and her mother alone, at Ryan's request. We made our way back to my study, and as we rounded the corner we both stopped at the sound of shouting.

"How the fuck could I breach his mind if he isn't related, Sophia?"

"I don't know, Dominic!"

"Don't fucking lie to me, Sophia—not about this. Who is he to *me*?"

"I don't know!"

"Stop fucking lying! You know more about that kid than anyone. You recognized him the day he turned up with Ryan. Who. Is. He?"

"How am I supposed to know, Dom? He told you himself he was raised in a cell." Lucian rushed around the corner, and I followed after him. Dom and Sophia stood outside my office, glaring at each other. As soon as they realized we were standing there, they both turned toward us. Dom looked pissed while Sophia looked fearful. Before I could ask them what was going on, Lucian spoke.

"How do you know me, Sophia? I saw the look on your face, as well, the day I arrived with Smurf."

Sophia dropped her gaze to the floor. "I don't know who you are, y-you just reminded me of someone."

"I don't need Jackson to be here to know you're full of shit, Sophia! Tell me the fucking truth!" I snapped my gaze to Dom, who was glaring down at my sister.

"Don't fucking talk to her like that!" I roared.

"Stay out of this, Nicky boy," Dom warned.

"What the fuck is going on between you two?" I looked between my sister and Dom, waiting for one of them to answer me.

"Dom and I, we kind of—"

"SIRE!" I spun around to see Cyrus and one of the other guards running toward me.

"What is it, Cyrus?"

"The alpha sent word; they are under attack *now* sire. The queen's sister has located the portal." Fuck, the war at Jackson's was a distraction, I just knew it.

"Ready your men, take them to the alpha, and do as he says until your king gets there, Cyrus. Eric, go retrieve the queen from her mother and bring her to the king's study."

Fucking hell, Sophia was like a drill sergeant. Both men stood there, looking at me, waiting. I nodded, and they both took off to fulfill their tasks.

"Nico, we need to go now. If she's found the portal, we don't have long!" I could hear the panic in Dom's voice. He was right; we would need to split up.

"I'll go with Ryan—" Dom was shaking his head before I could even finish.

"Randall has the blood of Jackson's father, Ryan's father, and Ryan's blood. You need to be at the compound to help us take him down if he's there. Ryan has to go to her sister on her own." I was already shaking my head.

"She won't be alone; I'll be with her." Dom and I turned to face Lucian. I knew the kid was powerful, but I didn't trust anyone aside from myself with Ryan's safety.

"Trust me, I will keep her safe, I swear it."

"I'll go with them."

I turned to my sister. "You can't, Soph. We need as many magic wielders as we can get to stop the witches." My gut filled with unease. I needed to be at Jackson's to help with Randall and the witches. I had no choice but to trust Lucian to keep Ryan safe.

The sound of footsteps pounding the floor drew all our attention. Ryan and Eric rounded the corner.

"What happened?" she asked, panting.

"Your sister. We need to go, now!"

CHAPTER 57

Ryan

We all ran from the castle like it was on fire. Once we breached the forest and made it to the clearing, Nico stopped me. He looked down at me with such anguish.

"I'm sending you to your sister, love." He wasn't coming with me. "Lucian will go with you to help, but we must go to Jax and Kai and help them." I nodded my head, this was it. "Stay alive, Ryan, do you hear me?" He clasped my face between his hands.

"I will. I'll save Farrarie, Nico. I promise." He leaned down and kissed me then pulled back and leaned his forehead against mine.

"Come back to me, love."

A stray tear leaked out the side of my eye. "I swear it."

Nico pulled away and released me reluctantly.

"I'll open a portal to your sister, love," Dom said, and began chanting. A portal opened beside me. Sophia gave Lucian and me a quick hug. I turned and smiled at Nico, who looked like he was two seconds away from saying fuck it and coming with me. Before Lucian and I could enter the portal, Dom stopped us.

"Trust in yourself, Ryan. You can do this. Lucian will help

you, but you need to trust him to be able to bring you back from the brink." Dom then turned to look at Lucian. "I don't know who you are kid, but don't die."

Lucian didn't reply, he just grabbed my hand and led me through the portal. I turned back just before we disappeared and saw Dom and Sophia holding Nico back.

"I love you!" I yelled. I hoped he heard me.

Lucian and I exited the portal in the middle of the woods. I knew these woods so well. I can't believe I never put it together before.

"Where the hell are we, Smurf?" I smiled. Kai told me years ago this place was the closest he could get to being home.

"Follow me." Lucian and I quietly made our way out of the woods, which was no small feat given the heavy underbrush. I resigned myself to the fact that my sister would know we were here.

I turned to Luce and said, "She would already know we're here, may as well just get this over with." We tromped through the rest of the woods, and when we emerged, Lucian gasped.

"Welcome to Lake William, Luce." I scanned the area and spotted Stevie standing at the end of the dock. Her back was to us, and I made my way down to her. I motioned for Lucian to stay back. He reluctantly nodded and waited on land.

As I walked toward Stevie, I noticed how thin she had gotten. She had leather pants and shit-kicker boots, with a black tank top. Her bones protruded in ways I'd never seen on her before. I cautiously approached her and stood beside her at the end of the dock, looking at her out of the corner of my eye.

She had her eyes closed. I could see black lines dancing under her skin. This darkness was killing her from the inside out. I couldn't think of her as my sister right now; if I did, I would never be able to do what needed to be done.

"I didn't think you would be ballsy enough to come, sister," she sneered.

"You plan on killing my people and harming the ones I care about. Of course I would come."

"You should have run while you had the chance, you stupid fool. Now you will die."

"It doesn't have to be this way, Stevie. If you let me, I will try to banish that evil inside you." My sister laughed, the sound like nails on a chalkboard. I turned to face her, and when she turned toward me, I gasped. There was no white around her pupils; her eyes were inky black.

"You and all those you hold dear will die today."

I wasn't prepared for what came next: a blast that hit me straight in my chest. I went sailing through the air and crashed into the water of the lake. I felt like a bowling ball had torn through my chest, and black spots were dancing in my vision.

The pain was unbearable. I focused on trying to push past the pain and get myself to the surface, I broke the surface of water, gasping and coughing. I had no time to recover; magic wrapped around me like a rope and pulled me from the lake.

Black swirls of magic were wrapped around me, and my arms were anchored to my sides. I looked down and saw my sister at the end of the dock with a cruel smile on her face. I jerked my eyes to the shore and icy dread went down my spine. Lucian was being held down by at least five vampires, and there were many more on the shore, at least fifty.

"You stupid bitch, did you really think I would come here alone? You really are naïve." Stevie was right; we had banked on them sending all their soldiers to Jackson's and her coming here alone. We were fools, and our stupidity had cost us greatly. I could barely breathe, let alone fight. The magic that held me immobile began to squeeze, and I gasped.

It was getting harder and harder to take a breath. The black spots were spreading throughout my vision, and I could see Lucian struggling against the hold of the vampires.

I was going to pass out.

"You will die in the place that you hold so dear to your heart," my sister hissed.

The magic tightened around me, and the pain in my chest intensified.

"Smurf! Fight it! You're stronger than her." I turned my heavy head toward Lucian and smiled a sad smile. I wasn't strong enough to beat my sister. One hit from her and I was down already. With one last deep breath, I blacked out and began falling toward the lake.

CHAPTER 58

Nico

Sophia, Dom, and I emerged from the portal at the back of Jackson's land. There were people everywhere; some of them were dead on the ground, and others were fighting to get the elderly out of here. Jackson was supposed to evacuate his compound the week before the attack: all elderly, and children or pregnant mothers were to leave here and go to safe houses until the attack was over. My blood began to boil when I looked down and saw a young boy with his throat torn out. He couldn't have been more than eleven years old and here he was lying at my feet dead. I growled and ran toward the fight, Sophia and Dom behind me. I launched an energy ball at a vampire attacking a shifter, launching him a few feet away. Dom and Sophia were throwing balls of energy at anyone who wasn't a fae or a shifter.

"We need to find Jax and Kai!" Dom yelled, and we took out as many witches, warlocks, and vamps as we could as we made our way toward the back of the property.

We huddled close to the building, and I peeked my head around the corner. There were witches and vampires everywhere. I couldn't see Jax and Kai among the warring supernaturals, but what I did see had my blood turning to ice. Without waiting or warning the others, I took off toward the four vampires who had Dom's father on his knees. The vampire with the black hair was going for the kill shot. I built the biggest energy ball I could in my hand and launched it at the unsuspecting vampire, who was knocked off his feet. Energy balls whizzed past my head, and I knew Dom and Sophia were behind me.

"Get the fuck away from him!" Dom roared.

I was throwing energy balls at one of the vamps, but he kept dodging. As I neared Mr. Silver, the blond head vamp engaged me in hand-to-hand combat. He was fucking strong, I give him that. I dodged his fist that was coming straight for my nose and landed a blow to his gut, but he recovered quicker than I would have liked. We traded hit for hit for a few moments before I called on my magic and punched him as hard as I could in the chest. My magic exploded out of my hand and blew the blond vamp to pieces. Vampire juice coated me from head to toe.

"Dad!" At the sound of Dom's panicked voice, I turned to see he and Sophia had taken out the other two vamps and were now kneeling in front of Dom's dad. "What happened? Are you okay?"

"If I was okay, Dominic, I wouldn't be on my fucking knees." Dom gave a half-hearted chuckle at his dad's attempt to lighten the mood. "They took Jax and Kai."

"Who?" I demanded.

"Randall Cane and his minions. He took the shifter and fae elders as well." How the hell did he manage to overpower the elder council?

"Why?" Sophia asked.

"I don't know, sweetheart, I feel like we're missing something. They attacked out of nowhere. Almost like they knew Ryan wasn't here. I think we have a rat." Mr. Silver sounded so weak; I have never seen this bear of man ever look as defeated as he did now. I looked around us to see the battle still raging on. These vampires were stronger than any I have ever encountered before.

"Where are Tyler, Aurora, Mya, and Ryan's cousins?" I asked.

"They were heading toward the lake; Tyler said there was something different about these vamps. They're stronger than any I have ever fought." I could hear the anger lacing Mr. Silver's tone.

"They drank her blood."

"Drank whose blood, Sophia?" Dom snapped.

"Ryan's! She said they were taking her blood three times a day. Randall gave her blood to his vamps so they would be stronger. That's why they're here during the day; her blood gave them the ability to walk in the daylight as well as extra strength." Oh my God, she was right. It hadn't even registered to me that it was daylight and vampires were here. They have Ryan's blood in their system.

"We need to find Kai; he will know how to stop them." They all nodded their heads. Dom and I helped Mr. Silver to his feet, then he waved us off and told us to go.

Dom was reluctant to leave his dad. "Go, son, go help the others. I have it under control here, the other packs were notified. They will be here as soon as they can." Dom nodded to his father and followed me and Sophia back toward the woods.

I knew where Randall would be taking Kai and Jax. I opened a portal to Lake William as soon as we entered the woods. I guess I would fight side by side with my wife after all.

CHAPTER 59

I felt weightless and free, and I didn't feel any pain. It's a bit of a relief, honestly. I thought dying would hurt.

"*Ryan, wake up.*" I knew that voice.

"Dad, is that you?"

"*Yes, darling, I need you to wake up now.*"

"I can't do it, Dad, I'm not strong enough."

"*You are strong enough, daughter. You just need to believe it. Trust in yourself and your power. If you don't wake now, you will die! Many have lost their lives today, don't let your fear cripple you.*"

"She's too strong, Dad. One hit and she already took me down!"

"*Remember your training, remember what your grandfather taught you. The whole supernatural race is counting on you Ry, now WAKE UP!*"

My father's scream jarred me awake. I was smart enough to not drag in a lungful of water. I scrambled to swim to the surface, my lungs burning from lack of oxygen. I broke the surface of the water, gasping, and pulled in lungful after lungful of air.

My head was cloudy from lack of oxygen and I tried to quiet my breathing so I wouldn't be noticed. Stevie was on the docks, arms outstretched, shooting black magic into a portal that wasn't there before I blacked out. I turned away from her to search for Lucian. He was on his knees with his arms behind his back. I looked past him and gasped.

Kai and Jax were kneeling behind Lucian. Randall-fucking-Cane stood behind them with a smug smile on his face.

"Don't pout boys, the half-blood bitch didn't stand a chance." I could hear the laughter in Randall's voice from all the way out here.

"Fuck you! I will kill you." A guard rained blow after blow on Kai for his outburst.

"You will all die for what that crazy fuck did to Smurf!"

Stevie stopped shooting her power into the portal and turned around, shooting a lighting-shaped blast into Lucian's chest. I screamed out as his eyes went wide and he collapsed into a heap.

All eyes spun toward me. Stevie glared. I released all the pain and anger I had been holding onto for years. Stevie reached out to shoot me with her magic but was knocked off her feet by an energy ball. I turned to see Nico, Dom, and Sophia walking out of the forest. I didn't have the time to process their arrival or deal with fallout that their arrival would bring.

"You are strong enough, daughter, you just need to believe it. Trust in yourself and your power."

I replayed what my dad had said to me. I could do this. I forced the cage open that I had locked all my feelings inside; it was time to let them out. Pain, anger, hurt, love, joy, happiness all warred inside of me. I chose to focus on anger. I channeled my magic and used it to propel myself out of the lake, levitating over to the dock. My sister was on her feet, scowling at me. My body was thrumming with power. I could feel my own strength, and it was *intoxicating*.

"You little bit—" I didn't let her finish. I blasted my sister with my magic. She went flying to the end of the dock and landed with a thud. She was back on her feet in an instant; my blow hadn't even hurt her. I needed to channel more magic. I focused on anger and hurt and let those feelings come to the surface, then threw another blast of magic at her. She dodged and reached her hand out, sending a blast of inky black magic toward me. I quickly erected a shield to stop the attack but I skidded back a few steps. Stevie was fucking strong.

She didn't stop her attack but increased her efforts, lobbing one blast after another, blow after blow. Sweat broke out across my brow. We circled each other, my back now to the woods. I was getting tired, and I could feel the magic inside of me slowing. Stevie moved toward me, throwing black balls of energy, and I threw my own balls of energy back at her, both of us dodging the other's attack.

I heard a scream come from behind me, and I averted my gaze from my sister to see Sophia screaming at Randall. Randall had Dom's head clasped in his hands, ready to break his neck. I had a choice to make; I saw Stevie out of the corner of my eye, ready to launch another energy ball right at me. I could block her attack and save my own ass, or I could save Dom's.

I chose to save Dom. I released the energy ball in my hand that was meant for my sister and hurled it at Randall.

I prayed that my aim was on point, and it was. It hit Randall in the side of the head and he stumbled back. His hold on Dom dropped and he collapsed to the ground.

I spun back toward my sister to see the ball of energy coming straight for me. This blast would kill me, but I was at peace with the decision I made to save Dom.

Everything was happening in slow motion. I could see the elders were here. On my right I could see Nico screaming out to me, but I couldn't make out what he was saying. I smiled at my husband and mouthed *I love you*. I returned my gaze back to my sister and gasped at the site in front of me.

What the fuck? NO!

No, no, no! What the fuck was he doing? He sacrificed himself for me—*for me.* Why the hell would he do that?

The blast hit him in the chest, and he staggered a couple steps back and then dropped to his knees.

My sister let out a gut-wrenching scream. Black magic exploded from within her, and I jumped in front of Tyler and prepared myself for the blast. I pulled all the magic I had inside of me and released it, creating a shield around everyone on the shore. I didn't want to protect the vampires, but I didn't have a choice. In order to save all of my friends, I had to save everyone on the shore.

My sister's blast of magic rattled my shield, and the power of her blast had me gritting my teeth. Stevie's pixie-cut hair was whipping around her face. The amount of power she was releasing would weaken her greatly. The trees around us began to crack and break. Stevie was leveling the forest with her power. I felt someone approach and saw it was Nico, he was covered in blood and panting. His shirt was no longer white and was barely hanging on by a thread.

"You need to take her out now, love. Her power is traveling

through the portal to Farrarie and killing our home." I turned back toward the dock; I could see black magic traveling through the portal.

"You have to do it now!" I looked down toward Tyler, his head resting in his sister's lap, Jackson beside her.

I knelt down and gripped Tyler's cold hand in mine.

I could see his life slowly draining from his eyes. Tears began to gather in my own.

"You got this, little hybrid," he wheezed out.

"Why did you do it, Ty?" I choked out.

"I lied. There was never a cure for me surviving my mate dying. Now go, before she kills your world and ours." I let my tears fall freely as I leaned forward and placed a kiss on his cold, clammy forehead.

"Thank you for being our alpha when we needed you most. You are the brother I never had, Ty. I love you, and we will meet again someday. You have my word that I will look after our pack. Run free and run wild Ty. I got this." A smile tugged at his lips, but I didn't wait for him to respond. I stood and walked away.

Just as I was about to pass through my shield, Nico's hand clamped down on my wrist.

"Let me help you," he begged. I didn't have time to waste. I turned and placed a chaste kiss to his lips and then sent a shock of electricity through him when I placed my hand on his chest. He dropped to his knees, a look of betrayal crossing his face. I would deal with his anger later. I pushed through my shield, knowing it would still stand without me in it, but I kept a piece of the shield around myself.

I pushed against my sisters magic; it felt like I was trying to move a boulder. Stevie was strong, stronger than any of us thought. I needed to get her and stop her before she destroyed both worlds. Focusing on my emotions, I sifted through them. I focused on my happiness. A voice inside my head was telling me my darker emotions wouldn't stand against my sisters darkness. I was light, and Stevie was dark. I focused on happiness and how happy I have been to be with my cousins, finding Kai and then Nico. Having Dom and Jax in my life as well, I met the girls through them and found friends. I found Lucian and Tyler. I loved all of them, and they loved me. Nina was getting help, and getting better. My dad loved me and wanted me to succeed. I married the man of my dreams, and I wanted to save the lives of all the people I cared for and loved. For the first time in my life, I had a family. And a future.

The weight I had felt on my chest earlier started to dissipate. My chest still hurt from Stevie's blow, but I would deal with that pain later. I started to feel weightless, relishing the thrum of the power inside of me, begging me to let it take control. Resigned to the fact I couldn't kill my sister on my own, I let the power inside of me take control.

It didn't burn; I didn't even feel warm. I just felt...content. The power coursed through my body, and I felt like a battery that was just recharged.

I didn't protest or fight the feeling, I embraced it, and I accepted the power inside of me.

I finally accepted who I am and what I am.

I leaned my head back, stretched my arms out wide and roared to the heavens. A blast so strong, stronger than the night of my wedding, shot out from within me. I snapped my head forward and stared at my sister. She was glaring right back.

My blue light was fighting and pushing against her black magic, against her darkness.

I moved one foot in front of the other and pushed with everything I had in me. My sister began to do the same and was making her way over to me. She wore a look of determination and rage.

We were closer to each other now. I felt sweat dripping down my brow and spine. Pushing against her magic had worn me down a bit.

"You will pay for what you have done, you bitch."

I smiled at my sister. I had gotten under her skin.

"I will walk away from this sister, but you will not."

Stevie grinned from ear to ear, she looked so deranged. "You are weak, and I have nothing left to lose. If I am to die today, I will make sure I take your precious fae realm with me."

CHAPTER 61

Nico

I'm still on my knees, watching her fight against her sister's blast. She has blue energy encompassing her. I'm pulled from my thoughts by Aurora's screams. I turn to see her clutching her brother's lifeless body. Tyler's gone.

Stevie killed him. He sacrificed himself to save Ryan. I heard what he said to her, that he lied to her about being able to save himself after she killed Stevie.

Tyler spent the past few months training *my* wife to kill *his* mate. Tyler was selfless, and he didn't deserve this end.

"She is using too much power, we need to find Lucian." Kai's voice pulled me from my thoughts, and I nodded. He was right. Ryan was pushing waves of power out, and I knew she needed to exude more power than she ever has, but I was worried now that she wouldn't be able to rein it back in. I jumped to my feet and looked around for Lucian, but I couldn't see him anywhere.

"There, he's out there!" Dom said, appearing at my side like a ghost. Lucian lay on the ground by the docks, and he wasn't moving. Stevie and Ryan were both using so much power that I

wasn't even sure he would be able to withstand the amount of energy out there.

We were all trapped inside this dome. Without Lucian, we were all fucked. He was the only one who could bring Ryan back.

"What the hell are we going to do? She can take Stevie out, but if Lucian doesn't wake the fuck up, Ryan could take us all out!" Dom was right, but I didn't have a plan. I didn't know what to fucking do because my wife had, once again, left me behind.

Ryan

Stevie and I were so close that the only thing separating us was our magic. Black smoke surrounded her, and I assumed I looked the same but blue. Stevie had a murderous look on her face, a look that promised pain.

"Stop your attack, Stevie, it doesn't have to end like this." A manic laugh escaped her, the black lines slithering beneath the surface of her skin like worms. I shuddered. I knew in my heart Stevie was too far gone; there was no saving her. I had to give her a chance to surrender, though. My conscience wouldn't allow me not to.

"You're fucking pathetic! I would rather die than live in your shadow; I have been second to you my whole life. That changes now!" Stevie launched a ball of fire at me—actual fucking fire!

I deflected it using my magic to push it aside. How the fuck could she throw fire?

We began to circle each other. I was now with my back to the dock, and Stevie had her back to the armies fighting behind her. I could see Nico, Dom, and Kai standing there, staring at

me. Dom was furiously pointing to something near me, but I couldn't afford to look without Stevie attacking me.

Thank God I didn't risk it. Stevie hurled fire ball after fire ball at me. I needed to do something, now. I focused on my connection with nature; I was surrounded by it. Grams had told me all witches draw their power from the land. I was half witch, so I needed to focus on that side of my being.

"Help me...help me fight her." I didn't know if asking Mother Nature for her assistance would work, but I had to try.

Stevie was stronger than we had all anticipated; I needed to use both sides of my power in order to beat her.

"Call the water to you, Ry." I heard my father's voice inside my head, and I didn't hesitate or question it. I stretched my arms out wide and commanded the lake water to come to me. In a flash, balls of swirling water were hovering over my palms. I didn't stop to dwell on it.

I launched them at my sister's fire balls.

I needed something stronger than these water balls; they may be extinguishing Stevie's fire but they weren't slowing her down.

"I need more, I need you to shoot water." I sounded like a mad woman, talking aloud to myself, but I had no idea how else to ask the elements for help.

Water shot from the lake like a cannon, the pressure so hard it knocked my sister back a few steps. She tried to dodge the blast to no avail. Stevie's black magic stopped pulsing out of her; she tried to erect a shield to shelter her from the blast, but the strength of the water broke through her shield.

I knew this was the moment—while she was down and distracted, I needed to make my move and end this once and for all.

I called all of the magic inside myself and channeled it into a bright blue orb. It hovered over my palm. The more magic I pulled from within myself, the more unstable I felt. I was losing control.

I needed Lucian, but he was nowhere to be found, and I didn't have time to waste thinking about how to bring myself back from the brink. I walked toward my sister with purpose. She was struggling to her feet, and when she finally stood and spun around, I was directly in front of her.

I could see the shock on her face, which quickly turned to rage.

"I'm so sorry, sister." I said as I pushed the magic orb into her chest, tears rolling down my cheeks. Stevie's eyes rounded like saucers, pain reflected in her eyes. She stumbled back several steps, screaming. Blue light illuminated under her skin, and it was like a rat race, blue chasing black. Blue was winning, for a moment, but the black worms inside my sister started to fight back.

I reached out with my hand and sent a stream of blue light into her chest. She screamed in agony, but I didn't stop pushing my magic into her until she dropped to her knees.

Tears were flowing down my cheeks freely as I watched my sister shake and shiver on her knees. I knelt down in front of her, cupping her face between my hands. When my gaze connected with hers, a sob broke free. Hazel eyes now stared back at me. The darkness inside of her was gone, and tears rolled down her cheeks. She was gasping for air.

"Stevie, I am so sorry. I'll fix this, I swear." I looked around for someone to help me—anyone. They were trapped behind the shield I had created. I pulled the magic from the shield back into me and it disappeared, just like popping a bubble. Nico came running, falling to his knees beside me and looking between me and my sister.

"She's dying Nico, help her, please." Nico looked to my sister, and she started to shake her head.

"I...can't...b-be...saved...Ry." She was in so much pain, I could see it in her eyes.

"I can take the pain away." I looked up to see Mya standing next to us, and I nodded without hesitation. She placed one of her hands on top of Stevie's head and whispered in some language I didn't understand.

"I have made her comfortable, but she doesn't have long, Ryan, her heart is slowing."

"Thank you, Mya." I turned back to my sister, who still looked weak and pale but no longer in agony. "I am so sorry, Stevie, I didn't want this to happen—"

Stevie cut me off. "Shhhhhhh, it's not your fault, Ry. I have been fighting against this power for so long. The darkness consumed me and I let it." I could hear the embarrassment in her voice. "I need you to know, Ry, I did not kill our father. Randall Cane did and blamed the fae." Stevie turned to look at Nico, so much regret and shame shone in her eyes. "I am sorry for all the harm I have caused you and your people. I let my grief consume me and blamed the wrong race."

"You are forgiven, coven queen." My heart bolstered at the respect and kindness in Nico's tone. He didn't have to formally address my sister, not after everything she had done, but he did it anyway, for *me*.

Stevie turned her gaze back to me, tears clouding her vision, she smiled a smile that didn't reach her eyes, she lifted her hand and cupped my cheek, I could see how taxing it was for her to hold her arm up.

"Don't cry, little sister, I am finally free. It was always going to end this way. I tried to fight as long as I could against it, but I was tired and—"

Stevie started coughing, blood spluttered out of her mouth. I brushed her hand away and shifted us so her head was resting in my lap. I knew deep down she didn't have much time left.

"Live your life, sister. Live for both of us." She coughed again, this time more blood spluttered out and her breaths came in short pants. "L-love...you...Ry," she choked out, then her eyes went wide and she sighed.

I watched the life leave my sister's eyes. A crushing weight slammed into me. My heart felt like it was on fire, and power like never before surged within me. I felt like a bomb, ready to explode.

"GET THE BOY, NOW!"

CHAPTER 63

Nico

I can see her struggling. If we don't get Lucian to her now, she will level this whole place and take out everyone in it. Dom and Kai pretty much carried Lucian toward us.

"No, no, no, no! What have I done? Stevie, please come back, please!" Tears are falling down her face like rain. Her grief is palpable, and it's crushing her. I try to comfort her by placing a hand on her shoulder, but she shrugs my hand off and glares at me.

"This is your fault!" I reel back; how is this my fault?

"Little one, I never wanted this to happen." Her glare turns from anger to rage, and I dart my gaze past her to search for Lucian. They're nearly to us, I just need to keep her occupied for a bit more. She gently places her sister's head on the ground and stands. She looks down at me with hatred. I don't get time to process that look before her magic wraps around me like a vine and I'm lifted into the air. I am man enough to admit that my wife scares the shit out of me right now.

I'm suspended at least five feet off the ground, hanging there like a limp noodle, my arms trapped at my sides. The magic wrapped around me starts to tighten its hold.

"You could have stopped all of this! You could have killed me as a child. My sister would still be alive if you did!" she screamed. She launched a ball of energy, and it happened so fast I didn't even have time to prepare for the attack. I went sailing through the air and landed on the hard ground with a bone-rattling thud. *Fuuccckk,* that hurt.

I had no time to process or calculate if I had any other injuries, because magic wrapped around me again, lifted me into the air, and pulled me back toward her.

This time she deposited me on the ground in front of her, her magic still wrapped tightly around me. I flinched as the magic squeezed me tighter.

"I blame you, I blame you for everything!" I couldn't bear to stare into her eyes any longer, the hatred and disgust in her gaze broke me. I hung my head in shame. She was right. I couldn't kill her, even after I knew Kai had failed. She is my *hugacko* and killing her would mean killing my soul. I saw a blue orb hovering in her hand, but I didn't protest or plead. I just waited for her to attack.

"Don't do it, love! You're angry and you're hurt. Killing him won't take the pain away." My head lifted to see Dom, Kai, and Lucian standing behind Ryan. Dom was trying to appeal to her humanity, but right now it looked like she had none. Her gaze was burning holes into me. If she needed someone to blame I would be that person, but I couldn't stand by and watch her lose herself to the power inside of her. She was glowing blue, but this time it was different, it was like she was encompassed in flames.

"If you need to hate someone or hurt someone, I will be that person. I love you, Ryan Stone."

"I am not Ryan Stone, Nico. I am a fucking Knox." She let out a scream so powerful it knocked everyone at Lake William to their knees; her power was like a wave of destruction. Wave after wave of power battered us. I Looked to Lucian, and his gaze met mine. We both knew if he didn't stop her, she would kill us all. Lucian closed his eyes and shouted out a spell I had never heard of before.

"*Braka incontinu faylinga prowess, bundunu!*" Lucian never hesitated; as soon as he was free of Ryan's power, he jumped to his feet and tackled her to the ground. The barrage of power stopped immediately. Lucian flipped her over so she was on her back then straddled her and clamped her arms by her sides.

"Get the fuck off me, Lucian."

"Never, Smurf. I can't let you do this, so don't fight it. It will only hurt the both of us. Just let me take it away. Let me take some of the pain away. The power inside of you is intensifying your pain. Let me do this for you, Smurf, please," Lucian begged.

"It hurts so much, Luce. Stevie is dead...my sister is dead." She broke into uncontrollable sobs.

Sophia, Alex, and Chase now joined us, all three of them heartbroken at her grief. I don't think any of us would have been able to do what she did today.

I moved toward my sister and wrapped my arm around her shoulders, grateful that I had her back in my life. Ryan made a sacrifice today that I understand all too well.

"I'm gonna take it away now, Smurfy. let it go. Release it to me." Ryan nodded her head, tears still streaming down her face. Minutes that felt like hours ticked by as Lucian funneled her power into him.

Finally, Lucian released his hold on her arms. A couple more minutes passed, and her head lulled to the side. She passed out. Lucian looked around to all of us, his strange eyes glowing brighter. "I can't hold this inside of me for long; the hit I took from her sister has weakened me. When she wakes, I need to start funneling the power back to her."

"Is there no way you could hold it longer?" Dom asked.

He shook his head sadly. "The longest I have ever held it was ten minutes." We all nodded. Lucian was injured, and we were all asking him to hold a bomb inside of himself.

"I hope she has calmed down by then. I mean, look around," said Kai. Lake William was destroyed. The dock was pretty much wood chips now, the forest was broken and bent, trees littering the ground. Bodies were all over the place, some injured, but most of them dead. So many had lost their lives today, all for the greed of another. Stevie was a victim of darkness, and I understood her part of this attack. Randall Cane had started all of this for power.

"Where the hell is Randall?" I asked the group. Everyone begun to spin in circles to see if they could spot the vampire king who had wreaked havoc on our lives for years.

"I haven't seen him since Ryan blasted him in the face," my sister answered.

CHAPTER 64

Ryan

I woke in a strange land, one I had never seen before in my dreams. I was on a beach, with crystal clear water lapping at the sand. I looked down and saw I wasn't in my usual white dress. I was wearing shorts, flip flops, and a yellow camisole. Where the hell am I? I heard a noise behind me and spun around.

"Daddy?" I choked out. My father smiled and walked toward me with open arms. I ran, slamming into him and wrapping my arms around him. He held me while I sobbed into his shirt. This must be heaven. I must have died, right? I don't remember dying.

"You're not dead, sweetheart. Your mind just needed to take a break." I pulled back from my father and stared at him. His soft green eyes held nothing but love and contentment.

"How am I here? Where are we?"

"You tell me, Ry, this is your dream, after all." I had no idea how I had called my father to me or where the hell we were. I wasn't going to look a gift horse in the mouth, though. I would enjoy this moment.

"Dad, I did something today, I—"

"Shhh, Ry. I know, and Stevie isn't mad. You freed your sister from a lifetime of misery." Tears began to fall from my eyes, and my dad wiped them away.

"I didn't want to do it, I didn't have a choice." A sob broke free, and I wrapped my arms around myself, trying to hold myself together.

"Ryan, you did what you had to do. Stevie is okay. She hated what she had become."

"You said I could blast the darkness out of her, but it didn't work! I killed her, Dad." My dad's face softened, and he cupped my cheek with one of his hands.

"It was too late, daughter, she had accepted the darkness inside of her. There was nothing you could have done, Ry." Wait —if my dad was here, then did that mean...?

"Is Stevie here?" My dad sucked in a breath before he answered.

"You're not ready to see her yet, sweetheart. When you are, she will come to you. Just trust me when I tell you that your sister is free now, thanks to you. She loves you, Ryan, and doesn't blame you." I broke out into uncontrollable sobs. I wanted to see my sister and tell her I loved her one last time.

"Ryan, I won't see you again, my dear."

"What, why?" Dad smiled down at me, but the smile didn't reach his eyes.

"I was granted the power to come to you from the elders of the past, to help you in this battle. Now that the battle is over, you must live and not dwell on the dead." I tried to butt in, but dad raised his hand signaling for me to shut up and wait.

"You have a long life ahead of you sweetheart, a long, happy life. When you return to your reality, let all the anger and pain of the past go. Your power overrode you today because you have never truly let go of your past. You cannot live in the past, Ry. Look toward your future and focus on that." Dad was right, but it was easier said than done.

"For you, I will try. I promise to try letting my anger go toward Mom and be happy." When Dad smiled down at me again, this time it did reach his eyes.

"I am so beyond proud of you, my daughter. I am sorry you had to do what you did today. I would never have been able to choose between my daughters. Because I was too weak to do what needed to be done, you were left with that burden." I wrapped my arms around my dad and hugged him. I didn't want to say goodbye.

"Go now, my daughter, live your life and be happy. We will meet again one day." Dad placed a kiss to the top of my head.

"I Love you, Daddy." As soon as I said that, everything went dark.

I awoke back at Lake William, with Lucian still straddling my legs. I turned my head from side to side to see everyone except Mya and Aurora staring down at me. I couldn't bear to meet Nico's gaze for longer than a second. What I did and said to him was disgusting. I let my pain and grief cloud my judgment, and I took it out on him.

"Smurf, I need to give it back," Lucian gritted out, and then I could see the strain on his face.

"I'm okay, Luce, I can take it," I said, smiling up at him. Lucian blew out a loud exhale and placed his hands on my chest. Power seeped into me at a slow pace, and I didn't feel any heat this time. It didn't hurt to have my power inside me now that I accepted it.

Once the transfer was complete, Lucian stood and helped me to my feet. Dom engulfed me a hug as soon as Lucian stepped back.

"Thank you for saving my life, love." I returned his embrace and smiled.

"It was never a choice between you or me, Dom." Dom held me tighter for a moment before he stepped back and nodded his

head then turned on his heel and left. I turned to face my cousins, both of whom hugged me and then left, saying they were going to help clean up. Sophia and Lucian followed after them. I was to chicken to turn around and face Kai and Nico.

"You can't avoid us forever, you know?" Kai was right; it was time to face the music. I turned around slowly and kept my head down, not having the balls to look either of them in the eye.

A hand lifted my chin, and I looked up to see the most mesmerizing gray-blue eyes.

Kai smiled down at me, but I couldn't return the gesture. Because of me, Kai now had to lead the race he hated most. Randall was gone, so now Kai was the king of the vampires.

"I'm so sorry, Melakai," I choked out.

"Don't be sorry for being a queen and making the hard decisions, *mi amor*." He called me *mi amor*! He hadn't called me that since he found out what I did to him. The words brought a smile to my face.

"You are going to be an amazing queen. The fae and witches are lucky to have you." Kai leaned forward and placed a kiss on my cheek. It wasn't enough for me, and I wrapped my arms around his waist and rested my cheek on his chest. Kai held me to his chest.

"Thank you for everything, Kai. Thank you for being my escape, my friend, and my protector. I love you." I felt his body soften at my words.

"I will always be here for you, Ryan. You will always hold a special place in my heart. If you should ever need me, all you need do is call." Kai and I broke apart, Kai bid Nico and I goodbye, and then left to help the others. It was time to face the music. I turned my gaze to Nico. He was looking at me with so much pity and shame in his gaze. None of this was his fault, and I was wrong to blame him.

"Nico—"

He cut me off. "You were right, you know, I could have stopped this. I could have killed you, saved my world and saved you from this pain. I couldn't do it, though, even after I knew Kai had failed. From the first moment I entered your dreams, I fell head over heels in love with you. Killing you was never an option after that; I would risk everything for you. You can be Ryan Knox or Ryan Stone. I don't really give a flying fuck as long as you are mine. I will never let you go, Ryan, you are mine. I am a selfish bastard, and I won't apologize for that.

"I'm sorry you had to go through what you did today, but I still wouldn't go back and change a thing if it meant I couldn't have you—"

I didn't let him finish his rant; I launched myself at him. We held onto each other and whispered words of love into each other's ears. We stayed like that for ages and only broke apart at the sound of someone calling my name. I turned around to see it was Victor, the leader of the fae elders.

It was time.

CHAPTER 66

Nico

I thought closing the portal and stabilizing Farrarie would be a lot harder. I mean, it looked easy from where I was standing, but in reality it was probably hard as shit. Ryan made it look so effortless. She didn't even need Lucian this time to help draw her power back. I honestly thought she would have been spent after exhausting so much power to stop her sister, but clearly I was wrong.

Farrarie now didn't need a portal to Earth to stabilize it. It could sustain itself now, thanks to Ryan. She truly was a gift to all of Farrarie and the strongest supernatural I have ever encountered. Many have tried to find another way to help my world, but no one succeeded but her.

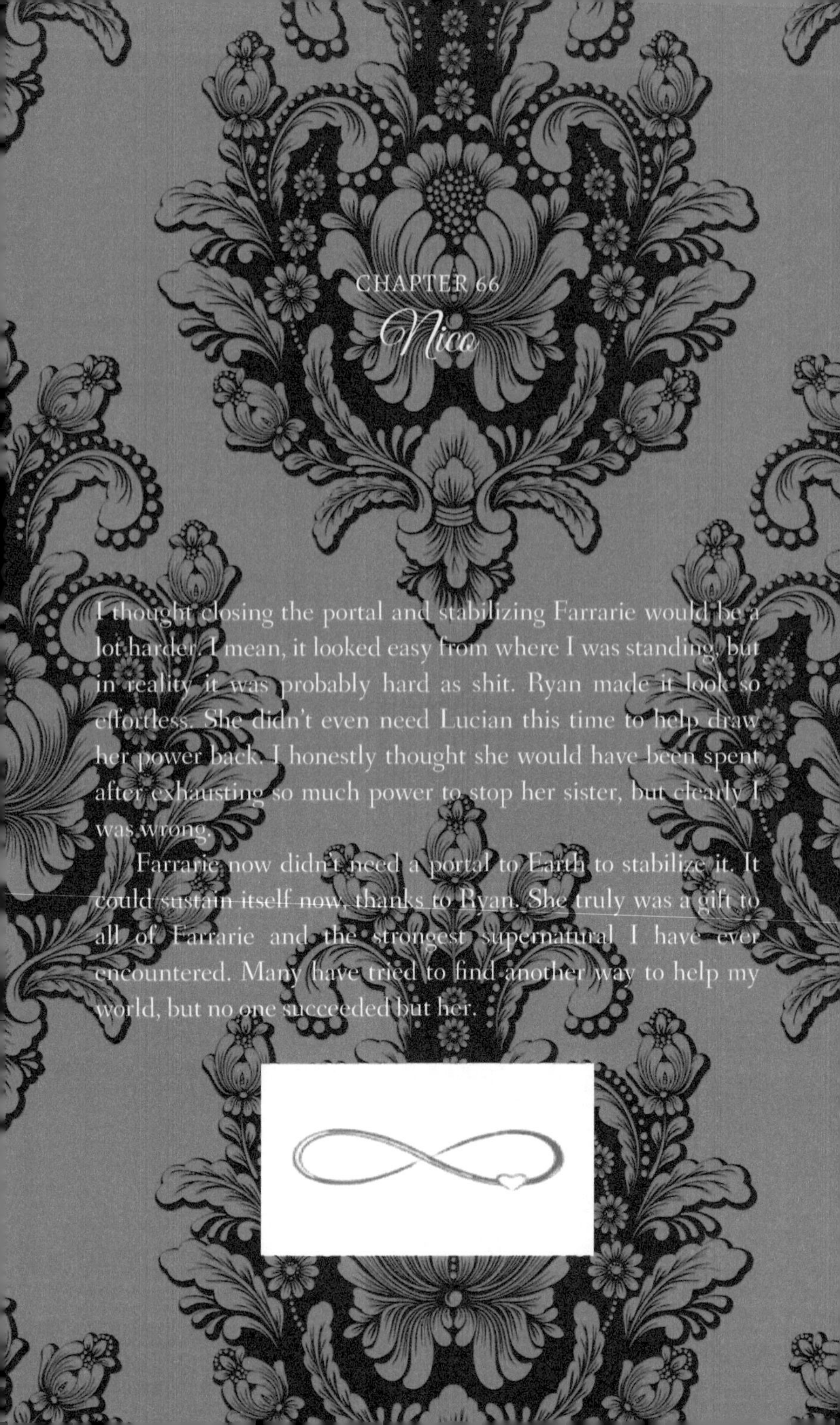

I left Cyrus and Larick back at Lake William to help with the cleanup and to bring the lost fae back to our realm so they could be buried with their loved ones. I carried Stevie back through the portal with Ryan at my side. She wouldn't look at her sister.

I didn't blame her; Stevie's chest had a charred hand print right where Ryan had pushed her magic into her.

Jackson's compound was in utter turmoil. Parts of the compound had been burned, and bodies littered the ground. So many had lost their lives today: fae, vampire, shifter, and witch.

I sent Maverick to retrieve all the fae we had sent over the world to let them know it was safe to return home. Half my soldiers were sent back to my realm to help with the burials while half remained to help restore order and clean up.

Ryan refused to send Stevie back to the coven until she had met with the witch elders. The witches didn't want her buried on the mountain with her ancestors. Ryan was not having any of that. We learned from her uncle that the witch elders' loved ones were being set free, thanks to Kai ordering the vamps to release them. Ryan also learned that her father wasn't buried in New Zealand; he was buried on the same mountain the witches refused to let her bury her sister.

I placed Stevie's body in the same room Kai had been in when Tyler first brought him back. Ryan and I were turning to leave the room to meet with all the elders in the mess hall when Jax and Aurora walked in. Jax was carrying Tyler, and at the sight of him, Ryan broke out into sobs and raced over.

She stroked Tyler's cheek softly and whispered, "Thank you for all that you have done, Ty. I hope you find peace now." Ryan leaned forward and placed a kiss on his forehead. Aurora cleared her throat and looked to Ryan. Ryan stiffened, and I know she was waiting for Aurora to lash out for her brother's death.

"I would like for Tyler to lay with his mate. I would also like to ask that she and Ty be buried together. Shifters are always buried with their mates."

"O-of course," Ryan stuttered out. She moved aside to let them place Tyler next to Stevie on the bed. Ryan went rigid when Aurora walked to the other side of the bed where her sister lay and placed her hand on Stevie's.

"I wish you peace, Stevie Knox. I hope that you and my brother find each other in the life to come." Tears leaked from Ryan's eyes. Ryan caught Aurora's arm as she went to leave the room.

"What you just did, I know it wasn't easy."

"I didn't do it for your sister; I did it for my brother."

As we entered the mess hall, I saw all the elders standing against the back wall. I swallowed past the lump in my throat. Before Nico could move further into the room to join the others, I stopped him. He looked down at me with concern.

"I just want you to know, everything I have done I have done because I love you. I need you to remember that, okay?" Fear passed through his eyes.

"What have you done?" he whispered.

"Miss Knox, would you join us, please?" I looked past Nico to see the leader of the vampire elders motioning us forward to stand with the others.

"It's Mrs. Stone," Nico growled.

"Of course, please forgive me," Lachlan muttered. Nico and I made our way over to stand with Kai, Dom, Jax, Sophia, Aurora, Lucian, and my cousins. Where was Mya?

"Let's not waste time, old friend, we have a lot to do and a lot to fix before this day is over," Dom's dad said to the vampire elder.

"Very well, first on our list, Melakai Cane, it has been brought to my attention that you are now a true blood heir of the late king?" I stiffened next to Kai, and Nico gripped my hand in his, offering me his silent support. I looked to Kai and heard him release a loud exhale.

"What you have heard is true. I am the rightful heir to the throne of the vampires." I could hear the strain in Kai's voice at having to say that out loud. My chest constricted at the pain I had caused him.

"Very well. I, Lachlan Inkwell, leader of the vampire council, accept your claim to the throne. You will be initiated as the king once we return to the mansion." Kai gave a stiff nod but said nothing.

My uncle David stepped forward next, a look of pity in his eyes. The elders were the only ones that knew the truth aside from me. We had to go through all of this political bullshit before we got to the truth.

"Ryan Knox, descendant of Ralph and Nina Knox, granddaughter of Marcus and Bethany Knox, do you accept the role of coven queen to the Knox coven?" I released Nico's hand and stepped forward, looking my uncle directly in the eyes.

"I, Ryan Knox-Stone, accept the crown and the role." Uncle David bowed to me and stepped back. I followed his lead and moved back between Kai and Nico. Next to speak was Victor.

"Do you, Ryan Knox-*Stone*, accept the role of queen of Farrarie?" The doors behind us opened, and I heard footsteps of many soldiers, guards from all four races surrounding the room. It was time for the truth to come out.

"What is the meaning of this?" Nico demanded.

"Dad, what the hell is going on?" Dom asked his father.

I turned to Nico and gripped his hand in mine. He looked down at me, and I could see it in his eyes—he knew what I had done.

"No." he whispered. I released his hand and stepped forward to face the council. I wrapped my magic around my friends, making them immobile. Lucian stepped forward to stand by my side. Luce now knew what I had planned. The look on his face told me he didn't like it, but he would stand by me.

"Ry, what the hell are you doing?" Chase shouted at me, but I ignored him and focused on the council.

"I, Ryan Knox-Stone, reject my claim to the throne as queen of the fae." I heard gasps and growls sound behind me, but I pushed on. "I Ryan-Knox-Stone, queen of the Knox coven, hereby abdicate my claim of the throne to my cousins. Alex and Chase Knox. Both have been studying the laws and the politics of the coven for months and have grown up knowing who and what they are. The Knox coven would be lucky to have them as their kings!"

"I don't fucking want it, Ryan! What the hell are you doing?" Alex shouted at me. I turned to face my cousins and then looked to my friends and my husband. Nico had a look of utter betrayal on his face and was looking around the room frantically.

"I have to answer for the crime I committed, Alex. You and Chase will lead the Knox coven as it should be. I was never going to be a good queen. All I ask is to please allow my sister to be buried with respect and honor. Stevie was as much a victim in this as anyone else who died today. Please let her be buried with dignity. I am sorry to all of you for lying to you about this. I knew none of you would let me go through with it, but the elders offered me a deal, and I took it to ensure all of your safety."

"Safety from whom?" Sophia asked.

"She took the lives of fifty-two supernaturals and some of those were elders. She must answer for her crimes." I lowered my head in shame at Victor's words.

"If any of you so much as *think* of harming her, I will kill every single one of you myself. Fuck your laws and fuck your rules! She is my wife!" Nico roared, and I flinched at the rage in his voice. Mr. Silver stepped forward to address the room.

"The elders will take some time to discuss the punishment and reconvene when we have made a decision. Your actions today and saving the fae realm will be brought into consideration, Ryan." Mr. Silver approached me and gestured with his hand to follow him out of the room.

"Dad, I swear to God, if you take her out of here—" Dom snapped at his father. Mr. Silver didn't falter in leading me out of the room as he spoke.

"I'm sorry, son."

Betrayal didn't come close to how I was feeling right now. How could she do this? As soon as she left the mess hall with Mr. Silver and Lucian, her magic evaporated from around us, and we sprang into action and fought our way out of the mess hall. The guards were no match against all of us. We ran through the compound, searching for her everywhere. She was nowhere to be found. I tried to feel for the bond she and I shared, and I deflated when I couldn't feel her presence anywhere. Lucian being with her is blocking her from being found.

"Where the hell did they take her?" Kai gritted out.

She gave up on me—on us. We would have helped fight the elders, what the hell did they have over her? In order for us to find a way out of this, we had to figure that out, and we also needed to find out what they planned to do to her.

"We need to find your father, Dom."

Dom was a picture of anger, just vibrating with rage, and his fists were clenched at his sides.

"Yeah we do. He and I need to have a little chat as well," Dom gritted out.

Hours had passed. We all congregated in Jax's office after we helped clean up. All of the people that lost their lives were returned to their pack, coven, or clan. Kai had to return to the mansion with the vampire elders to be announced as their king. Jackson had announced to his pack that they would do their burials tonight.

I refused to allow Stevie to be buried without Ryan present, so with Aurora's consent and Alex and Chase's okay, the witches cast a spell to preserve their bodies until that could happen. I thought it weird to have two dead bodies lying in a room, so we arranged for two caskets to be brought here and for their bodies to be cleaned and prepared for burial. Alex and Chase had to return to their coven, but they refused to take over leadership until they spoke with Ryan. I respected them for that; most people would jump at the chance to be a king, but not those two. They were loyal to my traitorous wife.

Dom, Sophia, Aurora, Jax, Mya, and I sat around Jackson's office, all lost in our own thoughts for some time. I got so lost in my spiraling emotions that I didn't even hear the door to Jax's office open. I was pulled from my thoughts by the sound of Lucian's voice. I turned to face him and Mr. Silver, who were now standing by the door.

Dom immediately strode over to them.

"I know your angry but—" Lucian didn't get a chance to finish what he was saying before Dom punched him straight across his jaw. Sophia shrieked and jumped up to stand between the two glaring males.

"It's not his fault, Dominic!"

"He knew what she was doing, Sophia! He could have told us, but he didn't. He is a fucking traitor!" Dom roared.

"I never betrayed anyone. I told you all I would always be loyal to Smurf. You knew that, Dom. I did what I had to in order to find things out. Now are you ready to listen, or should your father and I leave?" Lucian snapped.

"You have our attention, boy," I ground out. Lucian nodded and stepped away from Dom and Sophia. Mr. Silver remained quiet this whole time, which was unsettling. Lucian looked to Mr. Silver, who nodded his head.

"Is this room okay to talk freely?" What a peculiar question.

"Yes," Jax answered.

"Good, because I shouldn't be telling you any of this. I swore to always be loyal to Smurf and to always have her back, and I'm about to break that vow." I looked around the room to see everyone wore looks of shock. We all knew how loyal this boy was to Ryan, so for him to betray her meant something big was at play here.

"You should have a seat," Mr. Silver said.

"Smurf made a deal with the council when we were in Yukon at her grandparents. Her grandfather told her it was the only way. She contacted the leaders of the council. They told her if she didn't turn herself in they would come after all of us. She didn't even want me to know, but I was listening to her conversation with Gramps."

What the fuck.

"I would like to see them try!" Jackson said, his voice dripping with malice.

"Calm down, son, I was there when she called. Victor and Lachlan told her as the leaders of the fae and vampires, they would de-throne Kai and Nico and arrest them. They tried to get David and me to agree to do the same. They wanted David to arrest his own sons and for me to take over as head alpha and lock my son and Jackson away."

Those conniving bastards. I wanted to elect new council leaders at the next meeting.

"Mr. Silver is right. Smurf did what she had to in order to make sure you lot didn't pay the price for her mistake," Lucian confirmed.

"What do they plan to do with her, Dad?" Dom asked.

"Victor and Lachlan want her powers bound and her to pay with her life." The room erupted in chaos, everyone was shouting.

"QUIET!" Mr. Silver's voice boomed throughout the room, and the screaming trickled off. "David and I won't agree to that, and we are at a stalemate. They promised Ryan that she would stand a fair trial, and Ryan was under the assumption that she may face jailing. She has no idea they plan to bind her power. I personally believe that Victor and Lachlan always planned to kill her."

"What do we do in the meantime, then?" Mya asked.

"We wait for back up to arrive." Lucian had an evil grin on his face. What ace did the boy have up his sleeve?

"What back up?" Dom queried.

"They will be here shortly," Lucian smugly replied.

They?

CHAPTER 69

I couldn't shake the look of betrayal on Nico's face from my mind. I agreed to leave with Dom's father in order to not upset the others more by staying in the mess hall. Mr. Silver had driven me to a remote cabin in the mountains; he said this place was warded, meaning no one could track me or find me here.

He said there were clothes and food inside, and I should be comfortable enough until he returned. Lucian refused to stay; he was angry and felt betrayed. I couldn't blame him, but I had to answer for the crime I committed. Many good people had lost their lives because of me, and my conscience wouldn't allow me to run and not face my punishment.

After Lucian and Mr. Silver left, I wandered through the small cabin. There was a single bed with a metal frame, and a worn recliner that had seen better days. There was a small fireplace, a kitchen which was the size of a closet, and an equally small bathroom.

It was so quiet here, and there was nothing here to distract me from my thoughts. I tried to feel for the bond Nico and I shared, but felt nothing. I wish I didn't decide to do this on my own. I was here alone with my grief, which was overwhelming. I needed a distraction, I grabbed a coat from the end of the bed and left the cabin.

I walked around the woods aimlessly, and after a while I stumbled upon a small stream. It seemed so out of place, seeing this stream on a mountain. I sat down on a large rock, pulling my knees up to my chest and wrapping my arms around them, resting my chin on my knees. I sat there, staring out at the running water, tears leaking from my eyes.

I cried for my dad, at never getting to know him. How could you miss someone you didn't really know?

I cried for Nina. I felt for her. I wish I didn't, but I did. She had no control of her life for so long. She and Stevie were so much alike in that aspect. Neither of them had a chance to be themselves; they were ruled by a curse placed upon them. Thinking of my sister opened the dam and tears streamed endlessly down my face.

My heart felt like it had split in half. I looked up to the heavens and screamed. Why did it have to be me? Why did I have to be the one to end my sister's life?

"Why me?" I screamed to the sky. No one answered me, not that I expected a reply. I thought being a mystical hybrid might have its perks, but so far the only perk was finding my soulmate. A soulmate who I ridiculed for hiding things from me and yet here I was doing the same to him.

I kept making decisions on my own. I kept hurting him. I jumped to my feet, stretched my arms wide, and roared, a blast of power shooting out of me.

Screaming and releasing my power didn't make the pain go away or even lessen it. I dropped to my knees and sobbed on the forest floor, alone.

I couldn't blame anyone. I did this to myself. I chose to leave my friends and husband in the dark. This was my fault. I deserved to be alone and broken.

By the time I pulled myself together and wandered back to the cabin, it was getting dark and cold. I hoped I was going the right way. I would hate to get lost in this forest and starve or freeze to death. How ironic would that be?

I could see a dim light through the trees. Huh. I'm sure I didn't leave a light on when I left. I froze—did the elders find me here? Shit, what if it was one of the vampires, and they still held a grudge about what I had done to their former king?

"I know you're there, Ryan. I promise I come in peace."

CHAPTER 70

Nico

Everyone left Jackson's office after Lucian and Mr. Silver told us to meet back there after the burial of the shifters. I made my way back to my room and showered. I felt a minute amount better after showering. I sprawled across the bed. I had an hour before the burial started, but I didn't feel like meeting the others in the mess hall. I couldn't stomach the thought of food.

Lying here looking up at the ceiling, my thoughts got away from me. I wasn't angry with Ryan for doing what she did; given the same choice, I would have done the same thing. I was just pissed that she cut me out again. I would have helped her fight against the elders. I was, however, pissed as fuck that Victor and Lachlan were wanting her dead. What the hell was their end game?

What would they gain by killing her?

I hate that I can't feel her through our bond. I just wanted to know she was okay. Was she safe? For fuck's sake, I am 104 years old, and I have an eighteen-year-old woman reducing me to a teenage boy whose emotions are out of control. I smiled to myself. I have lived for over a century and not once in my life have I ever felt like this. Two years ago, when I decided to infiltrate her dreams, I did it for my own gain, and then that quickly changed. She changed me.

She didn't have a single bad bone in her body. She was self-less and kind. She would never hurt anyone intentionally. I know today had taken a huge toll on her. If I was exhausted from no sleep she must be wiped out.

All I wanted was to lay here and hold my wife in my arms and tell her we could be free and happy now. Most of all, I just wanted her back with me.

I met Jax and the others on the east side of his property; it was a half hour walk from the compound to where they hold their burials. Shifters didn't return their dead to the earth like the witches and fae; they burned their dead on a pyre.

There were so many dead shifters lined up on row after row of pyres. Cyrus was still tallying the lives of the fae lost in the battle, so far we were up two hundred and something. Jackson had lost nearly the same amount. Shifters from other packs had come to aid us in this battle and lost their lives.

I know from the message Jax had received from Kai that the vamps had lost nearly six hundred, and the witches had called covens in from over the world to help fight as well, under their queen's command.

Alex and Chase were dealing with the fallout of that. We didn't have a number yet for how many of the witches had lost their lives, but we did know that many of their kind had died as well.

I stood next to Dom, near the podium that Jax stood on, with Dom's father at his side. I looked around for the others, but couldn't see them.

"Where is Mya, Lucian, Aurora, and my sister?" Dom didn't turn to look at me. His silver hair was blowing in the wind and his eyes seemed so bright, but I could see anger lingering in the depths of them.

"Lucian is meeting the *backup* and Aurora refused to come. She wanted to stay with her brother. Mya was summoned back to the Knox coven, and Chase and Alex are trying to find a way to make her part of the coven again."

"What about Sophia?" Dom tensed at the mention of my sister, but he wouldn't meet my gaze.

"She left. I don't know where she went." His clipped tone pissed me off; he was being vague on purpose.

"I am asking you as my best friend, Dominic. What the hell is going on between you and my sister?"

This time, Dom turned to meet my gaze.

"It's my fault your sister was taken seventeen years ago. Randall never came to the fae realm. Sophia fled Farrarie to get away from me." I reeled back in shock.

"Why was she running from you, Dom?" I had a feeling I knew what his answer would be, but I needed to hear it from him. Dom's gaze held so much regret. I swallowed loudly. His answer was going to change things, I just knew it.

"Because I fell in love with her. Tyler and Stevie aren't the first to mate from separate races. Sophia and I are...your sister is my mate, Nico, and I...rejected her."

I knew that voice. I raced through the forest and emerged from the spot I entered through. On the steps to the cabin sat Sophia Stone, my sister in law. I made my way over to her.

She looked beautiful as always, long black hair tumbling around her shoulders, vibrant violet eyes focused on me. She looked so sophisticated, even wearing plain dark jeans and a long-sleeved shirt.

"You look shocked to see me." Laughter was clear in her voice.

"Well, yeah, Lucian and Mr. Silver told me no one would be able to find me here." Sophia laughed and I tilted my head to the side, confused.

"Oh, Ryan, you forget I can see peoples love lives. I saw you at the stream earlier in a vision, and I could see you in pain. Your heart is calling for my brother. Plus I know this cabin and that stream well, very well."

She sighed and then turned to look ahead. I leaned on the railing at the bottom of the stairs, looking at her, *really* looking. I could see so much sadness in her eyes, and I didn't like seeing that look on her face, Sophia was one of the strongest women I knew, so whatever has her looking this way must be bad. I climbed the stairs and plonked down beside her. She rested her head on my shoulder.

"You know, when I first learned about you and what you were to my brother, I was jealous." I looked down at her in shock, her gaze still facing forward. Darkness was in full effect now, the only lighting the porch light and the moon. It was a beautiful night.

"Sophia, why the hell would you be jealous of me?" She chuckled.

"Because you have your *hugacko*."

"You will find yours one day, Soph, I just know it." She shook her head.

"I already found mine." I pulled away, shocked, and she turned to look at me, a sad smile on her face.

"Who?" I felt excitement for Sophia bubble up inside of me.

"It doesn't matter. I'm here to talk about you, not me. My brother is hurt by your actions today. We all are."

I hung my head in shame. "I did what I had to do." I was proud that my voice didn't waver.

"We know why you did it; Lucian told us. We just don't understand why you did it alone. I know we have only known each other for a short time, Ryan, but I consider you a friend—a sister, even. I didn't have an easy upbringing. Mother didn't want me, and father couldn't stand the sight of me. Nico raised me. We are closer than most siblings. He would do anything for those he loved. He will stand by your side, Ryan, and weather any storm for you, because he loves you."

I could hear the truth in her words. Sophia loved her brother and thought the world of him. Here I was constantly hurting the man she loved so dearly. I didn't deserve her as a friend. I wrapped my arm around her shoulders and pulled her to me, and she came willingly. We sat there in silence for a long while, both of us lost in our thoughts. Then a thought struck me, and I looked around the front of the cabin. I didn't see a car anywhere.

"Soph, how did you get here?" She pulled away and grinned at me, a devilish glint in her eye.

"Promise not to tell anyone?" I nodded my head, eager to hear her answer. "My *hugacko* is a fae, so I can siphon some of his power. Meaning, I can portal myself anywhere." My mouth dropped open in shock. How fucking cool was that? Did that mean Nico and I could do the same? Sophia pushed my mouth shut with her hand, and we both giggled.

"The way I see it, you can stay here in isolation and wallow in your own self-pity. Or you can come with me back to the compound and help us find a way out of this situation you have landed yourself in. We will not allow the council to end your life, Ryan, with or without your consent."

What the fuck?

"What do you mean *end my life?*"

Sophia looked taken back. "You don't know?" I shook my head. "Lachlan and Victor are asking Ian and David to join them for a majority vote to have your life ended. David and Ian refused, so the elders have to include the other members for a vote."

Holy shit, what the fuck have I done? When I spoke with the elders, Lachlan and Victor didn't mention any such thing to me, those lying bastards. I stood and looked down at Sophia, who had a triumphant smile on her face. She knew she had me hook, line, and sinker with that bomb she just dropped.

"Let me get my things. I have a group of people to suck up to, a husband to beg for forgiveness, and a couple of asshole elders to deal with." Sophia stood and placed a hand on my shoulder, smiling at me.

"You are going to shake my brother's world upside down; I

can't wait to watch you drive him mad." We both broke into fits of laughter, and I quickly shut off the porch light and locked the cabin door. I made my way over to Sophia, who had a portal open and waiting for me. She clasped my hand and we stepped through the portal.

The burning of the shifters passed in a blur, I couldn't focus on anything aside from what Dom said. As soon as the service was over, I bee-lined it back to Jackson's office, I needed something to distract me, or I would go postal on Dominic.

I barged through the office door and came to a screeching halt. Lucian was there, with an older couple next to him. The man and woman looked so familiar, but I couldn't quite place them. I moved into the room and closed the door behind me, Lucian stood and the couple followed suit.

"Nico, I would like to introduce the backup, Ryan's grand-parents, Marcus and Bethany Knox. Gramps, Grams, meet Nico, king of the fae and husband to your granddaughter." I swallowed hard. I just fought a fucking battle for the life of my people and my home, and yet I was more nervous facing my wife's grandparents—well, her grandfather, to be more precise.

I walked over and extended my hand toward Marcus. His blue eyes held a challenge in them. We were nearly eye to eye, me just an inch or two taller. Marcus lowered his eyes to stare at my outstretched hand, and he had no intent of shaking my hand, I could see it in his body language. We worked together

once, and now that I was married to his granddaughter, he couldn't stand me. Great.

"Oh for heaven's sake, Marcus!" Ryan's grandmother placed her small delicate hand in mine and shook it; I met her kind, deep green eyes and smiled down at her. She seemed like a sweet woman.

"Please excuse my husband's manners, he doesn't get out much." I smiled wide at her attempt to lighten the mood.

She released my hand and reclaimed her seat, pulling her husband down with her. I sat across from them on the other couch.

I felt Marcus's gaze burning holes into me. The silence stretched in the room; it was awkward as fuck and the tension was worse, so much alpha male blood in one room wasn't good. I refused to back down to Ryan's grandfather. I was a king, and I would not show weakness in front of someone I once considered a friend. Well, in his defense he met me as someone else. I used a glamour when I met him many years ago. I helped Marcus gather all the intel he needed to make the first treaty.

"You tricked me!" There it was, the real reason he was glaring at me. He was still angry that I never revealed my true identity to him.

Before I could answer, the office door banged open and Jax and Dom walked in. Each of them looked from my couch to the other, a question clear in their gazes. With a sigh, I answered their unasked question.

"Meet Ryan's grandparents, Bethany and Marcus Knox, Founder and first king of the Knox coven." Marcus sneered at my introduction. Okay, so sucking up wasn't going to work. Dom and Jax bid them hello, and the old bastard smirked at me as he shook each of their hands. Jax and Dom took a seat next to me.

"So, what did we miss?"

No one answered Dom, so in true Dom fashion, his filterless mouth got away from him. "May I just say how beautifully stunning you are, Bethany. I know where Ry gets her hotness from now." Bethany turned a shade of red, and Marcus glared at Dom, his upper lip pulled back in a sneer. Lucian used his hand to cover his smile.

"Boy, I have heard stories about your smart mouth. If you wish to keep your tongue, you will not speak to my wife like that!"

The office door opened once again and in walked Dom's father, wearing a grin from ear to ear. He looked straight toward Marcus and said, "I have been telling him that for years to no avail, old friend." Marcus smiled his first smile since being in here.

Mr. Silver and Marcus embraced each other; clearly it had been a long time since they had seen each other. After they pulled apart, Mr. Silver embraced Bethany. He pulled back and looked down at the older woman, a soft smile on his face.

"You know the offer still stands; you could still run away with me."

"Piss off, Ian, and stop hitting on my wife."

"Pity, she could have done so much better than you." The three of them chuckled at their little banter. Dom glared at his father.

"Clearly your son takes after you, Ian. I think I may have to fill him in on some of our good old days." Mr. Silver paled. Oh, so he had some skeletons in his closet.

"My son doesn't need to hear about our glory days. Surely he has more important things to do than listen to stories about his father." "Actually, no, I don't. I have a lot of free time these days. Whenever you're ready to spill the beans, Grandpa, let me know." Jax and I both groaned. Dom was such a dick. Marcus pinned deadly eyes on Dom.

"It's Mr. Knox to you, boy, and when you learn some respect maybe then I will share with you." Dom didn't miss a beat, he just grinned at Marcus and winked. He fucking *winked* at my grandfather-in-law. I didn't know what to call him, so I was sticking with that.

Mr. Silver claimed the single seat, and I looked around the room, waiting for someone to speak. I didn't have to wait long.

"Marcus, Bethany, we need your help. Your granddaughter's life is on the line. I called you here because I found out a couple days ago what Lachlan and Victor were planning." So Mr. Silver was the one to call her grandparents here. Good to know.

"Why do they want to kill, Smurf, sir?" Lucian asked.

"Because she is stronger than all the elders, dear. Those two power-hungry knuckleheads don't want a being stronger than the elders around." Bethany's voice held a harsh edge; clearly she didn't like the elders very much.

"So you're saying Ryan is stronger than the elder council in their entirety?" Dom was awed by this fact.

"Yes, son. If what you saw today wasn't clarification enough, then I don't know what is. That girl stabilized a whole world in less than five minutes. She accomplished what many before her could not. Ryan Knox is not someone to be underestimated."

"It's Stone, not Knox," I blurted out. I didn't mean to, but it just flowed out of my mouth like verbal diarrhea. Marcus lent forward and rested his forearms on his thighs, glaring at me.

"You should have been named Loki with all the tricks you play, boy. My granddaughter is a Knox and will remain one." Hell no, he didn't get to try and push me around. I helped the old fool and thought highly of him, and now he wanted a pissing contest over my wife? Fuck that.

"You can hate me all you want, Marcus. I helped you at the risk to my own people. We all got what we wanted from that treaty. As for *my* wife, she wants her name hyphenated: Knox-Stone. She is mine, Marcus. Think of me what you will, but don't ever doubt my love for her. I risked the lives of my people and my world because I fell in love with Ryan. Do not question me about her again!" Marcus leaned back and stretched his arm across the back of the couch. He smiled wider than the Cheshire Cat.

"That's exactly what I wanted to hear, boy. I was never truly angry with you for deceiving me—annoyed, yes. I let that all go the moment my granddaughter told me what you meant to her. I had to test you, to see if you were worthy for her, and it seems you passed."

I exhaled a breath I didn't know I was holding. This whole fucking thing was a test. I see now where Ryan got her cunningness from. And also her temper.

Sophia and I arrived at the back of Jackson's compound. I looked down at my watch to see it was ten at night. I was wiped out. I needed to see the others and say sorry, then go to bed. I would deal with the rest of this shit tomorrow.

We made our way across the yard and entered through one of the many side doors. Sophia led the way, thank God, because I had no idea where I was going. I knew how to get to Jackson's office and the mess hall from my room, but that was about it. A few minutes later we stopped outside a familiar door. Sophia didn't wait or knock, just opened the door and strolled in, and I followed my sister-in-law's lead.

Seven pairs of eyes turned toward us, each and every one of them wore looks of shock.

"Surprise!" Sophia announced to the room. I moved toward my grandparents immediately, shocked but thrilled to see them here. They both embraced me in a three-way hug. Grams checked me over to make sure I had no injuries and was really fine. Gramps clamped a hand on my shoulder and told me to fill him in on what happened later. I nodded.

I embraced Luce quickly and then waved hello to Mr.

Silver. He didn't seem annoyed to see me here, which was good. I took a deep breath, steeled my spine and then turned to face the three alpha males sitting on the couch.

None of them would meet my gaze. Sophia gave me a nudge. I walked toward them and plopped down on the coffee table in front of them, and still the three of them avoided looking at me.

I turned back to Sophia, and she gave me an encouraging nod. I needed to suck up my pride and ask for their forgiveness and help. I looked from Jax to Dom and then settled my gaze on Nico, who found looking at the side of Dom's head more interesting.

"I know you're all mad at me." Jax scoffed, but I pushed on. "I did what I did to help. Well, I thought I was helping. I didn't mean to block you guys out. I thought you would have tried to stop me. I'm sorry." Jax glared at me, and the heat of his gaze made me jerk back.

"You *chose* to make this decision without us! We would have helped you, Ryan. You didn't just hurt Nico, you hurt all of us. We all fought together just hours ago and risked our lives together and then you go on a solo mission of your own? We wouldn't have stopped you; we would have helped you find a better way."

I blinked my tears away. I wouldn't cry, I needed to be strong right now. I turned toward Dom, who reluctantly faced me. Gone was my carefree friend. Instead his look had changed to one of sadness and hurt.

"*We* would have stood by you. *We* would have helped you, *we* would have protected you. Instead *you* chose to go it alone, and now we're all left picking up the pieces on how to save your life." Dom didn't give me a chance to reply; he just turned to gaze back out the window. I turned to the last of the three men, the one I dreaded facing the most. When he met my stare, my resolve cracked. No emotion was displayed on his face, his eyes gave nothing away.

"You chose to leave me—to leave us—again. What did you think would happen? You would come back and we would be happy? Of course we're happy to see you, but we're all pissed as hell at you as well. Now if you would excuse me, I would like to turn in for the night." Nico stood from his seat and left the room without so much as a look back, and Jax and Dom followed suit.

I sat there in shock. That certainly didn't go how I thought it would.

I couldn't leave things like this with the guys. I went to follow them but was stopped by my grandmother's words.

"Can you take us to see Stevie please, dear?"

I agreed to take them to my sister. It was Lucian, Grams, Gramps and me. I paused outside the door to the room we laid my sister in with Tyler.

I didn't know if Gramps and Grams knew about Tyler. I took a deep breath then pushed the door open. I paused as I entered the room. They weren't on the bed anymore. There were two caskets, both a dark wooden color, and neither had lids on.

I had to be strong for my grandparents. I couldn't break down, not right now.

"Why are there two caskets?" I looked at my Grams. Her eyes were welling with tears. They didn't know Stevie, but she was still their blood. I opened and closed my mouth several times but no words would come out.

"Tyler is laid in the other casket." Lucian saved me from having to say that out loud. Gramps didn't hesitate; he made his way over to one of the caskets with the rest of us trailing behind him.

I peered over the edge to see it was Ty in this one. He had been cleaned and changed into his signature shirt and jeans with his Doc Martins. He looked so peaceful that I could almost be fooled into thinking he was sleeping.

"You foolish boy." I flinched at the anger in Gramps' tone. How could he be so callous?

"Gramps—"

The old man cut me off before I could scold him. "How did he die?" I didn't hesitate to answer; Tyler was my hero.

"He died saving my life. He knew he wouldn't be able to live if his mate died." Gramps tore his gaze from mine to peer down at Tyler once more.

"I always knew you had it in you, son. You are a savior and a hero, and you will be laid to rest on Knox Mountain with your mate. I will make sure of it."

Tears welled in my eyes at hearing Gramp's declaration. I knew if anyone could get Stevie and Ty buried up on the mountain, it was Gramps. Gramps clasped Grams's hand in his and led her over to the other casket, where my sister laid. Lucian gripped my hand and towed me toward where my grandparents now stood, peering down at my sister's body.

Anxiety tore through me the closer I got to the casket.

I was the reason she was laying in there.

I took several deep breaths before looking at my sister. Tears fell immediately, because my sister looked so calm and peaceful. She had been cleaned and re-dressed in her favorite style, jeans and a T-shirt.

"I hope you find peace and happiness now, blood of my blood." I looked to Grams and saw tears rolling down her cheeks. "I didn't have the pleasure of seeing you grow. I vow to you now, Stevie Lee Knox, that I will not make that mistake with your sister. You have my word, I will protect her and care for her until my dying breath."

I choked back a sob at Grams's declaration. She leaned forward and placed a kiss on my sister's forehead. I looked out the corner of my eye to see Gramps blinking rapidly; he was trying not to cry.

"What happened shouldn't have happened. Your death will not be in vain, granddaughter of mine. Many will tell stories of your sacrifice, and you will live in the hearts of your family and in the memories of those you love." Gramps leaned forward and placed a kiss to my sister's forehead. "Until we meet again, little warrior," Gramps whispered as he pulled back.

I couldn't speak. There just weren't any words to follow that.

No sooner did I enter my room and plonk down on the bed did my door open again. Jax and Dom waltzed in and joined me on the bed. Each of us sat there quietly in our own thoughts until the door opened again. This time my sister walked in with a smug look on her face. I looked from her to Dom, wondering how I had missed the signs. Was I so self-absorbed that I didn't know my best friend was in love with my baby sister?

"Okay, so you're all angry and pissed off. I get it, but she did what she thought was right to save you three. She didn't want you to give up any more than what you had already given. She was trying to protect you. If you ask me, Kai got the raw end of the deal, not you." I glared at Sophia. She could be a real pain in the ass at times.

"Who died and made you queen?" Dom snapped.

"Nico's sister-in-law," she deadpanned. I flinched at the reminder of Stevie's death.

"Cut her some slack, brother, she loves you—"

"She has a funny way of showing it!" I snapped at my sister, who just grinned at me.

"You are over a century old and here you are pouting with

your cheer squad in your room. How pathetic. You are a fucking king, Nicholas, start acting like one! Jackson, you are the alpha of all alphas, pull your head out of your ass and act like it. Dominic...well, you really don't have a job, so stop fucking sulking like a child." Dom glared daggers at my sister.

"What would you have us do then, sister?" Her grin turned conniving, I knew that look. Whenever my sister had that look in her eyes, heads always rolled.

"Listen up and listen good, boys."

I awoke the next morning feeling more refreshed and more like myself. I didn't go to Ryan or try to find her last night, and she didn't come to me either. That's a good thing; we needed her away from us if we were to pull off this plan of my sister's.

I went about my morning ritual of showering and changing before setting out to find the others at the mess hall. No sooner had the doors opened then my ears begun to ring from all the noise. I loaded a plate full of food and made my way over to the others. I sat next to Dom. Our group had shrunk. It was only Dom, Jax, Aurora, Sophia, and me now.

We all ate in silence until another body joined us at the table. I peered up from my plate to see it was Lucian. I bit my tongue so I didn't demand he tell me how she was or what she was doing. He must have seen the unasked questions in my stare.

"She slept on the floor next to her sister. She isn't doing too great. Her Gramps has placed her on house arrest while he and Grams go to the Knox coven to try and help David and her cousins come up with a plan."

"I feel for Ryan, this must be so hard for her." We all turned our gaze to Aurora. She wouldn't meet any of our stares, and that's when it hit me.

"You knew what she was going to do, didn't you?" She still wouldn't meet my gaze, even when she answered.

"Yes, yes I did. It had to play out like this in order for a different ending."

"What the hell does that mean?" Jax demanded. She kept her eyes down, focusing on her untouched plate.

"If you had intervened, she would have died. Her doing it the way I told her to is what is going to save her life." We all sat there, mouths agape, while Aurora stood and left the room. I shook myself out of my stupor to face Lucian.

"Did you know about that?" I queried.

"No, I guess you're not the only ones Smurf left in the dark." Lucian sounded hurt that Ryan had left him out of the plan.

"She's doing what she thinks is right." Four heads turned to Sophia, but she didn't cower under the pressure of our gazes.

"You knew, too, didn't you, little dove?"

Sophia held her head high, and looked Dom directly in the eyes as she answered.

"Yep, sure did."

CHAPTER 75

Ryan

Three days had passed, and I had been holed up in my room for most of that time. The only time I left my room was to visit my sister and Ty. I didn't eat in the mess hall; Gramps said it was too risky in case the elders sent someone to try and take me out. I had two guards that followed me wherever I went. I had two more guards stationed outside my door. Having them here made Gramps feel better, so I just put up with their presence.

I'm sprawled out on my bed, bored out of my mind. I can feel myself going down the rabbit hole of grief and shame. Before I can get lost further in my own mind, a knock sounds at the door.

"Yeah?" I call out.

"You have a visitor," one of my guards shouts back. I sit up and stare at the closed door.

"Who is it?"

"D!" I smile. I know that voice.

"D who?" I call back.

"Deez nuts in your mouth!" I burst out laughing then stop when I hear a hard thump.

"What the fuck was that for?"

CHAPTER 77

Ryan

Nico and I made love for hours. My muscles were aching and tired, but in the best way. We finally fell asleep in the early hours of the morning. I thought I would fall into a dreamless slumber since I haven't been having any dreams for months now.

That was about to change.

I woke on the same beach I had seen my dad on days ago. I spun around looking for him; he said I wouldn't see him again. I turned back toward the ocean, confused. Why was I here?

I saw something...no, it wasn't something, it was someone coming out of the ocean. I squinted against the sunlight to see who it could be, then I cried out and then took off running to the water's edge. I slammed into her, wrapping my arms around her neck, and she wrapped her arms around my waist. I clung to her like my life depended on it. Sobs wracked my body. She was here! I thought I would never see her again.

"Shhh, little sister. It's okay." I pulled back to look at Stevie.

"That's my fucking wife you're saying that shit to!" I jump from the bed and run to the door, swinging it open in one fluid motion. Standing on the other side of the door is none other than Dom, Jax, and Nico. Nico looks delicious in his white shirt and skin tight jeans. I run my gaze over him. Fuck, he is gorgeous. A throat clearing snaps me out of checking out my husband.

"We're standing right here! Can you make those fuck-me eyes when were not around, please?" I grin up at Dominic; he smiles and shoots me a wink.

"Can we come in?" I look to Jax and nod my head, stepping aside so they can enter.

The three giant alpha males step inside my room, and I close the door behind them and lean against it. I feel nervous and unsure now that they're here with me. They all stand at the end of my bed, facing me. I can feel each of them looking me over, for what I'm not sure. I chance a glance up at Nico to find his gaze locked on me. I sucked in sharply.

He has desire and anger swimming in the depths of those beautiful violet eyes. I pull my gaze from him to stare at Jax, and his eyes soften toward me. Those beautiful chocolate brown eyes can lull you like no other. I look to Dom and gasp—he cut his hair! It's short on the sides and longer on the top. His beautiful silver locks are gone. His eyes still hold a hint of mischief in them, though.

I look to Nico and see a smirk on his face. He was waiting for his turn to be checked out.

His jet-black hair is slicked back, not a hair out of place. His eyes are burning into me with intensity.

"Let's get this over with so they can fuck. The sexual tension in here is making me horny." Both Jax and Nico turn to glare at Dom. He shrugged his shoulders and winked at me. I smile at his teasing. I have missed his humor. I've missed Jackson's smarts, and Kai's brooding, and I've just missed Nico, plain and simple.

"I'm sorry," I blurt.

"Sorry for what, love? Come on, be more specific now. We're grown ass men and were reduced to putty in the hands of an eighteen-year- old woman. Stroke our egos a bit, aye?" Jax and Nico's features soften at their friend's words. I straighten up and do as Dom said.

"I am sorry for cutting you all out. I am sorry I went behind Kai's back and did what I did. I'm sorry I didn't bring you guys in on the plan. I didn't want you all to give more up than you already had. If I could go back and change it, I would. Please forgive me." Each of them looked at each other, their expressions unreadable.

"Did you know the council had planned to kill you?"

"No, Jax, I didn't, I swear."

"What did they tell you?" I looked Jackson in the eye and answered.

"They told me that if I came back and turned myself in, you would remain alpha, Nico and Kai would still be king of their races, and Dom would be free. They also promised that I could hand over leadership of the coven to anyone of my choosing. They told me I would stand trial, and if found guilty, I would be sentenced to jail." I let out a whoosh of air, it felt good to get this all out in the open.

"You would risk your freedom—your life—just so we could go on living as we always have?" Dom sounded so surprised that I would do this for them.

"Of course I would. If I didn't Sophia would lose her brother. Aurora would lose Jax. Kai would be a slave, and you would be forced to become alpha of your father's pack."

"And what would you lose?" His voice sent shivers down

my spine. I pulled my eyes from Dom to stare at the man of my dreams. I wouldn't lie to him, he deserved the truth.

"You." My voice didn't waver, and I mentally high fived myself.

"Thank you, Ry. We'll leave you two alone now, Dom?" Jax looked to Dom expectantly.

"Oh come on, we're just getting to the best part!" Dom whined.

"For fuck's sake, Dominic, grow up. Let them have some privacy!" Jax growled.

"They don't mind if I stay and watch, do you Ry?" Dom was going to get slapped again, I could feel it.

"So help me God, Dominic, I haven't beaten the shit out of you about my sister, but I will gladly do it now if you don't fuck off!" Nico ground out.

Jax and Dom made their way toward me, Dom pouting like a child. I stepped aside and opened the door for them, and Jax gave me a hug and left. Dom stopped and looked down at me with a mischievous smile on his face.

"You know, there are other ways you could thank me, love?" I burst out laughing again while Nico yelled.

"GET THE FUCK OUT, DOMINIC!" Dom's laughter followed him as he left the room, closing the door behind himself.

Wow, the tension in the room just went up by several thousand notches.

Nico and I stood there staring at each other, neither of us willing to back down.

I didn't want to fight with him. I didn't like this tension between us. I sucked up my pride and made my way over to him. I clasped his hand in mine and led him over to the single chair by the window. He didn't protest when I pushed him down into the seat.

As he looked up at me, I could see the smile in his eyes. I didn't want any space between us, so I sat across my man's lap. He wrapped his arms around me and pulled me to his chest.

I sighed in contentment. He ran one of his hands through my long hair, and I moaned at the feeling of him massaging my scalp.

CHAPTER 76

Nico

This was proving harder than I thought. Holding her to me and rubbing her hair had turned into me massaging her scalp. Her moaning was driving me *and* my cock crazy. She's so relaxed in my hold, and her eyes are closed, her full kissable lips on display. I couldn't hold it any longer. I leaned down and claimed her mouth. She opened for me instantly.

God she tasted like honey and home. I missed her. I missed *this*. I lifted her so she was straddling my lap and cupped her face between my hands, looking directly into those beautiful green eyes with that peculiar yellow ring.

"No more hiding from me, no more blocking me out. I can't and won't go through this shit again. You're my wife, my partner. We're a team." Tears shone in her eyes, and she brushed my hands away to lean forward and place a quick peck on my lips before meeting my gaze again.

"I swear on my life, Nico, no more. I promise. These past few days without you have been hell. I need you." That's all I needed to hear. I wrapped my arms around her waist and stood. I carried her to the bed and laid her down, crawling slowly up her body, taking my time.

"Oh, I have missed you, little one," I said as I popped the button on her jeans. A second later I pulled the jeans from her body and helped her out of her shirt. She laid there beneath me in a blue lace bra and panty set. Fuck me, my cock sprang to life. I kissed my way up from her bellybutton to her mouth, then I trailed kisses back down to her plump, luscious tits. I pulled the cups of her bra down to expose them, and her nipples pebbled as I blew across them. I sucked one of them into my mouth and squeezed the other. She was a writhing mess beneath me, just how I like her.

"Nico, please." I released her nipple with a pop and gazed up at her. Her cheeks were flushed and her eyes glassy.

"Please what, love?"

"I want you."

"Want me where?"

She growled. "Don't fucking make me beg, please."

"Please what?" She leaned on her elbows, glaring down at me as I toyed with her nipples.

"Please fuck me. Dick inside me. Is that clear enough?" she snapped.

"You didn't need to shout, babe." I leaned back and smiled down at her.

I made quick work of shucking off my pants and shoes. I didn't bother to peel her panties off; I tore them from her body instead.

"Are you wet for me, love?"

"Fuck yes!" was all the answer I needed before I slammed my hard, aching cock into her pussy.

We both cried out. Her pussy was fucking heaven. God, I missed being inside her. I pumped in and out of her while I used my thumb to rub her clit. Not two minutes later, I felt her pussy start to tighten around my cock.

"Ohhhhh, God," she cried out.

"Not God, love, just me." I wasn't going to give that bastard the credit for making her feel good.

"Nico, I'm gonna come."

"Come all over my fucking cock, baby, I want to feel you on my dick." She screamed my name as she climaxed, and a few pumps later, I joined her in ecstasy, calling her name as I came undone. I was a little embarrassed that I didn't last longer, but we had the rest of the night to make up for that. I flopped down beside her and pulled her into my arms, and we lay there both panting for the longest time.

I felt content to just lay here and hold her.

"I could stay like this forever." I chuckled at her lustful tone. This woman was a little vixen under the covers.

"We have the rest of our lives together, love. I plan on fucking you every night before we sleep and every morning when we wake." She giggled, a sound that had my heart soaring.

"I can't wait." I turned my head and captured her lips. My cock started twitching; the little devil was ready for round two.

Her wet hair clung to her face, and she was in a polka dot bikini. She smiled at me, and she looked...happy.

"Are you okay?" I choked out between sobs.

"Yeah, Ry, I am."

"I'm so sorry, Stevie, I—"

"Shhh, none of that now. You did what you had to do, Ry. I don't blame you, I'm thankful for what you did." Huh?

"Why are you thankful?"

She sighed and stepped back, gesturing behind me. I spun around to see two beach chairs with an umbrella in the middle of them.

They weren't there a moment ago. I followed Stevie to the chairs and sat down on one while she sat on the other. She met my gaze and smiled a sad smile.

"I grew up with an evil inside me. I fought it as long as I could. The older I got, the harder it was to ignore. Losing Dad and thinking that the fae were behind his death was when I gave up the fight. I need you to know the things I said and did, I never meant. I was a passenger in my own body; I could see and hear everything, but I had no control. All I felt was the need for death and power."

"Stevie I know you would never hurt anyone intentionally. I just wish I could have done more for you."

She reached over and grabbed my hand.

"You gave me the greatest gift of all, Ryan. You set me free. I am able to be me now without fighting something inside of me every day." Tears continued to trail down my face. My heart ached at the daily battle my sister faced her whole life.

"I-Is Ty, with you?" Stevie's smile reached her eyes, and a blush coated my sisters cheeks. Oh my God, Stevie is blushing!

"Yeah, he's here with me. He is fucking aaaamazing, Ry, and don't get me started on what he's like in bed. His di—"

"Stooooopppppp. Please, Stevie, I look at Ty like a brother. I

don't want to be picturing his manhood, thank you very much!"
Stevie broke out into a fit of laughter. Hearing her laugh and
seeing how happy she is gave me a form of relief. I was still heart-
broken I wouldn't see her every day, but seeing her now and how
she is, lessened the burden of what I had done to my own sister.

"I needed that laugh."

"I didn't think I would see you." Her expression sobered and
turned serious in an instant. I tensed.

"You weren't supposed to see me for years, but your grief
called me to you, Ry. I'm here because you need me."

"What? I didn't call you."

"Your subconscious did, sister. I also needed to come to you
and tell you some hard truths."

"What happened, Stevie?"

"Randall Cane isn't dead. Lachlan and Victor are planning
to kill you and take the four guys out so they can lead with
Randall. Randall promised them that he would make them head
of each of their chosen races if they helped him take you out.

"The reason Randall's body was never recovered the day of
the battle was because Victor sent him through a portal to some-
where. Victor and Lachlan must be dealt with, Ry. I know some
things that will help you." My sister and I sat there for hours
talking over what she had learned about the elders and how
fucked up they really were. The sun had started to set when
Stevie stood and pulled me to my feet. We stood there holding
each other's hands, tears shining in both our eyes.

"I don't know how I'm supposed to say goodbye to you,
Stevie."

"Then don't say goodbye, say see you later." She tried to smile
but failed.

"I'm gonna miss you so fucking much!" We wrapped our
arms around each other and held on.

"I'll never truly leave you, Ry, I'll always be here watching

over you. Go be great, sister, and kick some ass. Show those old fuckers what Knox women are really made of. Oh, and tell that husband of yours I'll be checking in to make sure he treats you right." I laughed at her attempt to scare Nico.

"I love you, Stevie," I sobbed.

"And I you, Ry, now go. I can hear that brooding king calling for you."

CHAPTER 78

I woke to Nico looming over me and shaking me awake. I blinked up at him and saw worry lines across his forehead.

"What the hell happened, Ryan?" I pushed away from Nico and sat up, clutching the sheet to my chest.

"I saw it all last night love," he replied at my need to shield my body. I poked my tongue out in response.

"What happened, love? You were screaming and crying. I couldn't break into your dream." I smiled. My sister told me she blocked him out.

"I was with Stevie." Nico cocked his head to the side, confused. I quickly filled him in on what had happened and everything that Stevie had told me.

"We need to find the others and tell them." Nico jumped off the bed and started picking up his clothes off the floor. He chucked my clothes at me, and I growled.

"I am showering before we meet with the guys; I am not going near them without washing *you* off." Nico spun around and grinned at me, still naked as the day he was born.

"Fine, you shower, and I'll call Kai and your cousins. I'll send Dom to collect them, it will be faster." I agreed and kissed

Nico goodbye before he left. I headed for the shower to prepare myself for Operation Take Down the Lying Asshole Elders.

Nico returned to collect me from my room and we made our way to the bat cave. I chuckled at my new name for Jackson's office. Nico peered down at me like I was losing the plot, and I shrugged my shoulders.

I didn't knock or wait for Nico I just opened Jax's office door and walked right on in like I owned the place. Two seconds inside the bat cave and I was plucked off the ground and bear-hugged by none other than my cousin Chase. After he was done he passed me over to Alex, who didn't squish the life out of me when he hugged me.

"Don't you ever pull another stunt like that again!" Being scolded by Alex was like being told off by your parents.

"Yes, Dad." I tartly replied and moved away from him to say hi to Mya. I looked around to see Kai standing by the window. I didn't even think or hesitate; I made my way over to him. He opened his arms as soon as he saw me approaching. I ran to him, clinging onto his shirt. I missed this. I missed him.

"You really didn't have to come, you know," I mumbled into Kai's chest.

"When Nico told me it was urgent and you needed my help I dropped everything. I told you I would always look out for you. Plus, my skill set will come in handy today." Oh my gosh, how could I have forgotten? Kai had the power to control people's moods and emotions. He really was the perfect person to have with us today.

"You know, Tink, I'm proud of ya. Not once have you growled or thrown a tantrum about *your* wife being in another man's arms." I groaned, Chase really was an ass to Nico.

I pulled out of Kai's embrace to see him smiling down at me. He was enjoying Chase teasing Nico.

"Awwww, my baby is all grown up. I feel like a proud father." Chase cracked up laughing at Dom, and Nico glared at both of them. I made my way over to my husband and huddled into his side. He wrapped his arm around my shoulders, pulling me in closer.

"And I feel like a proud brother, knowing you have finally come out of the closet, Dom. You and Chase will make an amazing pair." Dom jumped away from Chase like he had shocked him, and everyone broke out into fits of laughter. Dom glared at each and every one of us.

"I'm enjoying seeing Dom squirm just as much as the rest of you, but I have to ask: Why are we here, brother?" Kai asked.

Nico looked down at me. "Would you like to tell them or should I?" I looked around the room and smiled. These guys weren't my friends; they were my family. Dom, Jax, Kai, Alex, Chase, Aurora, Mya, and Sophia. Wait—

"Where is Lucian?" I asked.

"He's collecting Dom's dad and your grandparents. They will join us momentarily." I nodded. I didn't want to have to repeat myself, so I turned to Aurora. She deserved to know how her brother was. She looked so lost, and she had dark circles under her eyes.

"Aurora, I need to tell you something." She lifted her broken eyes to me. I smiled, trying to ease her discomfort.

"I'll explain how I know all of this when Luce gets here, but

I need you to know Ty is happy." She looked shaken and taken back.

"H-how do you know?" she stammered out. I didn't get to answer, as the office door banged open. In walked Luce, Grams, Gramps and Mr. Silver. I guess it was showtime.

Everyone claimed a seat and listened intently as Ryan explained everything her sister had told her about the elders. To say everyone was shocked would be an understatement. Her grandparents were livid to find out the elders had ulterior motives; we needed to be smart about this.

We would only get one shot at bringing down the leader of the elders. The elders were made up of the strongest of each race; no one has gone up against them and lived to tell about it. I was beyond aggravated to learn about Victor's involvement in this. I thought Lachlan was one of the good ones, as well. Clearly I was wrong.

We were to meet with the elders in two hours; they had finally made a decision. We needed to come up with a plan and fast. If we failed, they would take us out. Dom and I weren't strong enough to take on the elders, not even with half of them being dead. We learned from Ryan's grandfather that her uncle had told him the elders were recruiting new members, and they would be with them today. David also told his father that the witches had spelled all council members so Kai's *gifts* wouldn't work on them.

I didn't like our odds; we had no other choice, though. If we had an eyewitness to the leader of the fae and vampire elders' nefarious dealings that would help, but we didn't. All we had was the word of a ghost who tried to kill us.

"I don't mean to but in, but when you saw your sister, did you see my brother?" Aurora's bottom lip was trembling, and she was on the verge of tears. Ryan straightened in her seat next to me and met the seer's gaze.

"No, I didn't see Ty. Stevie told me they were together and that they were happy. She tried to fill me in on what they had been up to, but I didn't need that mental picture." Everyone around the room let out a light chuckle.

"Stevie wanted me to pass on a message to you, though." Aurora steeled her spine, and her lip stopped trembling. Stevie was her least favorite person. "Stevie told me to tell you, look to the night sky, look two stars to the left and there you will see—"

Aurora cut Ryan off, finishing the sentence for her.

"The star that will lead us to Neverland." Aurora broke out in tears. She was smiling, though—did she have a mental breakdown?

"A-are you okay?" Ry cautiously asked. Aurora nodded her head vigorously.

"That message wasn't from your sister, it was from Ty. He used to tell me that when we were kids. It means he found his happy place." There was not a dry eye in the room. Hell, even I felt choked up.

We all left Jackson's office as one.

No one spoke as we made our way to the back of the property where the chapel once was. How cliché that the elders wanted to meet there. We knew they had asked for the leaders of each race to come; alphas from all over had flown in. Leaders of each sub coven had come. Vampire leaders from different seethes were here as well, and they were given fae blood from the elders so they could be outside for the meeting. The only faes that would be here would be Cyrus, Maverick, and Larick, as fae didn't have sub clans; we all lived as one and only had one ruler—*moi*.

The closer we got to the back door, the clammier Ryan's hand became in mine. She was nervous. I couldn't fault her for what she had done to save us. What she didn't know is that when she left earlier to go to the bathroom, we had staged a coup behind her back, in case things didn't go our way.

We stopped in front of the door that led us to the back of the property. Mr. Silver turned back to look at Ryan, and after taking a deep breath, she nodded her head. She was ready to face this shit, and we all had her back. She saved all our asses and sacrificed so much; we all owed her a debt.

She didn't expect anything from us. Hell, she tried to talk us out of coming with her to this meeting. She didn't want her grandparents to be outed, as all the elders, aside from Mr. Silver and the witch elders, thought they were dead.

Her grandfather refused to stay hidden any longer. There

was no need for them to hide now that Stevie was no longer a threat.

Mr. Silver and the others were at the front of our group. Lucian and I stood on either side of Ryan, while her grandparents walked behind us.

Hopefully the shock of seeing her grandparents would make Lachlan and Victor back down. Marcus Knox was one powerful warlock, a warlock you didn't want to get on the wrong side of. He may be old, but he was far from weak.

Dom's dad pushed the door open and walked out with his head held high, his son on his right and Kai and Jax on his left. Chase and Alex moved to walk beside Dom. Soph, Mya, and Rora remained behind the guys and in front of us. I gave Ryan's hand a reassuring squeeze as we made our way outside.

CHAPTER 80
Ryan

I gasped at the sheer number of people here—there must be over a hundred at least!

Why did so many people need to be here for this? I began to regret my decision; I never should have agreed to their terms. Gramps had told me the elder council were honorable people and upheld the supernatural law, and that they could be trusted.

I bet Gramps was regretting telling me that now. I should have trusted the others enough to go to them as soon as I arrived, and come clean about the deal I made. I thought I was saving them, but in reality all I did was piss them off and sign my own death warrant.

As we walked toward the chapel, I felt dozens of pairs of eyes on me; it made my skin crawl.

I knew some of these people had lost loved ones the night of my wedding. I didn't blame them for hating me, and I didn't think badly of them for wanting my death.

In the last seven months, my whole life has been flipped upside down. I left my home to be with my sister. I flew to a new country, met new people, got married. Got locked up and beaten, found my grandparents, fought a war, and lost my sister. My life was out of control.

I looked to Nico and whispered, "I'm so sorry for not coming to you with this. I should have brought you in on this from the start. Whatever happens today, just know I love you." His steps never faltered as he looked down at me with determination in his gaze.

"Don't do that. This is not goodbye; I will not live without you. I will fight till my dying breath if need be."

"Preach, brother!" came from Lucian, and I smiled at both of them. The closer we got to the chapel—well, the charred remains of what used to be the chapel—I noticed the shocked and confused looks on people's faces.

I followed their gazes, and that's when it clicked. They were shocked to see my grandparents alive and well.

A minute later we came to a stop. I couldn't see the elders as the guys had formed a wall in front of us.

"Ian, what is the meaning of this show of force?" one of the elders asked.

"No show of force, just leading the young lady out is all." Mr. Silver answered.

"Where is she?"

"She is here, but first I think David of the Knox coven has something to say." Mr. Silver nodded his head, and I assume that was my uncle's cue to speak.

"Yes, thank you, Ian. I, David Knox would like to hand over leadership of the witch and warlock elders to its rightful leader —" That same voice cut my uncle off. "You cannot do that!"

Chase stepped forward to address the elders.

"Actually, yes he can. If you look in the bylaws, it states that if a leader has not been removed or relinquished their role, they may return to said role at any time."

"There is no other leader, boy!" a new voice roared. I was

ninety percent sure that voice belonged to Lachlan. Gramps moved from behind us and walked to stand beside Chase. A collective gasp sounded from the elders in front of us.

"I think you should watch your tone on how you speak to my grandson, Lachlan. It is my right to lead the elders, and my son David has graciously offered to step down."

"Very well," Lachlan gritted out. "Now, step aside so the accused can be seen by the elders."

The wall of bodies in front of me reluctantly moved aside so I could step forward with Lucian and Nico either side of me. Before me stood all the elders. They had added more members. I counted each faction and saw that there were thirteen in each group. Lachlan, Victor, Gramps and Mr. Silver all stood in front of their council members. Gramps gave me a small nod; he was with me till the bitter end.

"Ryan, queen of the fae and rightful heir to the Knox coven, you stand before us today on trial for the murder of fifty-two supernaturals." Victor spoke so robotically that he sounded gleeful at speaking the number of lives lost. "The elders have met and come to a decision that—"

"I wasn't part of that meeting, so I regretfully have to say that the witches and warlocks cannot back your decision," Gramps smugly replied.

"I must agree with Marcus, I was not present either. So the shifters will not be able to back the fae or vampire's decision." Mr. Silver's facial expression gave nothing away. Victor growled at both of them.

"Your presence was requested four days ago for a formal elders meeting!" Lachlan snapped.

"Well, I couldn't be there four days ago. You see, I got a phone call from an old friend beseeching my wife and I to return to Alaska, because the elders wanted my granddaughter's life forfeited." I heard dozens of people gasp around us.

Lachlan darted his eyes around at the people gathered. He smiled sweetly at them, trying to placate them and their worries.

"A decision wasn't reached until late last night, Marcus. We took longer than we originally thought to reach a decision. Whoever you *dear friend* is, they were misinformed." Lachlan was trying to be diplomatic but was failing miserably.

"So the elders are not here to end my granddaughter's life then?" Gramps volleyed back.

"I cannot say at this moment, Marcus," Lachlan snapped.

"Why not?" Mr. Silver asked. Victor turned to glare at the leader of the shifter council.

"You know why Ian. Until we have reached that part in the trial, we cannot say."

"Oh so this is a trial, Victor? I thought it was a meeting?" Both Lachlan and Victor turned to glare at Mr. Silver.

"Enough of this, we are wasting time. *All* elders that were present at the meeting came to a decision—that you will pay with your life for the lives that you took!" I gasped. Lachlan's eyes held so much hatred toward me—why?

"Like fuck. She will not be dying for you or anyone else today. We know you have been planning this from the start," Nico yelled.

"Planning what, king?"

"Cut the shit, Victor, we know you and Lachlan planned to have my wife killed from the start of learning who and what she is. We also know that you two worked together the night of our wedding to make sure that not everyone got away from the chapel." Victor smiled at Nico.

"Do you have any proof of this? Was someone there to witness these heinous crimes you say we committed?" Nico tensed next to me. We didn't have any witnesses. I was going to sound mad, but I had to act fast.

"Yes, we do."

All eyes turned to me. Lachlan and Victor exchanged a glance between each other before schooling their features and facing me. I gulped. Everyone was going to think I'm crazy.

"And who might this witness be, my dear?" My skin crawled at his term of endearment. I pushed my shoulders back and looked directly at both men that were vying to have me killed.

"My sister." More gasps rang out around us, and Lachlan and Victor were visibly taken back.

"Your sister?" Lachlan queried, and I nodded.

"As far as I am aware, you killed her days ago, and her body lies inside the alpha's compound." I flinched at his cold and detached way of speaking about Stevie, like she was nothing more than a distant unpleasant memory.

"Y-yes." I cleared my throat and took a deep breath before continuing. "Yes, my sister is dead, but I have seen her and—" Lachlan cut me off with his boisterous laughter, and I looked to my friends to see them all glaring at the leader of the vampire council.

"So let me get this right. You have seen your sister's ghost, and she is the one who told you about this preposterous scheme?" I ground my teeth together.

"Yes, she also told me Victor was the one to portal Randall Cane out of the battle field so we couldn't kill him." That wiped the smile off both those asshole's faces. Just as I started to feel like we had the upper hand, they knocked us back down.

"Well, can Miss Knox join us now and tell us this herself?" Victor's smile was victorious and evil. They both knew I couldn't just bring Stevie out and have her defend me. They had me right where they wanted me. I had no other back up plans. I was fucked and probably going to die.

I saw her deflate, a look of defeat plastered across her face. I looked to my three brothers, and they each nodded.

It was time for us to try save my wife. If this failed we would battle our way out of here and run. My wife would not die by the hands of these lying, callous bastards. I released Ryan's hand. I felt her gaze on me but I couldn't look at her.

As I stepped forward, my brothers flanked me on either side. We stood there staring at the elders. The vampire and fae elders looked confused while Mr. Silver and Marcus looked proud.

I spotted a figure out of the corner of my eye trying to catch my attention. I squinted and saw it was Cyrus. He gestured to the person standing next to him. I was shocked, what the hell was she doing here?

"What is the meaning of this?" I pulled my gaze back to the elders and glared at the sons of bitches. Mr. Silver and Marcus moved to stand either side of the two dickbags.

"We want to make a trade," Jax bellowed loud enough for everyone around to hear. I heard a gasp behind me. I chanced a look back to see Ryan held back by Lucian and her Grams. I smiled at my wife.

"What kind of trade, Alpha?" I could hear the intrigue in Victor's voice from here. I don't know how I was fooled for so many years by these two. I thought they were trustworthy men—how wrong was I?

"For the life of Ryan Knox-Stone, I, Jackson Marshall, will step down as *the* alpha." Everyone gasped, and Lachlan looked gleeful.

"I, Melakai Cane, king of all vampires, am prepared to step down from my position, and allow the elder council to lead the vampires—*if* Ryan is freed of all charges!"

Kai sounded like a true king, brave and confident. I was beyond proud of my brother; he never wanted the title or to be a part of the vampires, but here he was falling into the role like a pro. Lachlan was grinning from ear to ear; this was what he wanted, to rule the vampires.

What I still couldn't figure out was where Randall was.

"Well, I don't have a fancy title, but, I, Dominic Silver, hereby swear that I will fulfill my destiny and claim the title of alpha of the New York pack. My terms are the same as the others: as long as Ryan goes free." Ian Silver stood taller and looked proud; his son has finally agreed to accept his fate, but why was there so much sadness in his eyes? Dom has never wanted to lead; he just wants to be free to live his life. It was my turn, and I took a step forward.

"Nico, no, please, you guys can't do this," Ryan begged. I turned and smiled at my wife.

"Isn't it obvious, love? We would give it all up for you, without having to be asked."

Love shone in her eyes, but so did shame. She was blaming herself for what we were doing, what the elders wanted from the start. I turned back and faced the four leaders of the council.

"I, Nicholas Stone, will renounce my claim to the throne and hand it over to Victor *if* my wife is set free." Victor's eyes said everything, he wanted the power and the title of *king*. I knew then we had the elders. Marcus and Mr. Silver's gaze's raked over us; they were proud of us.

They knew what we were giving up for Ryan. Jax and I were giving up our birthrights, Dom was finally falling into line, and Kai was going to be homeless.

"We will discuss this—" Lachlan cut Marcus off.

"There is no need for that, my friend. I am sure we all agree that this is a fair exchange."

"Yes, I agree, I think we can close this matter and release the girl from her crimes." Murmurs began to break out around us. The leaders that had gathered for the trial weren't happy. Either they wanted my wife's head on a platter, or they were pissed we had just handed over control of all our races to the council.

"Quiet!" Lachlan yelled, and everyone stopped talking. "Well now that the matter has been settled, we will need you four to fill out and sign over—"

"Actually, my son-in-law and his friends will not be giving anything up, and you will not be charging my daughter with anything!"

All eyes turned toward the slender woman walking toward us, her long hair billowing around her. The closer she got, the more I could see the determination in her brown eyes.

Nina Knox had an ace up her sleeve.

CHAPTER 82

Nina looked like a badass. She held her head high and walked with purpose. She even looked the part, in shit-kicker boots, black skinny jeans, and a form-fitting white shirt. She looked ready to fuck shit up. I was shocked. I have never seen her look so put together, but what the hell was she doing here?

"How dare you interrupt us!" Victor shouted, and Nina smiled back at the uptight bastard.

"Now, as the mother-in-law to the king of Farrarie and mother to the queen of the Knox coven, I believe I have a right to speak." Nina looked toward Gramps and asked, "Am I correct, Marcus, may I speak on behalf of my daughter?" Gramps looked at Nina for a long moment.

"Yes, you may speak." Lachlan and Victor turned to glare at Gramps. Nina made her way over to stand by Nico and the guys. Nico looked down at her and whispered something in her ear, but I couldn't hear their private conversation.

When Nina whispered back in Nico's ear, his body went tense, then he turned to look at me. The look on his face was relief. What the hell was Nina up to?

"Get on with it then, woman!" Victor growled.

"Don't be like that, Victor. I mean, we were friendly once, weren't we?" The leader of the fae turned a shade of crimson, anger was evident in his eyes. "You should know, Victor; all those times you thought I was too high to understand or remember things, you were wrong." Nina moved to stand directly in front of Victor. He glared down his nose at her. Nina spun around, her hair slapping Victor as she did.

She looked around the clearing to each and every one gathered. Then her gaze settled on me as she spoke.

"What my daughter said is true! The leaders of the vampire and fae council wanted her dead long before the night of her wedding. They were working under the orders of Randall Cane.

"Randall promised them they could each lead their race if they helped him set my daughter up. Victor erected a shield around the fifty-two people that died. He told them the shield would protect them. When the blast from Ryan emerged outside of the chapel, he dropped the shield, killing those that were inside it. They knew the punishment for this would be death for my daughter."

"How do you know this?" Mr. Silver asked.

"Because Victor and Lachlan raped me while I was held at Randall Cane's mansion. When they were done with me, they would shoot me up with drugs, thinking that it would make me more compliant. They would make phone calls or discuss the battle while still in the room with me, and I heard every fucking word they said!" Nina spun around so fast then slapped Victor clean across the face.

He raised his hand to strike her, but before he could, a blast of purple light shot him backward and he landed on his ass. I looked around to see who had done it and gasped when I found the culprit.

"If you ever try to lay another hand on my daughter-in-law, I will fucking kill you where you stand, Victor! That goes for you as well Lachlan, you piece of shit!" Gramp's tone sent chills down my spine; I have never heard him so angry.

"There's the man I married." I looked to my side and smiled at my Grams. She loved seeing Gramps so riled up.

"Cyrus!" Nico called out, and a moment later Cyrus and four other guards appeared in front of Nico. "Arrest them and detain Victor and Lachlan in the alpha's cells."

"You cannot do this! We are the elder council leaders. That woman is nothing but a liar and a common whore!" Lachlan shouted, but Nina never missed a beat.

"A common whore who bit your dick when you tried to put it in my mouth? Or the common whore who was present when you and Victor made plans to eliminate my daughter?" Lachlan looked around, shocked, clearly expecting the other members of the council to help.

"You're right, Lachlan, as leaders we cannot arrest you." Lachlan smiled, and as soon as Victor was on his feet again, he had a triumphant smile on his face as well. "The only way we can do that is if the other members of the council agree with us."

My stomach sank. What if they didn't believe Nina? We would be back to square one with my head on the chopping block.

I looked to each of the council members to see them speaking in hushed tones among themselves.

"The shifter council is in agreement. We vote for their arrest and for their lives to be forfeited." Lachlan and Victor looked murderous at Mr. Silver's words.

"The covens are in agreement." Gramps spoke loudly so everyone could hear. I looked to the fae and vampire council members. A young woman from the fae council stepped forward and bowed her head to Nico.

"The fae council is in agreement with the coven and shifters." She looked to me and smiled, and I mouthed a thank you. All we needed was for the vampires to be on our side. It felt like it took hours but in minutes a young man from the vampire council stepped forward. The young elder gulped loud enough for everyone to hear before speaking.

"We agree with the other council members." At his words, Lachlan and Victor began to fight and struggle against the guards.

Uncle David looked to Kai and nodded his head, and Kai made his way over to Lachlan and Victor. He placed a hand on each of them, two seconds later both men stood there with confused expressions. They didn't struggle or fight against the guards as they led them away. Uncle David must have removed the spell that blocked Kai.

Nico spun around and plucked me out of Grams's and Lucian's hold. He spun me around in circles, stopping only when I threatened to puke on him. He placed me on my not-so-steady feet and cupped my face between his hands.

"We did it. We're finally free to live our lives, little one." I blinked away the tears that threatened to fall and stood on my tiptoes to place a kiss on his lips.

"Do I get a kiss as a thank you?" Nico and I pulled apart to look at Dom. I smiled and hugged him.

I thanked each and every one of my friends and my cousins. Without these guys, my ass would have been dead several times over. There was no doubt in my mind about that.

"Dominic, we need to talk." We all stopped talking and turned to face a solemn-looking Mr. Silver. Dom rushed over to his father.

"Dad, what's wrong?" Mr. Silver tried to smile but it didn't reach his eyes.

"I'm so sorry, son."

"Sorry for what, Dad?"

"What you did today—" Dom cut his father off.

"Don't sweat it, old man. I still get to be free and be me." I could hear the happiness in Dom's voice.

"No, son, you won't get the life you want." Huh. Why the fuck not?

"What do you mean?" I could hear the slight shake in Dom's voice.

"Son, you made a vow and swore it today. You can't undo what you have done. You have no choice but to return to New York with me and become alpha."

"Dad, no! I didn't mean to...I can't...I don't want to!" Mr. Silver had so much sadness in his eyes; he didn't want to do this to his son.

"I'm sorry, you made a vow, and if you don't honor it, your wolf will override you. Wolves are bound by honor, and you vowed here today to take over for me."

CHAPTER 83

I left the others to go search for Nina. I found her around the side of the compound, speaking to my grandparents. I hid behind a tree to listen. Yeah, I know I was being nosy, sue me.

"I'm so sorry, I never meant to hurt Ralph. I loved him!" I could hear the anguish in Nina's voice.

"We know you loved him Nina, it wasn't your fault he died." Bless Grams for being so sweet.

"What you said back there—I didn't like hearing it, but I think you were very brave." Oh. My. God!

Gramps just gave Nina a compliment. She chuckled nervously.

"I'm glad I could help. I just wish I would have been brave enough years ago. My daughter may live, but she will always hate me, and I can't blame her for that."

Nina's words hit me in my heart. It was time to let go of the anger and the hate. Nina was sick, and I couldn't hold that against her anymore. My mother had just saved my life, after all. I didn't want to overthink this anymore. I moved out from behind the tree.

"Mom?" My mom spun around so fast she nearly lost her footing.

My mother stood there staring at me, mouth agape in shock.

"Y-you called me Mom." Her voice was shaky from trying not to cry.

I shrugged my shoulders. "Well, you did kind of save my life, so I thought I owed you one." Mom walked toward me and stopped directly in front of me.

"You owe me nothing! I did what any parent would have done for their child." She dropped her gaze, and I sighed. It was now or never.

"I'm so sorry for what those assholes did to you. I swear I will help you through it." She brought her gaze back up to mine, so many unspoken questions swirling in her eyes. "I'll never forget what happened to me as a kid, but I will move past it. You're all I have left. Dad's gone and so is Stevie. I want to make this work between us." My mom nodded her head vigorously and then crushed me against her, sobbing into my hair. After the shock wore off, I wrapped my arms around her. It felt strange to be hugging my mother. Right here, in this moment, all my anger and resentment toward her vanished. I knew she would do better and be better now. I was excited at the prospect of getting to know my mom.

The next day we all traveled in a convoy to Knox Mountain. Today was the day my sister and Ty were being laid to rest.

No one protested when Gramps said Stevie and her mate were to be buried with our father. Standing up here and looking at both caskets was a bittersweet feeling. I knew Stevie and Ty were together and happy, but I still missed them both. When a witch or warlock is buried, his or her power is taken from them and then passed onto their chosen one. I had no idea about this until Grams told me this morning.

"It is time; I will now say the sacred spell to transfer Stevie's power onto her chosen one." I looked around at all the people gathered here, wondering which one of them would inherit my sister's power. Would they inherit the darkness as well?

Nico's hand squeezed mine as he leaned down to whisper in my ear.

"So help me God, if you get any more power, I think it would crush my ego." I giggled at my husband's goofiness.

I gasped as I watched purple power rise from Stevie's casket, tears sprung to my eyes. That was my sister's essence, and now it would go to someone else. I hoped Stevie chose well.

"Seek your chosen vessel, granddaughter," Gramps whispered to the purple magic swirling above my sister's casket. The magic shot to the left of me, and I thought it was going to my mom, who stood beside me, but then gasped when I realized its target.

"Oh my God, Stevie chose you!" I said in awe as I looked at a shocked Mya. She was running her hands all over her chest in disbelief.

Stevie gave her power to Mya.

"Welcome back to the Knox coven, Mya. I couldn't have picked someone better to inherit my granddaughter's gifts." Gramps was happy to have Mya back in the coven. Mya opened and closed her mouth so many times, but words wouldn't come out.

I guess Mya was going to be one strong-ass witch. Mya

looked to me; she looked scared, like I was going to be mad. I leaned around my mom and gripped Mya's hand.

"I am so glad it's you; this is my sister's way of righting her wrong. I know you will do her proud, Mya." Mya relaxed at my words.

"I swear, Ryan, I won't let you or Stevie down. I'll use this new power to help the others track Randall."

It had become a mission assigned to a select few from the council to track down Randall Cane. Kai, Jax, Aurora, Mya, Alex, Chase, and a few others were dead set on justice being served.

Dom wasn't able to join them, as he would have to leave with his dad to go to New York. Sophia and Lucian were returning to Farrarie with me, Mom, and Nico. Sophia had promised to help Lucian find his parents.

Epilogue

RYAN

Standing here in my empty pink room at my father and Stevie's house was bitter sweet.

I only spent a couple days here, but it had a feeling of home. I had put off packing and selling my sister's house for as long as I could. My sister's childhood home was now sold to a family who would make their own memories here.

I smiled at the thought of my dad and sister playing and laughing in this house. I took one last look around the room that was supposed to be mine. I would have loved living here. Growing up with my mother was traumatizing, but it also made me the woman that I am today.

My mother had been speaking to a healer back in Farrarie who was helping her; it was a long road for my mom, but she was prepared to put in the work. I even saw a healer as well, to help me heal from the trauma of my wedding night. Nightmares still plagued her, and she said it was karma's way of punishing her for what she had done to me. I didn't blame her anymore for my childhood; I managed to get past all of that. The healer was helping her deal with what those bastards did to her.

After the council bound their power and banished them to the human world, my mother finally started to relax, and she knew then that they could never hurt her again.

Victor and Lachlan were banished from the supernatural world, never allowed back again. Nico, Jax, Kai, and Dom, with the help of Gramps and Mr. Silver, had both the traitors placed inside a human prison where they would live out the remainder of their days in solitude. I don't know how they managed to pull that off, but I was thankful.

"Are you ready, love?" I was pulled from my thoughts and turned to see my sexy-ass husband by the door. Nico still took my breath away. He stood there in dark wash jeans and a form-fitting black shirt that clung to his skin. His jet-black hair disheveled, like he had just run his hand through it, and those violet eyes always made me weak in the knees.

He sauntered into the room and stopped in front of me. I craned my head back so I could see his eyes. He smiled down at me. I know that look.

"If you keep looking at me like that love, I'll have to defile you in your childhood room."

I shivered at the huskiness in his voice, and the desire in his eyes sent liquid pooling between my thighs. He leaned down to capture my lips in what I'm sure was to be a heated kiss but stopped his descent at the sound of Lucian's voice.

"Eww, you two were about to fuck, weren't you? Do it when you're dreaming or something." I stepped back and smiled.

I moved toward the door where Lucian now stood and patted him on the chest. "You really need to find yourself a girlfriend, buddy. Your always cock-blocking me, and it's not cool for me or my coochie." Lucian reeled back like I slapped him, and I grinned. Nico and I learned that Lucian was the reason Nico couldn't come to me in my dreams. After returning to Farrarie, Lucian learned to control his power and removed his hold on mine, completely. Nico had a hunch that he was blocked because of Luce; that night Nico tried and managed to enter my dreams. It felt good to have him with me again in my dreams. It was like the final piece had been put back in place.

"I could have gone the rest of my life without knowing what your lady bits needed." I burst out into a fit of laughter. Living with Lucian has been an experience. We have been trying for months to track down information on his parents, but have had no luck. Sophia is with us in Farrarie, as well, and she has been nothing but amazing toward Lucian. She has been teaching him to read and write, and she was even the one to help Lucian to sleep on his own, in his own room.

Sophia hasn't smiled a full smile since Dom left for New York six months ago. Those two needed to sort their shit out and admit that they loved each other. I don't know what the history is between them, but I know there is a story there; Sophia just won't spill the beans.

We don't hear from Dom much. We've seen him twice since he left. Nico has tried to reach out and ask if we could visit, but he always has some excuse as to why we can't.

Dom is being weird and cagey, and I don't like it. Mr. Silver has even reached out and said he was worried about Dom. Nico and I are planning to visit him very soon and get to the bottom of whatever the hell is bothering him.

"All right, you two, let's lock up and get out of here. We still have to stop in Wonder Lake to see Jax and Aurora and get an update." Nico's words pulled me from my happy moment. Kai and Mya were in Chicago; they got a tip from one of the packs there that they had spotted Randall.

Kai is still king of the vamps, and Mya was welcomed back

into the coven. With Stevie's power transferring to her, the link to the coven was restored.

Kai was doing great at being king, and he was even more happy now that I managed to break Nico's spell on Farrarie that wouldn't allow vampires to enter. All this power was finally able to heal something instead of hurt it.

Alex, Chase, and Lucian helped me with that—it took us a couple weeks to figure it out, but with the help of my brainiac cousins, we did it.

Chase and Alex agreed to take on the role of kings of the Knox coven. Gramps and Grams stayed with them for a few months to help them settle in before returning back to the Yukon. I speak to Grams and Gramps at least twice a week. Everyone was doing well, even Jax and Aurora, who were starting to take things slow. Aurora still refused to mate with Jackson until the threat on his life was dealt with.

"I'm ready to blow this joint; what about you, Smurf?"

We made our way down the stairs and I paused to look at the wall that used to have photos of my dad and sister all over it. I was taking all the photos with me back to Farrarie, along with a few other things. The rest I donated to charity. I lived in a freaking castle now, so I had no need for any of the other stuff.

I pulled my gaze from the wall and smiled down at Nico and Lucian, who were waiting at the bottom of the stairs for me. A sense of déjà vu hit me: falling down these stairs over a year ago is where my adventure really started. I wasn't that same naïve eighteen-year-old girl anymore, that's for sure.

"Yeah, Luce, let's get out of here." I made my way down the remainder of the stairs and clasped Nico's hand in mine. We passed through the foyer and out the front door. Once we were at the car, I stopped before getting in and turned to take one last look at the house.

I smiled.

So much has changed since I first arrived at this house. I was not that same girl anymore. I'm a queen, a wife, a granddaughter, and a friend. I thought my life would always be *A Beautiful Nightmare*, but with a bit of luck and *A Twisted Fate* my life has become *A Beautiful Dream*.

Click the link to continue reading Dom and Soph's book
Redemption.

Also by Samantha Barrett

Mafia Romance

Murdoch Mafia Series

Played By The Bishop

Tormented By The King

Tortured By The Knight

Tempted By The Queen

Turned By The Pawn

Ruined By The Rook

Murdoch Mafia Novella

Stalemate

Memento Mori Series

Reign Of Royal

Broken By Sin

In Havoc Lays Chaos

Godfathers of the night

London has Fallen

Damned By His Angel

Re Della Strada

Shattered Soul

Fractured Heart

Tainted Essence

Fairytales With A Twist

Condemned Beast

Secret Society/ Bully

Filthy Few

Forever Filthy

Filthiest Of Them All

Masked Men Novella (Pure Smut)

Dirty Priest

Dirty Daddy

Sports Romance

Playing For Keeps

Offside

Touchdown

End Game

Hail Mary

Blindside

RH Sports

Hate Us Like You Mean It

MM

Love Me Like You Mean It

Paranormal Romance

The Veil Of Obsidian

Of Time And Carnage

Curse Of Fate

Dream

Fate

Nightmare

Redemption

Anarchy

Brutal Savages

Savage Lies

Brutal Truth

Savage Beast

Brutal Beauty

Acknowledgments

Wow, where do I even begin?
I have to say writing the final book for The Dream Trilogy was something else. The energy and emotional strength it took to this one was intense.
This trilogy has taken me on a journey, it has taught me so many different things and shown me dreams are achievable!
Ryan and Nico will always be a part of me and I hope you enjoyed their journey as much as I did writing it.
This trilogy isn't just words on paper for me, this trilogy is the start of a career I never thought I would be blessed enough to have.

I want to say thank you to my amazing support team, my family. You have all supported me on this journey, even when I felt like giving up your support and encouragement helped me push through all the self doubt.

To my amazing husband, Mark. My gosh, without you this trilogy would never have come to pass! You are my inspiration, my muse and my *Nico*. Thank you for pushing me to chase my dreams and supporting me throughout this journey. There aren't enough words or even the right word to explain how grateful I am for you.

Last but certainly not least, my amazing readers!
Without you, all of this wouldn't have been possible. There are

no words to describe how important you are to me. You make this dream of mine possible and allow me to live the life I have always dreamed of. I love you all dearly.

If you enjoyed A Beautiful Nightmare, I'd love it if you could leave a review on **Amazon**, **Bookbub** or **Goodreads**, it would mean a lot to hear your feedback.

Xxxx
Sam

About the Author

Samantha Barrett is originally from Auckland, New Zealand but living in Brisbane, Australia.

Sam writes all things dirty dark and delicious with a side of twisted mind fuck.

She is a lover of all things red flags and an anti-hero is a must.